BUSY

PATRICK ANDERSON

BODIES

A Novel

SIMON AND SCHUSTER

New York   London   Toronto   Sydney   Tokyo

Simon and Schuster
Simon & Schuster Building
Rockefeller Center
1230 Avenue of the Americas
New York, New York 10020

SIMON AND SCHUSTER and colophon are registered trademarks
of Simon & Schuster Inc.

Designed by Levavi & Levavi
Manufactured in the United States of America

10 9 8 7 6 5 4 3 2 1

Library of Congress Cataloging in Publication data

Anderson, Patrick,
Busybodies : a novel / Patrick Anderson.
p.   cm.
I. Title.
PS3551.N377B8   1989   89-19656
813'.54—dc20   CIP

ISBN 0-671-69004-3

For
Jim Gordon
Joe Goulden
John Greenya
Rod MacLeish
Les Whitten
Good writers, good friends

1.

The campaign was always out there that spring, rumbling over the horizon like thunder, far-off and ominous, but we in the Capital did not often heed its distant drama. We glanced at bulletins from the front—skirmishes in snowbound Iowa, guerrilla warfare in grim New Hampshire, shoot-outs in the dusty streets of Texas— and we chatted about polls and primaries, but no one except the political reporters and campaign staffs really cared. Most of us in the "media elite" were rooting for Don Allworth, our White Hope, who was young and au courant, but we knew the fate of other White Hopes over the years.

Mostly, our thoughts were closer to home, for there were juicy divorces that year, spectacular and sordid affairs, memorable parties, bizarre scandals, bloodbaths in the White House, vicious battles for major editorships. On such matters, Gentle Reader, do we focus in the Capital of the World; presidential elections come and go, but good gossip is forever.

I was watching the "Today" show when the phone rang, and only reluctantly did I tear my eyes from the box. Reluctantly, because Jane Pauley was smiling out at me, and Jane's a sweetheart. She's so damn wholesome it makes you want to cry.

"Yeah," I growled, to make my mood clear to the unwelcome caller.

"Oh, don't be a bear," Gloria said.

I gulped and shifted gears. Gloria can call me anytime, even if Lady Jane is inexplicably dancing the cancan while Willard and Bryant go at it with switchblades.

At a tender age, just out of Miss Hockaday's School in Dallas, Gloria married an oilman forty years her senior. "My little angel," he called her. Then his little angel proceeded to torment him until he sought refuge with his ex-wife, whereupon she gave the poor fellow his freedom in exchange for five million dollars and the second-largest house in Georgetown.

For most women, that would be the end of the story; for Gloria it was only the beginning. She took a succession of Senators as lovers (Supreme Court Justices mutter in Latin, she said, and Congressmen all look the same) and in time turned her talents to that last refuge of scoundrels, novel-writing. Gloria's novels were so depraved, so shameless, so blatantly libelous, so totally lacking in literary value or moral concern, that she produced three best-sellers in a row and made more money than Bob Woodward and Kitty Kelley combined. (Kitty hates Gloria the way Sinatra hates Kitty, but that's another story.)

Me, I like Gloria. She is great to look at, her books are funny, if you aren't in them, and she is loyal to her friends. I am among that elite, mostly because I am the only man she knows who is in her class gossip-wise. Gloria truly loves gossip; she calls it the ultimate oral sex.

"You're up early, doll," I ventured.

"Tommy, what do you hear about Donny Allworth?"

Zap, she hit me with it, and it was a big one, or she wouldn't have called so early and gotten to the point so urgently. Usually Gloria savors the foreplay.

"I've heard nothing. *Nada.* Give me a hint."

I picked up a pen and wrote "Gloria" and the date at the top of a notepad.

"Well, if you were clever enough to check his campaign schedule, you'd see that last Sunday was a down day. But he wasn't at home. And I have a source who saw him walking on the beach at Rehoboth with a woman who was not Polly."

"Rehoboth? It's a hell of a time to go to Rehoboth."

"Not if you want to be alone, it's not. Lovers adore those lonely, windswept beaches."

"What'd the woman-not-Polly look like?"

"Vague. She was wearing a windbreaker with a hood. White—her, I mean, not the windbreaker—and average-sized. Slender. Good legs. My source thinks they went back to the Seagull Inn after their walk."

I scribbled a few notes. "Shades of the Monkey Business—is that what you're telling me? Another great American heads oceanward and steps on his dick?"

"Could be," she said, and I imagined her arch smile, her glittery cat's eyes. We had been lovers once, an experience I would no more have missed than I would repeat.

"You know I can't touch it. A vague sighting—it could have been his daughter in the windbreaker."

"Stopping to play kiss-kiss six times?"

I sighed wearily. Why wearily? Do I grow old? Do I dare to eat a peach? "Okay, I'll check it."

"Check-schmeck. Would you use it?"

God, it was too early in the morning to confront a moral decision of that magnitude. Don Allworth was a friend of mine—as much as people in his profession or mine can burden themselves with friends. He was also the White Hope, and deep in my petrified heart I wanted to see him President, not one of those venal turkeys who were running against him. Please, God, give me the dirt on the turkeys, not on our White Hope.

But I was a man with a mission. If there was dirt out there, I had an obligation to my readers to shovel it up. Not to mention the publisher who paid my handsome salary and expected the worst of me.

"Tommy, I'm not saying you *should* use it. Maybe you should *talk* to him. What is this, a mid-life crisis? In the middle of the campaign?"

"Campaigns have been known to cloud men's minds," I mused. "My own keen mind was clouded once. But look, Don should know not to play kiss-kiss on a public beach. I deal in dirt, not fatherly advice."

"But you'll check it," she pressed.

"You're not going to give this to anyone else, are you?"

"What an insulting question, Tommy."

12

"Answer it."

"My lips are sealed."

"That'll be the day."

"But you will check it?"

"Oh, hell, yes," I growled. Then, in my Jimmy Durante voice I added, "What a revoltin' development *dis* is," and slammed down the phone.

Revolting indeed. What the hell was Gloria up to? Did she really want me to save Don Allworth from his folly, or was she setting me up—expecting me to do her dirty work and blow him out of the water? Did she love him for his enlightened leadership, or did she hate him because, as legend had it, he'd rebuffed her gin-fueled advances one starry evening on the terrace at Hickory Hill?

I hadn't the faintest, and that was what I loved about Gloria: she was so supremely Machiavellian that you could never be sure about anything she did, not anything at all.

Gloria's call, of itself, was no bombshell. Many lip-smacking tales make their way to me, but hard evidence is usually lacking.

No, what made the morning interesting was the call from Don Allworth himself—*that* was a juicy coincidence.

But before I relate Don's call, let me introduce myself.

Tullis is the name and gossip's the game.

Yes, I am that most depraved of ink-stained wretches, the vilest of the vile, a gossip columnist. A prattler, a tattler, a professional busybody.

Tommy Tullis, once an ambitious young reporter who dreamed of winning Pulitzer Prizes. Dreamed of writing novels, if the truth be known. But those dreamed-of novels were never written, because somewhere along the line I became a slave to that cruelest of masters, reality. I lacked the imagination to invent salacious tales, could only report numbly on the true-life horrors that passed before my disbelieving eyes.

Occasional speechwriting was as close as I came to writing fiction: while between journalistic jobs, I blundered into several presidential campaigns.

My reporting career was fatally handicapped by my inability to take the political world seriously. I came of age in the optimism of the Kennedy era, but then, so abruptly, those halcyon years were replaced by the crudity of Johnson, the outrage of Vietnam, the depravity of Nixon. When Nixon was elected a second time, Washington became surreal farce to me. And, God save us, eight years of the Gipper still lay ahead.

By my mid-thirties I was toiling for the mighty *Washington Post,* but I wasn't making anybody forget Dave Broder. I failed as a police reporter, failed on the business desk, failed as a feature writer, and finally was assigned to compile ("write" is too grand a word) the "Social Notes" column—I was the *Post*'s official garbage collector for what is laughingly called Washington society.

Give me credit. I tried to inject a spark of life into this shameful output of mine. One day I boldly reported that the Secretary of Agriculture arrived at an agribusiness convention alone and departed soon thereafter with Miss Soybean of 1979. The story was God's own truth, but Miss Soybean skipped town, and the Secretary threatened to sue, thereby upsetting my publisher and her craven lawyers no end.

Just then, with my future in journalism much in doubt, I happened upon Harriet Dingley at a NOW fund-raiser. Harriet was a goodhearted but somewhat crazed heiress with a fondness for young men and old whiskey.

"I'm going to start a newspaper," she announced. "And I want you to work for me."

"As editor-in-chief? The Ben Bradlee of the underground?"

"In your dreams," Harriet shot back. "I want you to be the king of down-and-dirty gossip. The Lippmann of the lowdown. The Bob Novak of who's fucking whom. That's what readers want, not this trade-bill crap."

"Interesting," I ventured.

"What are they paying you?"

"Sixty," I lied.

"In a pig's eye," Harriet replied. "I'll pay you seventy-five."

I saw the hungry look in her eye—the woman lusted for my byline. "Eighty," I said grandly.

"Sold, you bandit," she snapped. "And I expect you to earn it. We're gonna kick ass, make news, and sell papers. Kay Graham, you're history!"

Thus I cast my lot with the *Capital Vindicator*—Harriet's bizarre name for her new toy. Our feisty little weekly soon commenced publication, and if we didn't exactly bring the *Post* to its knees, we did have fun.

I had found my calling at last. I was the Hemingway of keyhole journalists, the Proust of P Street, the most hated and feared gossipmonger in the civilized world.

My coups were endless. After the *Post* ran a fawning profile of a certain African diplomat, I followed up with evidence that the ebony-skinned statesman had devoured several of his political opponents—literally, roasted on a spit, and served with A-1 Sauce. It was I who broke the news of the Mississippi Congressmen who gambled away their uncomplaining spouses in a drunken poker game, and the Supreme Court nominee whose wife was a man.

Amid storms of protest, Harriet stood by me like a brick. It is traditional in American journalism that newspapers are founded by men of courage and vision, who die young and leave their papers to their nitwit heirs to despoil. Harriet, in that context, was a saint.

We did have a small disagreement over what to call my column. Harriet proposed an inane play on my name: "Tommy Tullis Tells Us." But I, possessed of a grander vision, vetoed that. My column—my page, actually, page three, every week, all the dirt that fits we'll print—was headed "The Capital of the World."

Nice, eh?

But perhaps you're wondering if my column's name is serious or sardonic.

I'm glad you asked.

I love ambiguity the way other men love prepubescent girls. Is our Capital comedy or tragedy? Is Henry Kissinger a statesman or a war criminal? Is Ronald Reagan a political genius or a charming vegetable? Was Gatsby truly great, or only a cheap con man?

Or both? Or both? Or both?

And so we might ask, Is this monument-mad city of ours truly the Capital of the World—shining towers, the last best hope of humankind, a beacon to free people everywhere—or is it more truly a corrupt and corrupting factory town whose main products are red tape, secret wars, grubby scandals, and big salaries for the thugs and fools who bamboozle their way into office?

Decide for yourself, Thoughtful Reader. I could make a case either way. But The Capital of the World it is.

4o

Anyway, the phone rang again as I was finishing my breakfast of orange juice and yogurt. You may question the state of my soul, but my body I take care of.

"Tullis here," I answered, all charm again.

"Tommy, will you hold for Senator Allworth?"

I held, wondering what the hell? Could word of Gloria's gossip have gotten back to him already?

"Tom, how the hell are you?"

Don sounded disgustingly hale and hearty; he was probably just back from his morning run.

"I'm okay. Where are you? I thought you were down South."

"I'm in town for the day—a vote on the foreign-aid bill. How about coming by my office for lunch?"

I smelled a rat. "Anything special you have in mind, Donny?" I asked.

"Hey, we need to catch up. Of course, if you want some dirt on those jerks running against me, I'll try to oblige."

He laughed, ho-ho-ho. Humor was not Donny's strongest suit.

"What time?" I asked.

"One," he said, and clicked off.

Curiouser and curiouser. I called the manager of the Seagull Inn, a pretentious high-rise in Rehoboth, and asked if they'd had any celebrity guests of late. Well, Sean Penn's mom was in, he said, and the mayor of Wilmington.

"How about Senator Allworth?" I demanded.

There was a silence, then the lad got cagey. "Oh, you know Senators, they come and go."

"My friend, if you lie to me I'll close down that toilet you have the audacity to call a hotel."

With some people you can't be subtle.

"Well . . . ah . . . you see"—he was crudely working out his lie—"he was here, but he wasn't *staying* here."

"Was a woman with him?"

My informant gagged as if he'd swallowed a frog. "No . . . no woman . . . I don't recall a . . . but . . ."

I hung up, and made a note to check the sanitation-department reports on the Seagull. Still, I'd put Don on the beach, more or less, and it shouldn't be that hard to worm the truth out of him. What I would do with the truth was another question.

At noon I rode the Metro down to Union Station and braved a howling March wind on the three-block walk over to the Dirksen Building.

As I neared Don's third-floor suite, Mac McKenna, his long-suffering administrative assistant, steered me into his cubbyhole office.

"How goes it, Mac?" I inquired.

Mac looked like a man on the way to his execution. His face was lined, his hair was gone, his hands shook. He and I and Don were all about the same age, mid-forties, but Mac looked sixty. Don, meanwhile, was stuck at thirty-five. Clearly there was a Dorian Gray process at work here—Mac suffered for Don's sins.

"Not so good, Tom, not so good. It's rough out there. Lot of dirty money floating around. Craxton, where's his money come from? The Mob maybe?"

"Hey, you did fine in Iowa and New Hampshire," said I cheerfully.

Don had finished second to the better-known Governor Craxton in Iowa and second to native son Representative Fletcher in New Hampshire. Not bad, but he still had to prove he could win one.

"Second won't cut it," Mac said gloomily. "That damn Ratcliffe, what's he up to?"

Harris Ratcliffe was a political consultant who had been hired to manage Don's campaign. Mac of course thought that he, after a decade of loyal service, should have that honor. But Ratcliffe had the national experience. It's a problem whenever a Senator runs; his staff always hates and fears the "outsiders."

"How about South Dakota, you got a shot there?"

"Not a prayer," Mac declared.

"Tommy, whatta you say!"

The voice rumbled behind me like Dolby. I turned and found the candidate himself, roaring in like a hurricane, big and handsome and full of himself. He seized my hand in both of his and otherwise turned on the charm until I babbled incoherently.

"Still not married?" he tossed out, as he guided me across to his office, which featured a cozy fireplace and a choice view of the Capitol. Pictures, too, lots of pictures, of Don with Polly and the kids, with movie stars, with generals, even with Prince Charles, for God's sake.

"I tried it," I muttered. "Twice." But he wasn't listening. Like most Senators, he didn't listen much, not unless his vital interests were at stake.

He steered me onto the big leather sofa across from his desk. Cursed as I am with a dirty mind, I wondered how many times that sofa had been used for romance over the years.

"So how's it look?" I asked.

Don beamed, larger than life in a gorgeous pearl-gray suit. "Tom, I can be President."

I did not argue. Far more unlikely characters have been President in my time.

"It's a three-man race now. And look at the opposition. Craxton. A right-wing thug. And Fletcher. A left-wing nut. People are figuring those birds out."

I chose not to defend his opponents, although there were those who viewed them as honorable men.

"I don't have to be President," he added modestly. "Just so long as we elect somebody who's honest, who's bold, who's not afraid of new ideas." He shrugged. "But I look around and I don't see anyone else."

"You've got a lot going for you," I ventured.

"Right," he said softly. "Absolutely. But, Tommy, I have a problem."

You bet your ass he had a problem. His biggest problem, in my humble opinion, was what I call the Senate Syndrome. There are a hundred Senators, and at any given moment a majority of them think they ought to be President. I mean, they think it is *obvious,* written in the stars, that there is a conspiracy holding them back. What they never understand is that it's a million miles from winning in one state to winning nationally. Very few politicians are smart and tough enough to make that leap. That's what the primaries are all about, teaching a bunch of bozos the hard way that they don't have the right stuff.

Don, of course, just possibly did have the right stuff; that's why he was interesting.

"What's the problem?" I asked politely.

"What do you know about Wally Love?" he asked.

21

I thought a moment. "Some guy in Iowa?"

Don produced a clipping to refresh my memory. Love was a man from Oregon who had gone to Iowa to support Don with his own money. "He's a problem?" I asked. "You could use more problems like him, couldn't you?"

"Tom, how much do you know about the federal election laws?" Don asked.

"Not a lot. The most I can give you is a thousand dollars, right?"

"Right. But there's more to it than that. Let me give you a refresher course, okay?"

"Sure."

"Okay. Watergate was a lot of things, the break-in, the cover-up, but at bottom it was a money scandal. They had millions in cash floating around, people trying to launder it, trying to hide it, trying to steal it, a real mess. So, after Watergate, what does an outraged Congress do to purify our political process? We pass a law, of course. The Federal Election Campaign Act of 1974, controlling public financing of presidential elections and limiting contributions.

"But the next year, in the Buckley case, the Supreme Court got hung up on the idea that spending your own money is a kind of free speech. So the Court gave us this idiot compromise. You, as a citizen, can only give me a thousand dollars. But what about your free speech? That's where the Supremes went off the track. They created this loophole. You, as an individual—or, operating as a political action committee—can spend all the money you want on behalf of a candidate, *as long as you don't communicate with the candidate about it.*"

"I can only *give* you a thousand dollars," I said. "But I can spend all I want on you, as long as I don't talk to you about it. Right?"

"Right," Don said. "And, of coure, it's total bullshit. Because you don't *need* to talk to me. If I'm running, and you

22

want to help me, you *know* what I need. I need media. My face on the tube."

Bells were ringing, summoning the Senate to a vote, but Don ignored them.

"So what does all this have to do with Wally Love?" I asked. "He's just some clown, isn't he?"

"I don't know what he is. This guy turned up in Iowa. Driving around in a pickup truck, from county to county, placing newspaper ads. Ads that said what a great fellow Don Allworth is. Said I was for education and peace, said I had a wonderful family. . . ."

"No problem so far."

"Nice stuff. Nothing slick, nothing negative. Nobody in the media paid much attention. But we estimate this fellow spent at least thirty thousand dollars, big money in Iowa."

"Still no problem."

"Next he turns up in New Hampshire. Same operation. Except maybe he spent sixty thousand dollars there."

"Where's that problem, Don?"

"Dammit, wait. Now we hear he's been to South Dakota and then gone and opened an office in Texas. We hear he's having TV spots made. Whatever he's up to, the man is serious."

Maggie, Don's secretary, brought us club sandwiches and diet colas. Maggie is a sweet girl who weighs maybe two-twenty. No gossip there.

"Don, is it possible that this guy is for real, and you're the luckiest man who ever ran for President?"

"Sure it's possible. It's also possible that he's setting me up."

Paranoia in high places. "Setting you up how?"

"If Wally Love keeps going, he'll be running an unofficial Allworth for President campaign. People are going to think he's my guy—the more I deny it, the more they'll believe it. What if he goes negative? Or misstates my positions? Or turns out to be a crook?"

I shrugged. "Then you denounce him."

"That's too late. I have to know more about this guy."

I grew restless. "Well, send somebody to look him over."

"I *can't* send somebody!" Don responded. "My staff and I can't have any contact with him, or I'd screw the deal."

"Then send someone who's not on your staff."

Only when he began to grin did I wake up.

"No, Don. No, no, no. Not me. I'm not your private eye."

"Of course you're not. You're my friend. Plus, you're a journalist with a natural interest in the matter. Tom, the national media has not picked up on this guy, but he's going to be big news. The potential of this loophole hasn't yet been exploited. When and if it is, there could be shadow presidential campaigns twice as big as the official campaigns. It could destroy the system."

"How would I find this guy?"

"We hear he'll be in Baltimore next week. He stays at the Hilton, near the harbor. Give him a call."

"Maybe I will."

He started talking about his hot issue, the new trade-bill amendment. It was yet another threat to "get tough" with the Japanese before they bought the country out from under us.

"How's Polly?" I asked when he paused for air.

"Oh, fine, fine."

"What's she doing for the campaign?" I pressed.

Another frown. "You know Polly. She hates politics, always has and always will."

"A not unreasonable position."

"Except that her husband is running for President," he said grimly. "Dammit, she has to campaign a little, just so there's no gossip. You know—that we're not happy."

Perversely I said, "Speaking of gossip, I heard some you ought to know about."

"About Polly?" He seemed genuinely alarmed.

"No, you turkey, about you. That you were walking on the

24

beach at Rehoboth last Sunday with a lady who wasn't Polly."

Damn him, he began to laugh.

"Tom, where do you get all that garbage?"

"That's not the issue."

"My God, it's incredible that anything so innocent would . . . Look, I'll tell you exactly what happened. Mac and I drove over to meet with a big contributor. Ask Mac if you don't believe me."

Yeah, sure, ask Mac, who would swear that water flowed uphill if it served Don's interests.

"This guy wanted to take me out on his boat, drink a few cool ones, meet his friends. Big textile money. But there was a problem with his boat, and while they were fixing it, I went for a walk. And there was this girl on the beach, looking for shells. She walked along with me for a few minutes. How the hell could that get back to you?"

"You're running for President, pal," I reminded him. "My advice is, don't talk to girls on the beach. There is no such thing as a deserted beach."

Bells were ringing wildly. Two anxious aides burst in, proclaiming that the republic would fall if he was not on the Senate floor within seconds. Don smiled serenely and put his handsome face close to mine.

"Check on Wally Love," he whispered. "Nose around."

It is damnably difficult, in this bewildering Capital of ours, to keep one's eye on the Big Picture. If you're in the gossip business, you can go months, sometimes years, with hardly a glimpse of it.

Consider my talk with Don Allworth. The Small Picture it presented was tasty enough: Had Don met a lover on the beach, as Gloria believed, or was it only a chance encounter, as Don himself insisted?

Good gossip, yes, but the Big Picture kept intruding: Don Allworth was running for President, and I thought it was important to America for him to win.

Believe me, I dislike thinking in those terms. Historically, whenever I think it important that someone be elected President, either (1) he loses, or (2) he wins and proves to be a jerk.

And yet . . . and yet . . . maybe Don was different. Have I made him seem less than heroic? Did I suggest that he suffers from egomania, paranoia, and related disabilities? Well, okay, maybe he does, but all candidates are like that.

The Big Picture is that I know all the candidates and in my book Don is easily the best qualified of them. He's smart, he's honest, he's tough, he's well-intentioned, and he cares about this country. Damn my eyes, I'm talking serious again, but it's true.

So I cared about Gloria's tale, but not because I wanted to break the story. I wanted to protect Don. That was why I agreed to look into Wally Love's exploits, too; if the guy was out to screw Don, maybe I could prevent it.

That is why, as the campaign unfolded, I took strange, bizarre, and even dangerous steps on Don's behalf; to the rest of the world I may have looked nutty as a fruitcake, but in my own eyes I was a patriot.

Meanwhile, I had a column to write, one that kept me hopping for the rest of the week. Finally, my deadline met, I went home one afternoon, napped, showered, mixed a rum and tonic, played a Hot Five CD, and, thus sanctified, set off for Buzz Makito's party.

His real name was Yasuhiro Makito, but he called himself Buzz, and he was one of the most talked-about, sought-after men in town.

I considered Buzz a discovery of mine. Six months earlier his name had hit the street. Buzz Makito this, Buzz Makito that. Good works, good deeds, big bucks for charity and culture. A million dollars to keep a ballet company from going under in Ohio, computers to a school for the handicapped, a scholarship fund for black kids in Washington, generosity abounding.

Naturally I was suspicious. I gathered all the facts I could and then called the man. He received me in the grandiose former embassy he had leased on Massachusetts Avenue and we had a most interesting chat. He was a tiny man, boyish and high-spirited, with an engaging manner. But when pressed for details of his role in Washington, he alternated between modesty and mystery. He was no lobbyist, he said, no politician, simply a "businessman" who represented various "friends" yearning for better U.S.-Japanese relations. He wanted no credit, sought no publicity, but eventually he confirmed various good deeds I had already documented.

"Gatsby in Guccis," I called him, in what was for me a glowing column. A few weeks later the *Post*'s Style section discovered Buzz too, and their piece made him an official, certified celebrity.

I started getting invitations to Buzz's parties, which were ever more frequent and ever more lavish. A lot of media types turned up at Buzz's parties, and if a few hard cases grumbled that there was something unseemly, even sinister, about his extravagance, mostly we guzzled his champagne, gobbled his caviar, and praised his good taste. No one ever went broke by wining and dining the Washington media.

This evening's party happened to fall on the night of the South Dakota primary—that may have been the excuse for it, for all I know. When I arrived a band was playing Gershwin. A waiter sprinted up with bubbling Cristal. The party sprawled out before me in marble halls and gilded ballrooms.

Upturned faces greeted my arrival: some smiled genuinely, some falsely, some turned away. I do make enemies; one man's gossip is another man's heartbreak.

I stood there a moment, savoring my solitude.

Mine is a strange business in a strange world. I remind myself often that if I weren't writing my column, few of these people would remember my name. That's the Dirty Little Secret of Our Capital: you pretend they love you for your charm and wit, but lose an election, lose your column, and you can go sleep on a grate for all these people care.

My first Christmas as a columnist, I received hundreds of invitations to the fanciest parties in town. It made me so mad that I burned them all and stayed home every night. But of course I got over that.

I stood in the doorway, savoring our little world. Soon people drifted my way, for gossip is our Capital's true religion, and I was a prince of the church.

A reporter from the *Post* whispered that, as a result of a brief and disastrous affair, a certain editor was conspiring to have a certain columnist's work banished from the Op-Ed page to back among the want ads.

She was elbowed aside by a grizzled veteran of the Washington office of the *New York Times,* who related the latest body count in that Beirut of a bureau's never-ending civil war.

On and on my informants came, whispering of unspeakable acts at the Supreme Court, of devil-worship in the Pentagon, of a liaison between a Senator's wife and a female tennis star. A red-faced editor of *Human Events* was raving that Jesse Jackson was a Cuban agent, when I was saved by the belle:

"Tommy, darling!" It was Gloria, stunning in a wispy pink Valentino that must have cost three thousand.

She had in tow one Sammy Shiner, the junk-bond magnate who'd fled Wall Street one step ahead of the U.S. Attorney, taken refuge in Washington, bought the venerable old *National Beacon,* and proceeded to inflict his demented views on the American public.

"Well, Tullis, how's the gossip business?" chortled Sammy, an oily creep in built-up Ferragamo shoes and a phosphorescent Armani tux.

"Booming," I said.

"Don't you ever get sick of that stuff?"

"When you're sick of gossip you're sick of life," I said cheerfully.

"But what does it contribute?" he persisted.

"Not much," I confessed. "But at least I've never been accused of bilking widows and orphans . . ."

"Now just a moment . . ."

29

". . . nor indeed have I ever given aid and comfort to those fascists in South Africa. Moreover . . ."

"I don't have to listen to this," the pint-sized publisher declared, and slithered toward the bar.

"You must restrain yourself," Gloria sighed.

"How can you be seen in public with that pig?"

"With sixty million dollars, he advances from pig to social lion." She pulled me close. "Have you *heard* what happened?"

My ears pricked up, but abruptly Gloria looked past me to greet a new arrival. "Jeffrey, darlink," she cried in an odd, Garboesque accent. "How vare you?"

The man she was addressing, Senator Jeffrey Willingham, was generally the soul of composure. But as Gloria spoke he underwent an amazing transformation. A tic seized his boyish face. One shoulder began to jerk. His mouth flapped soundlessly. His agonies recalled the Wolf Man confronting a full moon.

"Arrrgh," he gasped, and stumbled away from us.

"What was that all about?" I asked in amazement.

Gloria flashed her cat-who-ate-the-canary smile. "I'll tell you tomorrow at lunch," she promised. "But haven't you *heard* what happened today?"

I laughed. "Look, I talked to Don about this woman at the beach. He says . . ."

"Never mind *him*. My God, you're allegedly a gossip columnist. Where have you been for the past four hours? In outer space?"

I shrugged. "I took a nap. What's up?"

She rolled her jade-green eyes in frustration. "My dear boy, the pudding has hit the fan. The scandal of the year. It's Mike Cunningham, your favorite anchorman. You won't believe what that fool has done. He . . ."

God help us, another interruption—she stopped in mid-sentence, and I turned and found Buzz Makito grinning at me. "So glad you could come, Tommy."

Gloria gave him a frozen smile. Clearly, whatever Mike Cunningham had done, she didn't propose to share it with our host.

"Gloria, a vision of delight, as always," he said grandly.

Buzz inquired solemnly about our health, nodded to a waiter to refill Gloria's glass, then said, "Tommy, my friend, if you could spare me a moment."

Gloria agreed to part with me—her sensational news about our anchorman friend still undisclosed—and I followed my host up the spiral staircase. We stood on the landing for a moment, admiring the beautiful people spread out below.

Down by the fireplace, a small, dark man named Joey Swink was turning his considerable charm on a girl half his age. His hands fluttered, his eyes glowed, and you could see the girl start to melt.

Joey was a somewhat shadowy political consultant who'd once worked in the White House and in recent months had made Buzz Makito his chief client. They seemed an Odd Couple, the elegant Makito and the slippery Swink, but perhaps Buzz's success was a tribute to Joey's skills.

"Looks like Joey's about to score," I said.

Buzz arched an eyebrow. "Joey is a salesman who can't stop selling," he said inscrutably, and guided me into his office. Modern art, neon sculpture, a stunning aquarium, and boyish Buzz behind a Louis XIV desk.

"I loved your last column. Did he really propose to leave his wife for the babysitter? Ah, Tommy, you don't write a gossip column. You write about the human comedy itself."

With difficulty did I restrain myself from flinging myself at this good man's feet. How often in life do we meet someone who sees us as, in our heart of hearts, we wish to be seen?

"Tom, I have an item to offer you," my friend continued. "It concerns a potentially delicate matter."

His "item" concerned the fact that some Japanese investors were about to buy a venerable old Washington country club.

31

A lot of visiting Japanese businessmen would use the golf course, there would be resentment, but the club would be saved from the wrecker's ball.

It was an item, but just barely. I was surprised he'd taken time out from his party for it. Or was it the pleasure of my company he sought?

"I'm sure you want to get back to your guests," said I tactfully.

"No hurry, no hurry," Makito said. "Tell me your news. Have you been following the campaign?"

"Not much. I had a chat with Don Allworth the other day. He's optimistic."

Buzz nodded sagely. "A most attractive and articulate young man," he said.

"Indeed," I said.

"What issues does the Senator seem to stress?" my host asked.

Ah, so! "Arms control. Education. And he thinks there's mileage in his trade-bill amendment."

Makito's mouth tightened. "As you know, Tom, I never involve myself in American politics, but many of my countrymen will be grieved if such an outstanding candidate takes that unfortunate approach."

"Tell him so," I said.

"We've never met," he said.

"You've never met Don? Call him up."

"I wouldn't wish to be so forward."

That put the ball in my court. "I could arrange something. Maybe the three of us could do lunch."

"I wouldn't wish to trouble you."

"No trouble at all," I said dutifully.

Soon we returned to the party. I found Harriet, my publisher, and boasted of my golf-course scoop.

"Chinks on the links," Harriet quipped.

"Don't be racist, dearie," I said. "Anyway, these are Japs, not Chinks."

"Japs in the traps," said my irrepressible, not to say drunk, publisher.

Gloria pulled me aside and finished the story she'd been trying to tell me earlier. Except now everyone knew it: you saw the news rippling around the room.

Mike Cunningham, the anchorman, had left his wife for a 23-year-old intern in his bureau!

Zowie! The network had spent millions promoting Mike as The Man We Trust and now he had fucked up on a scale that made Gary Hart look like Mister Rogers.

And the wife he had wronged, Adele Hopkins, Addie she was called, was herself a star in our firmament, a much-admired political reporter for the *Post*. One report was that Addie had already changed the locks and hired the formidable Joe Califano to crucify the errant anchorman.

Someone else declared that Mike's hands had shaken and his voice cracked as he read the news that night.

A network person said that was because Gloria had gotten through to him by phone, seconds before he went on the air, and shrieked, "You're finished, asshole!"

(Gloria had never forgiven Mike for calling her "the Tom Clancy of the bedroom" during an acerbic, on-the-air commentary on her screw-and-tell first novel.)

God help us, just as the Mike-and-Addie story began to die down, another bomb exploded. Television people were arriving with exit polls, which had Don Allworth upsetting Governor Craxton in South Dakota.

My mind was thoroughly boggled. Buzz Makito had flattered and befriended me. The million-dollar anchorman had left the admirable Addie for a girl of twenty-three. And my friend Don Allworth might indeed be headed for the White House, if he didn't blow it all by meeting women on the beach.

Shaken, I retired to the bar for serious meditation.

People lingered, clustered around two huge TV screens for the news from South Dakota, a place as distant as the moon. At one point, we viewed an unscripted exchange between the anchorman and the reporter in the field.

"Ah, Bill, what do you think accounts for this stunning upset by Senator Allworth over Governor Craxton?"

"Ah, well, Dan, ah, of course, many factors, but, ah, there may have been a joker in the deck. A man called Wally Love turned up here a few weeks ago from out of state, Oregon I believe it was, and began a one-man media blitz that may have put Allworth over the top."

Dan gulped, clearly alarmed at this news. "Ah, do we know how much this, ah, this man spent?"

"Ah, actually, we don't, Dan. And Wally Love seems to have left the state. But one thing is certain, the battle for the nomination is a real horse race now."

Ah yes, Dan, one thing is certain: nine out of ten political reports will end with a solemn One Thing Is Certain. An OTIC, as we call it in the trade.

I drank deeply of my host's expensive cognac. People came bearing gossip, but I was not listening. A woman took my arm. I'd avoided her all evening. A decade before I'd been in love with her, left home for her, then she dumped me to marry a big, loud, rich lawyer. I'd seen him that night, too, charming various women.

"He left with that German girl," she said. Tears glistened in those unforgettable eyes. "Take me to your place, Tom."

I shook my head. You make your bed, you lie in it. I was a million miles away.

"You bastard," she said, and looked about for another savior.

Seeing her had shaken me. As the party roared on, I stood aside, invisible, trying to reconcile myself to this world. Everyone was here, liberal and conservative, black and white, reporter and source, prosecutor and defendant, labor and management. We fought our nine-to-five battles and then we joked together over Buzz Makito's champagne and caviar.

I thought what a good life this was for all of us. Out There somewhere, people—union members, welfare mothers, corporate boards, newspaper readers, whatever—were counting on us. But all that mattered, here in the Capital of the World, was that *the game go on.*

There could be wars, assassinations, riots, scandals, tragedies without end, but these were only minor blips on our screen. We would report on them, appoint commissions to investigate them, punish an occasional wrongdoer, see an occasional colleague go down in disgrace, and we would gossip and tut-tut, but nothing Out There really mattered to us.

All that matters is that the game go on.

The Capital, to our elite, was like a candy store where the goodies never stopped flowing.

Someone, somewhere, paid the bills, but not us.

I thought all this, that night at Buzz Makito's party, groping toward a drunken epiphany.

I thought: *Men have died from time to time, and worms have eaten them, but not for love.*

I felt a sudden pain where once I had a heart, and then I was racing away from the music and laughter, away from the people who made news, the people who worshiped power, away from all that, stumbling out into the night, where a cold, cleansing rain embraced me like a lover.

omen tell me things.

Why?

Perhaps because I listen, because they find me sympathetic. When I was growing up, I found that I liked girls, liked them a lot; they always struck me as smarter than boys, nicer, more interesting, braver, more fun in just about every way.

So I listen, and they tell me their dreams and sorrows and secrets. They help me write my column, and if I had the talent I'd write something far grander with the wonderful tales they tell.

I went to see Addie the next morning. Addie Hopkins, the first woman I knew to keep her own name when she married. At forty-plus, Addie was fresh-faced, intense, nervous-thin, and not so very different from the girl I'd met two decades before, just out of J-school. She had never been a beauty, but she had a smart, sensible, no-nonsense look that I and many other men admired.

Addie and Mike and I had started at the old *Washington Daily News* together, and she'd been clearly the most talented of us. She could write, report, edit—Addie was a whiz.

Need I add I was soon in love with her?

But Addie married Mike, as all the world knows.

Mike Cunningham, what a boob! A gorgeous boob who couldn't write his way out of a paper bag. I can still see him, hunched over his typewriter, in sheer agony, trying to devise a lead for the weather story.

Addie would save him, of course. When the city editor slipped out for a drink, she'd sneak over and "suggest" a lead to him, and the next two or three paragraphs too. Mike could manage from there.

It was Addie who persuaded him to make the leap into TV reporting—she understood his talents far better than he did.

The rest, alas, is history.

Mike's relationship with the TV camera was chemical, all but obscene, like Elvis with a guitar, and he quickly shot up the ladder to his present ridiculous prominence.

Addie, meanwhile, joined the *Post* and broke through many old-boy barriers to become one of its top political reporters. A series she'd written on Don Allworth the previous summer had all but launched his presidential campaign.

On this morning, however, she was not a tough reporter but a woman wronged.

I went to the glass-walled mansion they'd built on a wooded hillside overlooking Rock Creek Park. The day was warm enough for us to have coffee on the deck.

"He's my Frankenstein monster," she said bitterly. "I taught him to walk, to talk, to dress. Even to read."

"The last time I saw Mike he was declaiming about Hemingway."

"I made a list. Books he absolutely had to read. *The Catcher in the Rye. Gatsby. A Farewell to Arms. Portnoy. Animal Farm.* Just the obvious ones. Others, the Russians, *Moby Dick,* the hard stuff, I summarized for him. He was like a virgin. But he learned fast."

"And now this monster you created is the asshole of the decade."

Her eyes flashed. "He always had that potential. He's so vain, a child, a puppy that wants its belly rubbed."

"We all want our belly rubbed. But that doesn't mean we run off with children."

"But he is a child, don't you see? She won't threaten him, won't criticize his neckties or correct his grammar. They can be twenty-three together."

"You don't want him back?"

"Not in a million years."

I wondered if she meant it.

"Tell me what happened."

Addie brightened. At twelve she'd been Oklahoma's Spelling Bee champion. I always saw in her the teacher's pet, getting up to recite.

"He came to me in tears. He said, 'Addie, I'm in love. She's an intern at the bureau. She's so sweet.' At which point I threw an ashtray at him."

"Hit him?"

"A near miss. The idiot, he didn't have to *tell* me about her."

"Poor Mike, honest to a fault."

"I gave him a choice. He could call the little bitch and tell her she could never see him again. Or he could leave our home for good."

"And he said?"

"Well, he blubbered some more. He said he loved us both. I said, 'You idiot, what is the network going to think of this?' And he said, 'Addie, I'm a superstar.' I'll swear to God, that's what he said—this noodle who never mastered the art of obituary writing."

"You never suspected anything before?"

"Oh, Tommy, I know what the world is like. He travels, he's gorgeous, I assume a little hanky-panky. I can live with that. Tit for tat. But when he rubs my nose in it—that's unforgivable."

Tit for tat? And what did that mean? If Addie played around, it would be vastly discreet, the kind of invisible affair you'd never guess at.

"What about the kids?"

One-hundred-and-two-pound Addie raised her chin defiantly. "Sarah's in college. Bradley is at Andover. They can handle it."

"Last night, at Buzz Makito's party, someone said you'd hired Joe Califano."

"Joe referred me to another lawyer. She's fine. Tough as nails."

"Scorched earth? No prisoners?"

Her smile cut like glass. "Tommy, I'm a wronged woman. I'm entitled."

"Addie, tell me, how do you feel about this? I know you're pissed, but beyond that."

"Repeat this and I'll kill you."

"Agreed."

"I *am* hurt. I *am* wronged. But I'm relieved too. Life with Mike was pleasant. He's a hunk, he's successful, he's good in bed. We have nice children and a good life. God knows, most women envy me. But I did get bored sometimes. Intellectually, we're miles apart. Somehow I could never see myself growing old with Mike. Now he's spared me that necessity."

She was so damned tough; I gazed at her in perfect awe.

"Addie, what do you want me to do?"

"I think you should write up what happened. There'll be items here and there, maybe something bitchy in *Time,* maybe a few others who want to take a shot at the network. But you could do the real story."

"Thus creating a favorable climate for your tough lady lawyer to zap your faithless husband."

She shrugged. "Just tell it like it is."

I knew I should do it. Their split was big stuff in our scandal-hungry Capital. And yet I hated it. Hated to interview Mike, that poor fool whose runaway dick had led him into this mess, never mind the girl, who I suspected would wind up the loser in this affair. In one corner you had the lovers, all glands and not a brain between them, and in the other Addie and her legal shark. You didn't have to be a genius to guess whose blood would make pink bubbles on the water.

"I guess I'll do it," I told her. "But now I've got to go. I'm late for lunch with Forrest Keel."

I gave her a parting hug. Not the professional thing to do, true, but it felt good.

My friend Forrest Keel is one of the nation's most successful political consultants.

He's also gay.

It took me a couple of years to figure that out, then a couple of days to forget it, because Forrest is one of my favorite people in the world.

We met a few years back when I wrote about one of his clients who was running for the Senate. Most political consultants are consummate bullshit artists—let's face it, bullshit is their stock in trade—but Forrest was a thoughtful, candid, cultivated, altogether delightful fellow.

As Forrest and I became friends, I did not at first notice that he did not have a girl around. The truth is, a lot of men in politics aren't all that interested in women. Sex, sure, but not women as people. I've been to dozens of political gatherings where beautiful women were absolutely ignored by

41

cigar-chomping politicos who'd rather relive the '76 Iowa primary than peek down a lady's dress.

Eventually I went for a drink at Forrest's townhouse on Kalorama Circle and met his friend Chuck, a wiry, balding, witty, very pleasant stockbroker. Still I didn't get it. I just imagined these two carefree bachelors sharing a super pad, until one day Forrest mentioned that he and Chuck were having their "third anniversary" and at last the light dawned.

But we never discussed his sexuality. Politics was our common ground, politics and pop culture. Forrest was a pollster who'd done some pioneering work with focus groups. That means you sit down eight or ten average voters in a room and ask them what they think, about the candidates, about the issues, about life in general, and you pay close attention to what they say. It's what politicians are supposed to do—listen to people—except today they're so busy raising money that they have to hire someone to talk to voters for them.

Forrest and I met for lunch at Joe and Mo's underground cavern on Connecticut Avenue. You couldn't throw a stone in Joe and Mo's without hitting a political consultant or reporter.

Forrest arrived and immediately announced that he'd watched *Nashville* the night before, and that led to a heated debate as to whether *Nashville* or *McCabe and Mrs. Miller* was Altman's best.

We went on like that, moving from Altman to Fellini to Woody Allen (was *8½* or *Stardust Memories* the greater work?) to the new Philip Roth novel. It was a ritual, based on our shared, decidedly deviant view that Altman and Fellini and Allen and Roth were at least as important as the South Dakota primary.

But, inevitably, we turned to Topic A, the Allworth victory.

"What do you think happened?" I asked. "Did Dandy Don's murky message finally take root in the rocky soil of South Dakota?"

"Does he have a message?"

"He's been talking a lot about Old Values and New Directions," I said. "Or is it Old Directions and New Values?"

"Doesn't sound like it was the message," Forrest said. "In my experience, when someone wins who wasn't supposed to win, the reason is always the same."

"Money," I said. "The mother's milk."

"The same."

"Some guy named Wally Love flooded the state for Don the last few days. Claims to be operating independently. I've been trying to reach him."

"He may have won it for Allworth," Forrest said.

"What do you think about this guy?"

"He's a story, but he's not *the* story."

"What's *the* story?"

"Money in politics. There's going to be backdoor spending this year like no one ever imagined."

"Bags of cash floating around?"

"Why bother? Cash is clearly illegal, and there're too many legal ways, or gray areas, to exploit."

"For example?"

Forrest grinned. He was a handsome, bulky man with thick black hair. He'd played ball in college and flown helicopters in Vietnam. But he never talked about Vietnam.

"The biggest scam this year will be soft money," he continued.

"Soft money?"

"Money you give directly to a campaign is more or less regulated. But there's another loophole. In '79, Congress decided to encourage state parties. The idea was to let them pay for bumper stickers and voter-registration drives. But both parties are using that to get around the spending limits. You simply have your fat cats give a hundred thousand, or whatever, to the state parties. We're talking tens of millions here."

"It really is an outrage," I said.

43

Forrest looked perplexed. "Is it? How can you tell people they can't spend their money on the candidate of their choice? I know a lot of rich gays who'll give a hundred thousand this year, because they're outraged by the government's inaction on AIDS. Is it a crime for them to spend their money on an issue that's literally life or death to them?"

Over coffee, Forrest brought up the story of a human rights worker in the Philippines who had been murdered by a right-wing death squad a few days earlier. A young woman with two small children.

"We sit here in Washington and we don't think about these things," he said. "But it's a war that's being waged all over the world. Mandela and thousands of other blacks in South African prisons. Those who disappeared in Argentina. Dissidents in China and Russia. Arabs on the West Bank. Women fighting for equality in this country."

"And gays," I said.

"Some suffer more than others, some risk more than others, but it's all part of the unending struggle of the human spirit for freedom. A war against the forces of greed and selfishness and brute power."

"Or is it the two sides of the human spirit at war with themselves?" I asked.

"I think there are good guys and bad guys. I think some people and some systems are no damn good."

"So what do we do? Elect Don Allworth?"

Forrest sighed. "We could do a lot worse. My God, think of the things this country could do if we only had the leadership!"

I found the subject both depressing and strangely exhilarating. But that was what made me enjoy Forrest so much. I knew damn well no one else in Jo and Mo's that day was worrying about the struggle of the human spirit for freedom. The struggle to afford a second BMW was more like it.

Still, he was human, and before we left he stooped to gossip.

"What's this about Mike Cunningham?"

"It's true. He thinks he's in love with a girl at the bureau."

"What a crazy thing to do. Addie is such a fine lady. A great reporter and a fine lady too."

"Love is strange," I reflected.

"Indeed," my friend said. "Indeed."

8.

I went to see Polly Allworth for the best of all possible reasons: because seeing her always made me feel good.

I found her in the barn behind their house, bent over her potting wheel, perfectly at peace. She was wearing jeans and a smock, she had mud up to her elbows and a scarf around her head, and she glowed.

She came to me, wiping her hands on a towel, and raised her face. I kissed her lightly on the lips.

"You look sensational," I told her.

"I'm a mess. But thanks."

"Still potting, I see."

"I do love it."

She washed her hands and I looked at some of her work on the shelves. Bowls, mainly, and plates, done in pale blues and browns, with flowers painted on them.

I'd known Don and Polly since we all attended our state

university, where I was the crusading editor, Don was the all-American boy, and Polly was a campus queen, despite herself. I say despite herself because all she did was walk around being Polly, and dazzled classmates kept electing her Favorite This and Most Beautiful That.

Polly is one of the truly sensitive people I know. She cares about beauty the way Keats did, as an absolute, an end in itself. She painted for a time, watercolors mainly, and eventually she moved into pottery, where she's worked contentedly for a decade.

She also married Don and raised three lovely kids, but somehow that never seemed to be Polly's real life. People often asked why so public a person as Don and so private a person as Polly had married, for she cares nothing about the world outside her home, and there's no question that her indifference to politics has caused Don problems.

Because the people who support a politician want many things in return, but mostly they want the illusion of intimacy, the kisses, the hugs, the flesh-pressing that make them feel they are close to the candidate's heart. And they want that illusion of intimacy with his wife too.

Some politicians' wives are able to play that game. Some have been destroyed trying to play it. And some, like Polly—and Jackie Kennedy, a generation earlier—simply don't try. They shut the door, they preserve their privacy, and their children's, and in return they are hated, resented, and endlessly bad-mouthed by the idiots they refuse to pander to.

Don, to give him credit, recognizes Polly's uniqueness, and protects her. But it's getting harder now that he's running for President.

"Are you selling your stuff?" I asked with my celebrated savoir faire.

She smiled an angel's smile; she knew my heart.

"A place on East Seventy-seventh Street in New York sells it for me. I earned enough last year to pay the children's tuition."

"Fantastic. How about in Washington?"

She shook her head. "I don't want my things for sale here. You know, it'd get political. Fat lobbyists with cigars would buy them. Wouldn't that be awful? I really want to keep my work separate from Donny's."

While we talked she fixed tea on a little hotplate in the corner, and then we settled at either end of an old ruby-red sofa.

"Does he have a chance, Tommy? To be President? It seems so unreal."

I shrugged. "As good a chance as anybody. He has a lot going for him. It's just . . ."

"What?"

"Is he devious enough? There's a certain agility needed. The best candidates shape reality to suit their needs the way you shape your clay."

She laughed uncertainly. What she saw as cynicism, I saw as realism.

"Anyway," I concluded, "I'm going by the campaign office later on, and I'll get the lowdown then."

"I went when they opened the headquarters," Polly said, "but I haven't been back. That awful Harris Ratcliffe." She began to laugh. "I just hate to *look* at him."

"A thing of beauty he is not," I agreed.

"A tub of lard is more like it. I hope he thinks better than he looks."

"Being a slob is part of his job. Nobody trusts a campaign manager who's neat and trim—observe yon Cassius, and all that."

"I feel pressure to do more," she said. "Not from Don, he says it's up to me. But the staff wants a candidate's wife who's *active*. They always make it sound like I'm neurotic because I want to stay home and do my own work. Whatever I agree to do, they want more. What should I do, Tommy?"

"Do what feels right to you," I told her. "You'll take some

heat if you don't campaign, but that's better than going places where you'll be unhappy and everyone will know it."

"I know," she sighed. "I'd feel like a fool, listening to the same speech over and over. You're supposed to look sort of *rapt*. But it's hard to keep saying no. The *Post*'s Style section wants to do a piece on me, and I've been putting them off. But then you wonder if the longer you make them wait, the nastier they'll be."

"Do you know who they've assigned to it?" I asked.

She shook her head. "I hate those profiles they do of candidates' wives. All the anonymous quotes and gossip and psychobabble. They always ask the wife, 'And what about the Women on the Campaign Trail?' It's a great do-you-still-beat-your-wife question. Am I supposed to say, 'What women?' like I'm a complete dummy? Or say 'Oh, but my husband is a saint'?"

She lowered her head. "It's so undignified. I suppose it's fine to live in the White House, but people do such degrading things to get there."

"Polly, if anybody ever asks you anything about other women, all you have to say is . . ."

"Donny told me what you said about the woman on the beach."

"He *what*?"

"This morning, at breakfast, when I said you were coming over, he said, 'Oh, Tom came to see me last week, with some crazy story about a woman on the beach at Rehoboth.' And he said it was just somebody he talked to for a couple of minutes."

"That damn fool," I raged. "Polly, I would never have mentioned it to you. I don't know why he'd bring it up. Look, for what it's worth, I hear a hell of a lot of gossip, and I've never heard anything about Don and other women."

"Oh, I trust him," she said. "If I didn't, I wouldn't live with him. It's just that, you know, rumors get into print, and it's ugly."

49

I left Polly as I had found her, at her potter's wheel, serene, not quite of this world. I hoped things would go well for her. The media is a big dumb monster that sometimes destroys people without meaning to. It was impossible to say what it might do with someone as fragile as Polly. But I thought the best, the only, strategy was for her to be open, be herself, and hope that reporters had enough sense to recognize a gem when they saw one.

Something puzzled me as I left their home in Great Falls. Why the hell had Don told her the story about the Woman in the Dunes?

Was our White Hope hell-bent to self-destruct? Had this been a preemptive denial, fueled by a guilty conscience? Could it be that Senator Cool was a touch nervous on that particular issue?

Or was that my dirty mind at work again?

Allworth for President was operating out of a crumbling old townhouse in Southeast Washington, near the Marine Barracks about ten blocks from the Capitol.

You entered to typical campaign chaos: a switchboard where the phones never stopped ringing, people fighting over the Xerox machine, volunteers jammed into tiny rooms like clowns in a Volkswagen, eager yuppies dashing about self-importantly, grizzled old pros muttering beside the coffee machine, and pretty girls everywhere.

"Allworth for President, can you hold? Allworth for President, can you hold?"

I waited patiently until the sweet young thing at the switchboard caught up, then she said, "Can I help you, sir?"

I said pleasantly that I had an appointment with Harris Ratcliffe, but I was wounded by that "sir." Okay, maybe there's a touch of gray in my hair, maybe I'm twenty years her senior, but I kept thinking that, just a few campaigns back, that girl would have winked at me and said, "Hi! I'm Susie, let's ball!"

That is, after all, what campaigns are all about.

What did you think they were about, Innocent Reader, electing candidates?

Yes, candidates are elected as a by-product of the process, and maybe (don't bet on it) the world is sometimes a better place because Tweedledum won a famous victory over Tweedledee.

But what mostly happens is everybody fucks like rabbits.

How could it be otherwise? There you are, a happy few, young and crazed, thrown together on a battlefield. No one knows what they're doing, you're all broke and scared, the rest of the world is against you, bombs keep exploding all around, so naturally you huddle together for warmth.

That's what a presidential campaign is, a movable orgy, floating from city to city, party to party, hotel to hotel, bed to bed, and don't let anybody tell you different. It's once in a lifetime, London during the blitz, eat-drink-and-be-merry-for-tomorrow-you-may-get-zapped, and you'd have to be a damn fool, or maybe a saint, not to seize the opportunity.

Speaking of saints, in all the campaigns I've been in there's always been endless speculation about whether the candidate was joining in the fun. I mean, if press secretaries and speech-writers have groupies, imagine how The Man Himself could make out.

In one of my campaigns there was a lass named Linda who was blessed with the most incredible body in recent political history. Soon the candidate, who was reputedly a saint, took a certain interest in her, and she kept being promoted. From licking stamps (which she did with heart-stopping aplomb) to assistant press secretary to chief adviser on women's issues. "She really understands people," the candidate kept mumbling, eyes unfocused, mouth ajar.

Well, we lost that election, and in its bitter aftermath there was much speculation that if the candidate had focused more on his message and less on Linda the outcome might have been different and the future of the Free World brighter.

Plus, we would all have had jobs.

"Tullis, come on up," Harris Ratcliffe bellowed from his office upstairs overlooking the street, by far the headquarter's grandest.

He lurked behind his desk, clutching a Coke, puffing a Marlboro, mopping his sweaty face with a dirty handkerchief. He had not shaved that day and a foul odor arose from the vicinity of his feet.

In my experience, all campaign managers are slobs, but Ratcliffe was outstanding, a slob's slob. He waddled, he reeked; his clothing was filthy, his manner crude, his language vile. You would not have permitted this obscene creature into your home, yet Don Allworth had chosen him to guide his march to the White House. A strange business, politics.

"How's it going?" I asked with a buddy-buddy grin.

"This is all off the record, right?" Clearly, buddy-buddy wasn't going to fly.

"Right."

"It's murder. Mac McKenna and that damn Senate staff, they don't want him elected President, that way they might have to give up their cozy little Senate scam and share him with new people."

I shrugged. "It's always like that."

"Yeah, I know. They just piss me off."

He scratched his head vigorously, creating a blizzard of dandruff. "I heard you talked to his wife this morning."

"That's right."

"Jesus, what's with that woman? Doesn't she know he's running for President? Doesn't she fucking *care*?"

"Have you talked to her?"

"Talked to her? *Can* she talk? She floated through here one day, did her Mona Lisa number, and disappeared in a puff of smoke. Listen, I wish you'd tell her, if you're on her wavelength, that the American voters don't elect candidates with weird wives."

"She's not weird, Ratcliffe, she's a special lady. She's got class. She can add something to the campaign. If you handle her right."

"Handle her?" he exploded. "I never see her."

"She said she was doing two events a month."

"Big deal. She ought to be doing two a day, like the other wives."

"Why don't you hire some woman Polly approves, to schedule her and write for her? I'll tell Polly she ought to do two events a week. Try to find things she'll be comfortable with. Museums, arts and crafts, whatever. You've got to bring her along."

"Jeez, am I baby-sitting the broad?"

I shrugged. All candidates' wives were a problem, most of them far more so than Polly. I thought Ratcliffe was a fool. If nothing else, he should know that campaign managers who offend the candidate's wife almost always live to regret it.

"What happened in South Dakota?" I asked.

"They got overconfident, we got lucky."

"I heard this Wally Love helped a lot."

"He's some bozo out for a good time."

"Don wants me to check him out."

"He's crazy. You stay away from the guy. Everybody knows you're a pal of Don's."

"I'm a reporter after a story."

"Well, don't even hint you're talking for us. If this guy is legit, let him keep spending his money. But he's probably some nut. Every campaign is surrounded by nuts. Politics is their natural element."

He groped past his Falstaffian belly and to my horror began to take off his shoes. The stench was life-threatening. As I grew faint, he opened his drawer, took out two paper inserts, and slipped them into his grimy, shapeless shoes.

"Odor-Eaters," he explained.

I stumbled toward the door, but Ratcliffe came squishing after me. "Hold it, Tullis," he growled. "What's this crap about some broad on the beach?"

"It's something I heard. Don said there was nothing to it. I take his word for it."

"You do, but there's others who won't. He's too damn pretty, so we get all this gossip."

"Who do you think is behind it?"

"Maybe that damn Makito," Ratcliffe declared. "Because of the trade bill. Sneaky little bastards. They steal our markets, tax our stuff, and think we're gonna stand there with our thumb up our ass. Don's gonna get tough and it's gonna win some damn primaries for him."

I edged toward the door, but he wasn't through with me yet. "What's the poop on Mike Cunningham?"

"He left Addie for a girl in the bureau."

"This on the level?"

"What do you mean?"

"Is the girl for real? Or did somebody put her up to it? A lotta people wouldn't mind screwing him and the network both."

"As far as I know, it's just young love. Weren't you ever in love, Ratcliffe?"

"What about the network?"

"They've got a lot invested in Mike. They'll probably wait and see how it flies."

"Hasn't he got a morals clause in his contract? Moral turpitude? The bastard must be crazy."

"Men have given up thrones for the women they love," I reminded him.

"Yeah, but nobody ever gave up being a *network anchor*. That damn Cunningham—I don't give a rat's ass about him. But I don't want Addie to get hurt. That lady's been good to us."

He punched me lightly on the shoulder. "Hey, buddy, you

come by anytime—we're gonna elect us a President, right?"

I fled down the stairs, wanting only to escape into the fresh air of Capitol Hill, and then a door opened, two sad brown eyes met mine, and a decade melted away.

"Tom!"

She kissed me, held me close. Her name was Dinah O'Shea, and three campaigns back we'd been lovers. It was bittersweet to see her now, the girl of yesteryear abruptly in her late thirties, heavier, with streaks of silver in her rust-colored ponytail.

"I thought you were working for the governor of Oregon."

"He got beat. Then the campaign came along." She shrugged. "You know me, a campaign junkie."

"Weren't you married?"

"It didn't work. He was great in some ways, but he had a roving eye. How about you? I read your column."

"I'm okay. Still single."

"Going with anybody?"

I shrugged. "The column takes most of my time."

We were standing by the front door, with people flowing past us. She took my arm and led me out on the steps. This part of the Hill was mostly gentrified now, the townhouses restored and brightly painted, the streets thick with BMWs and Audis. We watched as a bunch of kids burst out of the headquarters and raced past us.

"They're all so young," I said.

"Like we were."

Dinah laughed. She had a wide, funny mouth whose sweetness I would always remember.

"These kids, I don't know, they're so serious. Our campaign was a crusade. For them, it's more like something good for their résumés."

"I just confronted that great American Harris Ratcliffe."

"That pig."

"I thought you might feel that way."

56

"He knows organization. But he doesn't know anything about people."

"What're you doing?"

"Fund-raising. You remember how we used to look down our noses at the money people? But the longer I'm in politics, the more I realize that's where it's at."

A fire engine wailed past us, chasing a false alarm.

"How's the fund-raising going?" I asked.

Dinah looked around before she spoke. "Oh, we're doing great. We may be doing too great."

"What do you mean?"

"I can't talk now," she said. "Could we have dinner?" She gave me her address.

A young woman called from the doorway. "Dinah, Mr. Iacocca's returning your call."

"See you then, stranger," she said.

I hugged her, then I was running for a cab, late for lunch with another lady.

10.

Gloria and I buzzed over to Adams-Morgan for a late lunch at Hazel's. Hazel is a wonderful black woman who serves up cool jazz and hot, Southern-style food: honey-fried chicken, barbecued ribs, black-eyed peas, cornbread, the works. Clearly more than a couple of exiles from Dixie could resist.

"I do believe Ah've died and gone to heaven," Gloria cried, as we stumbled back into the blazing reality of Columbia Road. Across the street the authorities were booting some poor bastard's car. We picked our way around the bodies on the sidewalk, slipped into Gloria's Ferrari, and hastened back to the more subtle jungle of Georgetown.

Gloria lives on Thirty-first Street, my favorite street in Washington, perhaps in the world. A quiet, tree-lined, Georgian avenue only six blocks long, anchored on the south by Larry McMurtry's dusty, vaguely ominous rare-books shop, in the middle by the massive and brooding Chez Bingham, and on the north by the glories of Dumbarton Oaks. Along this seemingly placid street live not only Gloria and my intrepid publisher, Harriet Dingley, but a galaxy of heiresses, courtesans, and kooks too improbable to enumerate.

But, damn my eyes, I digress. At her place, Gloria checked her messages, kicked off her shoes, and opened a bottle of Le Montrachet—she refuses, on principle, to drink wine that costs under a hundred dollars a bottle.

There was a hell of a racket outside. Gloria was having a new pool put in. The old one was shaped wrong or needed painting or something. Gloria, like many women of means, endlessly and compulsively remakes her house and grounds.

In time she took a bejeweled antique box out of her dresser drawer.

"Want some?" she asked.

"The wine's fine."

She did two lines with fierce efficiency. "Why don't you do coke?"

"I did once."

She started a Violent Femmes CD, a song about a man throwing his daughter down a well. I tried not to listen.

"You didn't like it? The coke?"

"Loved it. For an hour I was witty, wise, lovable, everything I've always dreamed of being. But I was afraid I'd wind up like one of those monkeys."

"Monkeys?"

"In tests. They make them choose between cocaine and food. They do coke until they starve."

"Humans, being somewhat more reflective than monkeys, should be able to manage both," she declared.

"So you would think."

"So what's the poop on Mike and Addie?"

I shrugged. "I haven't talked to him yet. A network PR type called and appealed to my better self—personal tragedy, don't make things worse, et cetera."

"I trust you told him to bug off."

"Her. I told her I was deeply troubled. She hinted that poor Mike was reacting to Addie's carryings-on."

Gloria's eyes lit up. "Anything to that?"

"It's just the network's line, trying to protect their investment. They're such bastards."

"Stranger things have happened."

It pleased Gloria to think that other women's morals were no more elevated than her own. In truth, most women tended not to fling themselves into sexual adventures as recklessly as Gloria.

I had, just a year before, rescued Gloria from the burning building of one romance. She had been seeing an aging Latin American diplomat, an old roué with a waxed mustache and a girdle, whose appeal to her was purely novelistic: she was coaxing from him amazing tales of Rubirosa, Aly Khan, and other of his playboy pals in their prime. He swore, for example, that Rubirosa had gone to Lloyds of London and attempted to insure his erection for ten million dollars.

Anyway, the old bandit lived in a mansion in Potomac and insisted on sending his chauffeur to bring Gloria for evenings at his home. Well, it was a long, dull ride from Georgetown to Potomac, so Gloria seduced the chauffeur, who was young, creamy-skinned, and flat-bellied, and had the additional charm of speaking no English. ("The only man who never bored me," she said.)

Alas, one evening the diplomat discovered Gloria practicing her Good Neighbor Policy in the backseat of his Bentley; he proceeded to shoot the chauffeur dead, and very nearly did the same for Gloria. A bad scene, but I had some dirt on the U.S. Attorney and was able to keep Gloria's name out of the papers. Officially, the chauffeur died in a tragic accident, mistaken by his employer for a terrorist.

"What's with you and Sammy Shiner?" I asked.

Gloria sighed. "Nothing's with us. He took me to the party."

"No romance?"

"Be serious. He's gay."

"Gay? Wasn't he married?"

"That doesn't mean anything. He worries about his image. He wants to be taken seriously as a molder of public opinion. So he squires high-profile ladies."

"Incredible," I muttered.

"Thomas, for a man in your position, you can be enchantingly naive. There are scads of gay married men in our fair city."

"For example?"

She shrugged impatiently. "Jock Dugan."

"Hey, I just met his wife. At Buzz Makito's party. A nice lady, a shrink."

"He needs a shrink. She's his second wife. The first one caught on too late, and he had to buy her off. With this one, he cut a deal up front."

"Why would she do it?"

"Wake up, lover. There are certain amenities to being a Senator's wife. And there are precious few to being a single woman over forty."

"He's such a repulsive little dwarf."

"Beauty is in the eye of the beholder, ducks. She lives in a big house, she goes to nice parties, and he leaves her alone. Sexwise, he goes his way and she goes hers. The way I hear it, she favors her patients."

"Male or female?"

"Yes."

I changed the subject again. "What happened to Jeff Willingham last night? You spoke to him, and he went to pieces."

Gloria's chuckle was truly evil. "Tom, you cannot print this. I'm saving it for my next novel."

"Agreed."

"The charming Senator has the morals of a gerbil. He married two perfectly nice women, both for their money, and treated them both like dirt. More wine?"

"Sure."

She called downstairs and a moment later her Cuban girl arrived with another bottle of Le Montrachet. This is the wine Victor Hugo said should be drunk on one's knees. We live well, here in Gossip Central.

"A few months ago, Kristin Hope had Jeff to dinner. A lovely party. But what does our dashing Senator do? He spends the evening drooling over Kris's Swedish *au pair* girl, this child of eighteen. Bibi, she's called. Hardly the way for a man of forty-five to ingratiate himself with women his own age."

"Okay, but why the seizure last night?"

"Patience, doll. So the next day, Kris and I talk. She's Swedish, you know—Bibi's the daughter of a friend back home, which made it worse. And we hit upon a plan."

She sipped the wine; her tongue flicked in and out like a snake's.

"So Kris calls his Senate office. 'Tell him Bibi is callink,' she says, reverting to her Swedish accent. That got Jeff to the phone fast.

" 'Hello, my dear—I was just thinking of you,' says Senator Sexpot. I was listening on the other line.

" 'I thought about you all night,' Kris says. 'You're zo handsome and zexy. I'll die if I don't zee you again.' She should have been an actress—she sounded absolutely eighteen and mad to do it.

" 'When?' says our Jeff.

" 'Tonight. They're going away. I'll be here alone, dreamink of your beautiful body.'

" 'I'll be there,' he says. Tommy, he was like a dog in heat. I'll play you the tape sometime."

I shuddered. The guy is a jerk, but in this cruel and unequal war between the sexes I had to have some sympathy for my fellow male.

"She told him she would leave the back door open. He was to come to her room at the top of the stairs. 'I'll wait for you in zee bed, beautiful Mr. Senator.'

" 'Call me Jeff,' our Romeo says. So, that night, he parks outside, the house is dark, he lets himself in, he tippy-toes up the stairs, he reaches the door of the bedroom, and by the moonlight he can just make out a figure in the bed.

" 'Take hoff your clothes, darlink Jeff,' says this sweet Swedish voice. 'Oh, please hurry—I vant your beautiful body!'

" 'Don't worry, I'm coming, you'll have me,' he says, tearing off his clothes. She's moaning, 'Hurry, darlink,' and he's panting, 'I'm coming,' and finally he's naked as a jaybird. And guess what happens."

"Oh God, oh God," I moaned.

"So. The lights go on and six female voices are crying, 'Surprise, surprise.' It's not Bibi in the bed, but Kris, fully clothed and pointing a camera. The rest of us leap out from hiding. Flashbulbs are popping. And there is Senator Jeff, armed only with an impressive but rapidly wilting erection.

" 'Fuck us, darlink, fuck us all!' we cried, but Jeff wasn't up to the challenge. The boy turned tail, literally, hotfooted it down the stairs, still in his birthday suit, and leapt into his Jag to make his getaway. Meanwhile, one of the girls had tied tin cans to his bumper, and we chased him all the way back to the Watergate, honking the horn and screaming, 'Help, police, stop the mad rapist!'

"So, that's why Jeff goes to pieces when I say 'Hello, darlink.' It's like Pavlov's dog. A phrase or two in Swedish and he falls apart. Oh, and we sent him one of the pictures we took. Anonymously. He's running for reelection, and perhaps he has the idea that one of those prints might turn up back home."

"You wouldn't do that, of course."

Gloria tossed the shimmering mane of her hair. "Oh, probably not. But men like Jeff are such pigs. It is a joy to see one of them twist slowly in the wind."

I thought of a book I'd read years before about Indians. The worst thing that could happen to a white man was to be turned over to the squaws. The braves would scalp you, but the squaws would roast you over a spit, or skin you alive, or otherwise prolong your agony for days upon end.

"Gloria," I said. "Please do not ever become angry at me."

"You're such a sweet boy," she said, stretching like a cat.

I wanted to go, but Gloria was hitting her stride.

"You saw Claudia Simpson at Buzz Makito's party?"

"Yeah, she looked good."

"Her roots showed. But the point is who she was with."

"I didn't notice."

"Charlie Yawley, the Veep's press secretary."

"He goes with Claudia?"

"Wake up and live, lover. She's been the Veep's honey forever, and now he's thinking of running for La Casa Blanca, so the Veep dumps her, but gently, because she knows too much. Good old loyal Charlie is playing the beard. I hear he may marry her."

"What's interesting is if he wins," I said. "Does Claudia emerge as the Royal Mistress?"

"They say he's crazy about her," Gloria sighed. "I'm sure I don't know why. Not that he's any prize. I think she must do it in a basket."

The phone rang. As Gloria murmured to her caller—her use of the telephone was blatantly erotic—I studied her sleek, pitiless face. There is, I must concede, a dark side to my friend Gloria. Her early life in Texas was not easy; it involved a succession of foster homes, and at least two cases of rape by her pious Baptist guardians. When other kids tormented her about her ragged clothing, she responded by sending them anonymous death threats. By her early teens she had succumbed to kleptomania, a weakness that led her to two traumatic confinements in the Texas State Home for Delinquent Girls.

Neither her marriage to a millionaire, her success as a novelist, nor twelve years of analysis have cured her illness; I have twice been summoned to bail her out of jail for pointless thefts, both of which she stubbornly denied in the face of overwhelming evidence of her guilt.

Gloria is too rich and too beloved by the media to be ignored, but the Capital is filled with those who hate and fear her. I have often defended her against those who compare her to a vulture, a rattlesnake, or worse, and I have often been warned that in time she will turn on me as she has turned on so many others who tried to be her friend.

Yet I am drawn to her, not only professionally, as an invaluable source, but by a deeper, darker undertow. I find her unique, a work of art, a *monstre sacré,* as gloriously Gloria as Lennon was Lennon, Chaplin Chaplin, Reagan Reagan, or Picasso Picasso. Perhaps in her own good time the monster will devour me, yet she fascinates me, perfect in her imperfection.

When she put down the phone, Gloria's face held a look of absolute bewilderment.

"How totally bizarre," she said.

"What?"

"That was a man I know at State. He wants me to go to Cuba. They have a cultural-exchange program, leaving next week. I mean, I am not exactly Joyce Carol Oates, culturewise, but he said it would be fine."

"So go," I said impatiently.

I had a parting thought. "On Jeff Willingham, maybe I could carry a blind item. Something enigmatic. Say a few Swedish friends gave him a surprise party."

"Tom—you promised!"

"It would twist the knife, drive him bananas, and you'd still have the whole story for your novel."

Her eyes glowed with cocaine and malice. "Let me think about it."

"Of course."

She followed me to the porch. Men were painting the house across the street; normal-looking people strolled by on the sidewalk.

"Tommy, what do you know about The Boys' Club?"

I drew a blank. "Like the YMCA, you mean?"

"It's some men. I heard Sammy Shiner talking on the phone one night. They were going to have a meeting. Something about politics."

"What do they do?"

"I don't know. But when I asked him he was mad as hell. That's not like Sammy. Usually when he does something nasty, he brags."

I shook my head. "I haven't heard a thing."

"I've never seen Sammy so upset. He was truly ugly. He squeezed my arm, saying I was never to mention it again. He *bruised* me, the nasty little fag. I think you should check it out."

Something in her eyes made me shudder. "Sure," I said. "Sure."

She tilted her cheek for me to kiss—an imperial gesture, vaguely disdainful, as a queen might expect a courtier to kneel and kiss the hem of a royal gown—and then I fled to the relative safety of the Georgetown afternoon.

11.

Dinah lived with her cat, Chester, in a basement apartment in Adams-Morgan. We had a beer there and she played
Joni Mitchell's album *Blue,* the theme music of our long-ago
romance. But now the music depressed me, and so did her
little apartment, so I suggested we take a walk. The evening
was unseasonably balmy and people had flocked into the
streets. Adams-Morgan was hot, with chi-chi shops and
trendy restaurants everywhere and a brutal traffic problem.

We settled for coffee in a sidewalk café on Columbia Road.
Next door a fortune-teller was plying her trade from someone's front steps, and across the street a couple of Latinos
were parking cars in a vacant lot at five bucks a shot.

"It's like a circus," I said.

"It's real," Dinah said. "There's a lot of crime. It's changing
too fast. But I don't know where else I'd live. In Portland,

when I was married, we lived in the suburbs, and it was death."

We talked about her life. Things rarely went right for Dinah. She was still in high school when she was tear-gassed in Chicago in 1968. God bless her, in 1973 she was arrested on federal charges for stealing about a hundred of the special "No Parking—Presidential Inaugural Route" signs during Nixon's second inauguration. She still had one on her wall.

Such a good person, so much bad luck. Her lovers stayed married, her husbands ran around, her candidates lost. But she kept following her rainbow, imagining a pot of gold ahead. She told me about her son, who lived with his father in Portland.

"It's best for him now," she said. "Till I get my act together. I swear this campaign is my last one. If Allworth loses, America will have to save itself!"

I urged her to get a job on the Hill, where salaries were good and there was a measure of security.

"Oh, Tommy, the Hill is so bloody dull. If Allworth bombs, I might join the Peace Corps. Just go live in a mud hut, Africa maybe, for a couple of years."

I didn't argue. A mud hut in Africa might be a step up from her dreary little basement in Adams-Morgan.

"Dinah, what's going on in the campaign?"

She stirred her coffee glumly. "I don't exactly know," she said. "My end of it is solicitation. I call people and say, 'Hey, the train is leaving the station, better get aboard.' I look for supporters who'll max-out at a thousand dollars and get their friends to do the same. When the money actually comes in, there are other people who deal with it. The thing that bothers me is, I think there's cash floating around."

"Illegally."

"Sure. We can only accept up to fifty dollars in cash. More than that we have to send back. Serious donations are all by check now. Each check is photostated when it comes in and a copy goes to the FEC."

"I'd never thought about it," I said, "but those limits are unnatural. A thousand bucks is nothing for people who take politics seriously. There've got to be all kinds of people scheming to get around those laws."

"You know it," Dinah said. "And there are plenty of candidates who want their money any way they can get it. You never get enough money in a campaign. It's like getting enough love in real life."

"Dinah, what do you think is going on?"

"I think Ratcliffe has a slush fund for the field people. And he could be siphoning off some for himself. And some of our people think there's a pattern to some of the checks coming in."

"What kind of pattern?"

"I'm not sure. But it seems like some days we get a lot of checks from one city or state, like something organized that we don't know about. But, let's face it, if you send us a thousand bucks, we don't question your motives real hard."

Across the street a powder-blue Mercedes slammed into a black TransAm. A big ape with sideburns and tattoos jumped out of the TransAm with a baseball bat and started breaking windows in the Mercedes and calling its terrified driver various unpleasant ten- and twelve-letter words. A crowd gathered to watch.

"Have you heard about this guy Wally Love, who's running an independent pro-Allworth operation?" I asked her. The TransAm roared away, to cheers from the crowd.

"Sure, he's a legend. Like Robin Hood or D. B. Cooper or Kilroy."

"You don't sound worried about him."

"What's to worry? He's legal. As long as he doesn't talk to us. And, believe me, if he walked up to this table right now I'd be gone so fast it'd make your head spin. It's the illegal stuff that scares me. I don't know what to do. Keep my mouth shut? Go to Ratcliffe and maybe get fired? Or go to the candidate and maybe be wrong?"

"If you come up with hard evidence, I could go to Don with it."

"That'd be great," she said. "You know him pretty well, don't you?"

"I've known him a long time."

"What's he really like? I mean, I shouldn't be doing this, working for peanuts in another campaign at my age, but I think maybe Allworth is the one who can get the country back on track. Or am I crazy?"

There was a case to be made that she was crazy, but I didn't want to make it. People like Dinah need encouragement.

But what was Don Allworth really like? I didn't know what to tell her. Don was an impressive man. Maybe he had the potential to be a good President—I hoped so—but I didn't know what dreams or demons fueled his relentless pursuit of power.

Somerset Maugham once wrote that he'd known many actors and enjoyed their wit and vitality, but he never thought of them as human beings. I feel that way about politicians. Insofar as they are successful, they became larger than life: more than human, and less than human too.

But that was not what Dinah needed to hear.

"Don's intelligent, he's compassionate, and he might be a great President," I declared.

Dinah beamed, and I was glad. Who knows? It might even be true.

We stopped at Hazel's for a nightcap. The trio played "Secret Love," the Doris Day tune from the fifties. Dinah put her hand on mine and smiled a secret smile. She knew not to talk.

Outside her apartment, she asked if I wanted to come in. I'd been thinking about it. "I don't think so."

"Oh, Tommy, we're not too old, are we?"

"Too wise, maybe. It wouldn't be the same."

Call me a romantic, but I thought the memory we had was too nice to mess up.

She groped for her key, then looked up in alarm. "I almost forgot. Do you remember Doyle Kane?"

It was a name I hadn't heard in years. "Sure. From Don's Senate staff."

"That's right. A sweet guy and a whiz with numbers. He moved over to the campaign, but when Ratcliffe took over they had a fight and he went to work for Craxton. He called me the other day, really spooked. He thinks the same things are happening there that I think are happening in our campaign. I wish you'd talk to him. He's about to resign, he's so shook."

I might have pressed her for more details, but I was tired, the moment was past. "Have him call me."

"I will. Good night, Tommy."

We hugged for a long moment, then I left her there, in her basement apartment with her cat and her dreams.

12.

Wally Love was a pear-shaped fellow in his mid-sixties with a red face, a bulbous nose, a monk's thatch of graying hair, and blue eyes that truly did twinkle.

We met in a restaurant called the Rusty Scupper on the Baltimore waterfront. Wally greeted me warmly, recommended the crab cakes, and asked the waitress for iced tea. "I hope I haven't kept you waiting," I said.

"No, no, I just got here myself. I stopped by the Baltimore Museum of Art. All those wonderful Matisses. And that lovely Picasso of his wife and child. That's what this election is all about, Mr. Tullis, our children and grandchildren."

"Call me Tom," I said.

"Call me Wally."

"Wally, as I understand it, you've been spending your own money on behalf of Don Allworth in some of the primary states. But you haven't talked much to the media."

"I move around a lot, and reporters haven't seemed to catch up with me. You were more persistent than most."

I got out my notebook. "Would you tell me why you're spending all this money on Allworth?"

His blues eyes widened. "To make him President."

"I understand that. But why? Do you know him?"

"Never met the man. Don't intend to. The law says . . ."

"I know what it says. But why Allworth, instead of Craxton or one of the others?"

"Research, my boy, research. I've studied the candidates. Read their speeches, followed their votes. I've been entirely scientific. And my conclusion was that Senator Allworth would make the best President. I gave them all a grade, and he scored ninety-three out of a possible one hundred. Nobody else broke ninety."

"How much money are you prepared to spend on behalf of Allworth?"

"All it takes."

The waitress brought our crab cakes. Across the harbor, school kids were marching into the big new aquarium.

"How much money do you have, Wally?"

"Oh, I don't know. My accountant says if I give away more than twenty million I'll die in the poorhouse."

"I thought you were in the newspaper business."

"I was, for forty years. Editor and publisher of the *Parker County Gazette*. Finest little weekly in Oregon. We won twenty-three first prizes in statewide competition while I was editor. Should have won a Pulitzer, too, for exposing a crooked sheriff."

"Forgive me, but in my experience newspaper editors don't accumulate twenty million dollars."

Wally laughed. He was nicely dressed, in a brown tweed coat, gray flannel pants, a button-down shirt, and a regimental tie.

"You're quite right, my boy, quite right. You see, my grandfather was a pioneer in the lumber business. My father founded the paper. All these years, we've owned a good deal of land, harvested the timber, and not thought much about it. But then the cities grew out to our land. We started getting offers.

"But I never sold my land outright. I always took a percentage of the deal. Subdivisions, office buildings, shopping malls. It does add up."

"But why spend it on a politician? Why not collect art or go live in France or whatever your fantasy is?"

Wally's eyes twinkled. He was a homely little man and yet there was something radiant about him.

"Tom, I've got the biggest fantasy of all. I want to make this world a better place. I've got five children and twelve grandchildren. I can give them plenty of money when I'm gone. But what good is money if our air and water are polluted, if our country is blighted with poverty and hatred and the fear of nuclear war? I can't solve those problems, but I might be able to elect a President who can."

I was scribbling like mad. You didn't have to be a genius to know that Wally was a hell of a story.

"How much money have you spent on Allworth so far?"

A sheepish grin. "I haven't been counting. I'll file with the FEC on April 15, but I doubt if I'll add it all up before then."

"I heard you spent about thirty thousand dollars in Iowa and sixty thousand dollars in New Hampshire."

"That sounds high. But I won't deny it."

"Is this all on media?"

"Oh sure, it's the only cost-effective way to go."

"And you're starting to do TV spots?"

"Absolutely, that's the name of the game. Even an old country editor like me knows that."

"If Allworth wins, do you want some office? Secretary of State or something?"

Wally laughed until he was red in the face. "No, no, no," he said. "All I want to do is get home to my family, back to God's country. You couldn't pay me to live in Washington."

I pushed him as far as I could on his plans, but soon Wally was restless. "I've got a big afternoon ahead," he said. "A lot of money to spend."

The last I saw of Wally, he was marching briskly toward a GMC Jimmy, a tweed cap on his head, a walking stick in one hand, off to elect Don Allworth.

That Saturday, Wyoming held its primary, and Don won an unexpected victory, much like his upset in South Dakota. A few calls to Casper and Cheyenne convinced me that Wally's last-minute media buys had done more for victory than the ragtag Allworth organization out there.

As best I could see, Don Allworth was the luckiest son of a bitch who ever ran for office. Because it looked like Wally Love was for real, had twenty million dollars to spend, and was hell-bent to make him President.

13.

I reached my office Monday morning all primed to write my Wally Love piece, only to be blindsided by an unexpected call.

"Collect from Holly. Will you pay?"

I paid.

"Hi, Daddy."

"Hi, sweetheart. How are you?"

My guess was that I already knew the answer. I hadn't heard from her since she dropped out of school several months before, and if she was calling it probably meant trouble.

"Not so good."

"*Where* are you?"

"Laredo, Texas."

I shuddered. Nothing good could happen in Laredo, Texas.

"What's wrong?"

"The Border Patrol searched the car and found some dope and Vern's been busted. They say I can go if I make bail but I don't have any money."

"How much?"

"Two pounds."

"I mean how much bail."

"Five hundred."

"Where do I send it?"

"Western Union."

"I'll send a thousand. You catch the next flight to D.C. Or to Boston. I talked to the dean; they might take you back."

"I can't leave Vern."

Give me credit. I did not scream, "To hell with Vern!" at the top of my lungs. "Have you called his parents?"

"Oh, they're such jerks."

"Dammit, they're his parents!"

"Do you have to yell? I've had cops yelling at me for two hours. Not to mention the body-cavity search."

"Look, I'll send the money. But please get out of there."

"Thanks, Daddy."

"Baby, call me, let me know what's happening, okay?"

"I guess."

I put down the phone, torn by all the rage and frustration that is the lot of the fathers of daughters in this enlightened age.

A great story for someone, I mused darkly.

GOSSIP'S GIRL NABBED IN BORDER BUST

Funny as hell, if it wasn't you. I sent the money, brooded on my sins, and tried to focus on Wally Love, and the phone rang again.

This time it was Addie's lawyer with a tip. Mike was out of town, this was his girlfriend's day off, and I should talk to her while the getting was good. I jumped at the idea; anything to escape the endless torture of the telephone.

The girl's name was Robin. She had an apartment in Glover Park, a pleasant, tree-shaded community above Georgetown. I knocked on her door, identified myself as a friend of Mike's, and only when I was inside revealed that I was a reporter.

Robin was slender and lovely, with intelligent eyes, sun-streaked blond hair, and as bright a smile as I'd seen in years.

Not that she was smiling now.

"I don't want any publicity," she said, fingering her bangs.

"Robin, one of the most famous men in America has left his wife for you," I reminded her.

"I didn't want that."

"What did you want?"

"Are you going to quote me?"

"I'll paraphrase you. If I want a direct quote, I'll clear it with you."

That seemed to satisfy her, not that it should have. Quotes are someone else telling a story; give me the facts and I'll tell it my way.

She settled on the sofa with her long legs tucked under her. Out the window, we could see kids running around the playground at the Stoddert School.

"What did I want? To do my job, to enjoy Washington, maybe to get a regular job with the network later on. I love TV. It's so exciting. People kill for those jobs."

"So you met Mike."

"It was flattering. In his world I'm nothing. A student. My father works in a factory. But he was so nice to me. I didn't even think, you know, romance or sex. He was just this nice man . . ."

"Twenty-odd years older than you."

"He took me to Jean-Pierre and it was like royalty had arrived. He ordered this wonderful wine. We talked about journalism. About the famous people he knows. About writing, Hemingway."

"Mike's very literary," I said.

"I wanted to learn from him. About news, about my career. I thought he wanted to help me."

"You're a very pretty girl, Robin."

"I've never even dated anybody older than thirty."

"Did you fall in love with him?"

She nipped at a hangnail. "He came here one night. He said he'd never known anyone like me. That he'd never felt like this before. It was exciting. He is attractive, for his age. You know it's crazy, but you think, Okay, why not? No, not love. Curiosity maybe."

"You knew he was married."

"It didn't seem to bother him." Then, lowering her voice and her eyes: "Do you know her? His wife?"

"I've known both of them for a long time."

"What's she like?"

"Addie? She's wonderful."

"He made her sound, I don't know, tough."

"I'll bet he did. Robin, what do you want? To marry him?"

She looked at me in amazement. "Are you crazy? I've got a boyfriend at school who'll freak out if he hears about this. I just want to go back and get my degree. This is just, you know, something that happened."

She fought back tears. "Do you think I've been terrible?"

I shrugged. "Your only sin was being too young and too pretty. Although, as a general rule, I'd advise you to avoid married men in the future."

"No shit," she said bitterly.

I asked a few more questions, but Robin had said all she wanted to say. She looked confused, hurt. Part of me wanted to comfort her, but more of me knew better. Poor Mike hadn't known better. For a man our age a girl that age is a gift-wrapped bomb.

But that was not my problem. My problem was a deadline. Therefore I holed up at home for two days, took no calls, and knocked out my column and a separate Wally Love story.

When I returned to the real world, Super Tuesday had come and gone. Don had won four states, Craxton had won four, and no other candidate had taken more than one. Still a horse race.

My piece on Wally came out on Friday headlined ALLWORTH'S SECRET WEAPON?, and caused a stir. Reporters and political types called, wanting to know how to find Wally, or what the "real story" was.

Don Allworth called from Chicago. "It's all true," I told him. "The man has twenty million dollars and he's willing to spend it all to elect you."

"There's *got* to be a catch," Don grumbled.

"You scored ninety-three on his test. You're the best man. It's all scientific."

"Don't be sarcastic. It's too good to be true."

"Get it while you can," I advised.

I had a lot of calls backed up. Unfortunately none of them was from Mike Cunningham, whom I'd been trying to reach. Even his whereabouts were unknown; there were reports that he'd taken refuge at the Woodward Inn in Georgetown, but this was not clear.

I did, however, have three calls from Doyle Kane, the man who Dinah said suspected financial misdeeds in the Craxton campaign.

I remembered him, of course. It was strange that he would reenter my life now.

We met at my nadir. I had left a wife and quit a job. Broke, depressed, rootless, I took a furnished apartment on Capitol Hill and signed on to write speeches for a Senator.

Doyle and I were thrown together in a tiny, windowless Senate office. He was a small, nervous, vaguely handsome young man with a wispy mustache who worked in campaign finance. He wanted to be friends; I did not—that was the essence of our relationship. Doyle had an eager, puppy-dog quality that I found maddening. I treated him curtly, when I recognized him at all.

Then one bleak October day my candidate delivered one of my speeches in a cold rain; he was under an umbrella, I was not. I was soaked to the skin, and soon wracked with chills and fever. It was pneumonia, although I did not accept that fact. Given my loathing of doctors, not to mention my lack of money, I chose to tough it out. I stayed in bed, drank vodka, and told myself this "cold" would pass.

I was in my second day of delirium when Doyle appeared at my bedside. He came by on his lunch hour and persuaded the janitor to let him in. He took my temperature, made soup, let in air, called a doctor. For twenty-four hours, until the fever broke, he stayed with me. I awoke one morning and found Doyle asleep in a chair beside my bed, and myself weak but coherent again.

Over my feeble objections he stayed to fix my lunch, clean my apartment, change my sheets. He returned the next day to check on me. I thanked him, but as I grew stronger I found my aversion to him returning.

By the time I recovered, the Senator no longer needed my services, and I blundered into my job at the *Post*. Doyle called two or three times, suggesting lunch.

I turned him down.

I should have been kind to this person who had been so kind to me. And yet he unnerved me, set my teeth on edge. Perhaps I hated that he had seen me so helpless, I who took such pride in my precious independence, or perhaps I was repelled by his pitiful quest for intimacy.

For whatever reason, I saw no more of Doyle Kane, the Good Samaritan who perhaps had saved my life.

Now, nearly a decade later, he was calling, at Dinah's urging, to pour out some tale of campaign intrigue.

And I no more wanted to talk to him than I had after my illness.

I knew I should deal with him, should do my job. That was obvious. But I didn't *want* to, and one of the glories of the gossip game is that I jolly well make my own rules.

81

I told myself that Wally Love was all I needed to write about campaign finance for a while, that all campaigns were crooked and nobody gave a damn. People want to read about a colorful character like Wally tossing his millions away, but they didn't want to read about laundered money and fake bank accounts and all that CPA crap. And, even if they wanted it, I wasn't the one to give it to them.

I told our switchboard, therefore, that if Doyle Kane called again, I was permanently out.

14.

I was embroiled with a lissome Brit named Annabelle when news of the Polly flap reached me.

Annabelle was the happy ending to an otherwise grim week. My daughter's whereabouts were a mystery, I couldn't find Mike Cunningham, Doyle Kane kept calling, and some bastard stole the tape deck out of my car.

Then, at an embassy party on Saturday night, along came Annabelle: a Julie Christie lookalike soon to return to London and in search of happy memories. We exchanged meaningful glances, ditched the embassy party, caught the late show at Blues Alley, and soon hastened to my place to consummate our brief encounter.

The next morning, I asked if she wanted breakfast. "Just a hot roll with honey," she said lewdly, and I knew the honor of American manhood rested on my frail shoulders.

Did I explain that Annabelle was in publishing? Who says books can't corrupt a girl's mind?

The contest began, a veritable Bunker Hill of the bedroom, and after an hour, with me at the brink of a coronary and Annabelle crying, "Don't stop! For God's sake, don't stop!" the accursed phone rang.

Not any phone. The hot line. The unlisted number I give only to Major Sources.

I cursed but answered. Annabelle cursed too.

Astoundingly, a third person began cursing: "Tullis, you asshole, I hope you're happy!"

"What did he say?" asked alarmed Annabelle.

It took me a moment to recognize the unwelcome caller.

"What's with you, Ratcliffe?" I yelled.

"Don't you read the Sunday papers?" the campaign manager yelled back. "Look at the Style section. You're the one who said how great she'd be with the media!"

I raced to the front porch for the *Post*. Inside, my worst fears were realized.

Polly had given her interview to the *Post*. Oh boy, had she given one.

CANDIDATE ALLWORTH'S WIFE SAYS POTTERY YES, POLITICS NO

The story almost broke my heart. It was just Polly talking. Just Polly being sweet, irreverent, apolitical Polly, but the reporter had done nothing to give her a context. She had, instead, chosen the easier route of presenting Polly as a freak.

The lead was Polly talking about her potting, and all the fine craftspeople she knew, and how so much of the dishes and furniture that Americans bought was just "mass-produced junk." She confided that she'd be happier without a TV in her home because she hated to see her kids watching all those "idiot shows." And that her younger children had gone to private schools because "I've about given up on the public schools." Finally, she added, "Sometimes I wonder if it matters who's President, because we always seem to have wars and crime and poverty and all these problems."

Alas, poor Polly, she had spoken the unspeakable. Americans don't want to be told that their homes are filled with junk, that their favorite TV shows are designed for idiots, that their kids are illiterate, that their country is a mess.

I roamed the bedroom, reading the article, cursing and groaning. Annabelle, meanwhile, lay stiff as a board, a sheet pulled up to her chin.

Finally, I realized there was nothing I could do for Polly, but much that Annabelle and I still might do for one another. It took a half hour of flattery and sweet talk to rouse her from her sulk, but at last she was once again crying, "Don't stop! Don't stop!"

And then, God help me, the doorbell rang.

And rang. And rang. And rang.

"Bloody hell!" cried the lissome Brit.

Raving incoherently, I threw on my robe and marched to the door. If my own sainted mother had awaited me I might well have thrown her down the steps. Instead, I confronted a wiry man with sad eyes and thinning hair. In my rage, I did not immediately recognize him.

"Tom?" he stammered.

"Who the hell are you?" I howled.

"Don't you remember me? Doyle, Doyle Kane. I've called and called. About the campaign. Nobody will listen. It's just so awful."

I am not proud of what happened next. Clearly a man in my profession should receive informants day or night; that goes with the territory. Moreover, I was indebted to Doyle; I owed him my time and attention.

But *coitus interruptus* does not lead to good manners or good journalism; it drives men mad.

"I can't talk now!" I shouted. "Go away! Call me tomorrow!"

He pleaded, seized my arm, insisted it was urgent, life or

death, but I would not be moved. I shoved him away and slammed the door.

And returned to my bedroom.

Annabelle was dressed and calling a cab. I begged her to reconsider, but she was having none of it. "Seems rather a madhouse here," were her parting words.

I went to the kitchen, opened a beer, and turned on the radio. As I'd feared, Polly had made the hourly news. A pro-Craxton union president ranted about how Senator All-worth's wife owed an apology to every working man and woman in America for saying they produced junk.

Because it was Sunday, a slow news day, Polly's remarks were becoming a full-fledged controversy, not quite on a level with Jimmy Carter's "lust in my heart" confession, but right up there with Nancy Reagan consulting her astrologer and Governor Romney being brainwashed and Betty Ford saying she would not be astounded if her eighteen-year-old daughter tried sex.

I felt terrible for having urged Polly to be open with the media. It's such a rotten game. Reporters bitch about politicians who "manage" the news, but when someone like Polly tries to be honest and candid they get screwed every time.

Finally I called Polly. "I really blew it, didn't I?" she sighed. "It didn't occur to me that they'd only use little bits of what I said. It made me sound so dumb."

"It wasn't your fault."

"I don't know whose else it was. The reporter was so young and sweet. She kept smiling and nodding at everything I said."

"Never trust a reporter who smiles."

"Don't you smile?" she asked wistfully.

"Only when I'm about to screw somebody," I admitted. "What does Don say?"

"Nothing. He just read the story and left for the airport. I called his press secretary. He said they were going to have a meeting."

"Suppose I come over and we talk. I know what I think you should do, and I'm not sure those idiots at the campaign have any sense."

"I'd love it if you came."

When I parked in front of Polly's house that evening, two Secret Service agents stopped me. Polly hadn't told them I was coming, so I had to wait until she came and approved me. I was fuming by then. I've dealt with the Secret Service over the years, and I'm not real crazy about them. Basically what they are is bureaucrats with guns, a deadly combination.

Polly and I settled in the kitchen, and she opened a sensational Côtes-du-Rhône. Lobbyists were always sending Don wine, and neither of them drank much or knew good wine from bad.

We watched in dismay as her flap led the evening news. Don was shown, somewhere in the Midwest, saying, "My wife always speaks for herself."

Polly thought that was wonderful. I thought it was close as Don could get to saying he didn't know her.

When the news ended, I outlined my theory that she should go on the "Today" show, or "GMA", or Larry King's show, or whatever, and show the real Polly.

"But what if I've already shown the real Polly?" she cried. "What if I make things worse?"

I grew ever more eloquent as I consumed the wine. I declared that she should invite Jane Pauley to interview her in her potting shed. I proposed a media blitz that would make her more popular than Mother Teresa.

Polly began to laugh, and I decided I'd better quit while I was ahead. "Gotta go," I mumbled, and edged toward the door.

"Dear Tommy," she said, and took my hand. She was so incredibly gentle. You don't meet a lot of gentle people in Washington.

"Do you remember Doyle Kane?" she asked.

I gulped. "Sure. He's been calling me."

"He called me," she said. "He wanted to tell me something

about the campaign. I told him to come over here, but he seemed frightened."

"Did you know him well?"

"Not well. But back when he worked for Don, and I'd go to the office, he was always sweet."

"Did he tell you what was bothering him?"

"Something about money. He didn't want to talk on the phone. He was very upset. I remember him saying, 'It's bigger than anyone can imagine,' and, 'They won't stop at anything.' I thought it was, I don't know, melodramatic. You know how people in politics are. Everything is a conspiracy, a crisis."

"I'll call him," I promised her.

The campaign grew more bizarre each day. It so distracted me that I forgot my promise to call Doyle Kane.

One candidate caused a stir by endlessly bellowing, "God bless America!"

"God bless America!" his people would shout back, in the spirit of an old-time revival meeting. No other issue existed in their minds. Finally the candidate would demand to know why his opponents did not proclaim, "God Bless America!"

"Don't they believe in God?" he would roar. "Don't they love America?"

Other candidates were thrown on the defensive; one by one they began crying, "God bless America!" lest their love of God and/or America be cast in doubt.

Newsweek came out with a Wally Love piece a week after mine. Much as I had, it portrayed a lovable eccentric.

Forrest Keel called that morning. "You know what's happening?"

"God bless America!" I cried. "What?"

"Panic. You and *Newsweek* may see Love as a loony, but politicians are scared to death. Let's face it, this guy has carried three states for Allworth, and he'll carry more before he's finished."

"Good news for Don Allworth," I said.

"Not necessarily. The Law of Unintended Consequences comes into play. Wally Love has given Craxton and the others something to run against. Other people are starting up independent operations like Love's. A lot of political consultants are going into the business. The money is flying, like nobody's ever seen before."

We managed to get off politics for a while. I told him about a new group I'd caught at the Birchmere. "The Nashville Bluegrass Band. They're great. They do a song about the death of Jimmie Rodgers that'll break your heart."

Forrest made friendly noises, but he was more the chamber-music type. Abruptly, he said, "Say, did you know that fellow who was killed last night?"

"What fellow?"

"It's in the *Post*. He used to work for Allworth."

I threw down the phone and began tearing through the paper.

The story was on page 14.

CAMPAIGN AIDE SLAIN IN GEORGETOWN

Doyle Kane.
Stabbed in his apartment on Q Street.
Possible robbery.
The little man who'd once saved my life.
Who I'd turned away just days before.
Who'd been so frightened, who'd claimed to know who was corrupting the campaign.
Who I'd told Polly I would call.
Who now was silenced for good.
Of course it was coincidence. People were killed in Washington all the time.
Then why was I shuddering?
And wondering what he had wanted so badly to tell me?
I called a detective named Briley, whom I knew from my

days on the police beat. "What happened was, he brought home some rough trade," Briley grunted.

"Slow down, what are you saying?"

"The guy was gay. He brought home the wrong stud."

It took a while to sink in.

"Do you have any suspects?"

"Nah. It's a big apartment house. They could of come in through the garage and nobody seen 'em. The guy stabs Kane, tears the place apart, looking for money or drugs, then gets the hell out."

"What if it was somebody looking for something besides drugs?"

"Like what?"

"I don't know. Kane was working for the Craxton campaign. Maybe he brought home the secret papers."

"Yeah, and maybe I'm agent 007, wiseguy."

I caught a cab to Allworth headquarters, barged in on Ratcliffe, and found him stuffing his face with a pastrami on rye the size of a football.

"What the hell do you want?" he mumbled.

"What do you know about Doyle Kane's murder?"

"What I saw in the papers."

"Why did he quit the campaign?"

"He was a hardhead, a troublemaker. He didn't like our system, so he left. We run a tight ship."

"I heard he accused you of having a drawer full of cash, a slush fund—is that your system?"

It was a bluff, but worth a shot.

Ratcliffe heaved himself up. "Tullis, how about you getting the fuck out of here?"

I took the hint.

I looked for Dinah, but she was out of town.

Then I made a decision.

This was a case for Oliver Grundy.

15.

Grundy is insane; you start with that.

Everything about the man, from his mismatched socks to the mad gleam in his eye to the odd twitch of his shoulders to the irrational leaps of his mind, attests to that sad fact.

You then proceed to the equally indisputable fact that Grundy is one of the two or three great investigative reporters of our time.

There is, of course, no conflict between his genius and his madness; it is typical of the breed.

I have known most of the great reportorial snoops, and almost without exception they are seriously twisted, far around the bend, in one way or another. Bernstein, Whitten, Hersh, the notorious Mad Dog McClure—clearly not men you would want to meet in a dark alley.

I say "almost without exception" because of the strange case of Woodward, who was to Bernstein as McCartney to

Lennon, as Abel to Cain, who indeed to this day appears as normal as you or I.

But I digress. Oliver Grundy is a small, furtive, dark-skinned man who looks as if he should be selling dirty postcards and young girls in a Mexican border town. He is, rather, a Pulitzer Prize–winning reporter for a great American newspaper. His dedication to his cause is legendary and perhaps manic. He got himself sent to prison to expose conditions there, won prizes for the feat, and for an encore got himself committed to a mental institution. There are those who say Grundy never recovered from his four months in the New Jersey Home for the Criminally Insane, but he returned to Washington and became the scourge of Bert Lance, Ed Meese, Rita Lavelle, and the Wedtech Gang.

I met Grundy years ago, when we were covering the police beat for rival Washington newspapers. It was an unequal competition. Grundy used bribes, blackmail, flattery, guile, and threats to win all the good stories for himself. The cops recognized this sinister little man as one of their own, who if he were not a reporter would surely have been a cop or a criminal or both.

Grundy and I were out of touch for a decade, while he was winning fame and I was mired in obscurity, but after I began writing my column he called me for lunch one day.

As Grundy had guessed, we each had something to offer the other. He could give me scraps of scandal that he had no use for but wanted to see in print. For my part, I sometimes stumbled on hints of criminality that were too explosive for a gossip column but that might be grist for Grundy's relentless mill.

After Doyle Kane's death, I called Grundy and we met at One Step Down, a shadowy jazz bar on Pennsylvania Avenue. I love the jukebox there; it's the only place in Washington, perhaps in the world, where you can still play old Earl Bostic 45s.

I dropped all my quarters into the machine, summoning

up Bostic and early Billie Holiday. Grundy was muttering to himself.

"Whatta you know about the mayor?" he demanded.

I thought a moment. "The mayor does all available drugs, screws anything that moves, and is a great leader of his people."

"Yeah, but what about his poker games?"

"I know zip about his poker games."

"Okay, he plays every Wednesday night with the big contractors."

"It's heartwarming to see such friendships evolve in public life," I ventured.

"Fifty-buck openers, no limit. Four or five thousand bucks a pot."

"Must be exciting," I said. "I won a thirty-dollar pot once, in college. Drew to an inside straight."

"Not so exciting," Grundy continued. "The mayor wins every pot."

"Every pot?"

"Every blessed one. The son of a bitch is gonna give graft a bad name. He's raking in millions, tax free, and shipping it off to Bermuda."

"Where'd you get this?"

"From one of his poker buddies, where do you think? Got ripped with him the other night. He's pissed. He says it ain't fair—the rest of 'em ought to get to win one or two hands a night. They've got their pride."

"Big stuff if you can prove it," I said.

"Can't be done unless one of 'em talks, and they're all part of the scam. But I've got a plan." Grundy's eyes were agleam. I wondered why he was telling me all this.

"I want you to put an item about the poker game in your column."

"*What?* Listen, Grundy, if I put that in my column, somebody might put a bomb in my car. No, thank you."

"Don't be so chickenshit," he snarled. "You're not important enough to kill. They'll know I'm behind it. But it'll put pressure on 'em. A couple of the weak links might decide to save their own skins before the whole thing blows."

I was hurt by his assertion that I was not important enough to kill. "Okay, I'll do it," I declared fearlessly.

"Good deal," Grundy grunted.

I decided to do my business before he launched some new tale of corruption and deceit.

"Grundy, a man named Doyle Kane, worked in the Craxton campaign, was killed two nights ago."

"I saw it in the papers."

"He'd been telling people there was something wrong in the campaign. Dirty money."

Grundy shrugged. "There's cash floating around in every campaign."

"But this guy was about to blow the whistle, and somebody killed him."

Grundy shrugged, clearly not interested. I tried another approach.

"Have you ever heard of something called The Boys' Club?"

Grundy's little eyes gleamed with interest. "Maybe," he said. "Give me a hint."

"Powerful men. Political connections."

"Not by any chance a certain sleazebag with the initials 'S.S.' in the group?"

"Could be." It was, of course, Sammy Shiner's role in the mysterious Boys' Club that had aroused Gloria's curiosity.

Grundy shrugged. "I maybe heard a mention."

The waitress brought our hamburgers and we munched in silence. I was lost in the immortal "Billie's Blues" until Grundy belched and brought me back to reality. "The Boys' Club. Sounds like The Lodge."

"The Lodge," I repeated, as if that made perfect sense.

"Never told you about that one, did I?"

"Nope."

"Repeat this and I'll ruin you."

"Trust me."

Grundy got a faraway look in his eye and I settled back for the ride.

"The Lodge was some Senators who liked to go hunting once in a while. Except they didn't want to hunt real hard, if you get my drift."

"Hunt what, Grundy?"

"Look, what is the one thing your average Senator wants? More than he wants money, or power, or three minutes on the tube? What's the real reason he got into politics in the first place?"

"To get laid, obviously."

"Obviously. But not a quickie on top of his desk. He's done that. What he wants is for his fantasies to come true. A harem. Twelve-year-old girls. Orgies. And most of all . . ."

"Impunity," I suggested. "No leaks, no kickbacks, no problems."

"Precisely. But it ain't simple. That's where The Lodge came in. That's what they called themselves, pot-bellied old farts in their fifties and sixties, but powerful as hell. That's what drives 'em crazy, when they've got all that power, they can snap their fingers and spend a billion dollars, but they can't get laid."

"I know the feeling."

"So, two or three times a year they'd say they were going hunting, going to The Lodge, and they'd slip off to this cabin north of here."

"Where did the girls come from?"

"That was the clever part. Most of these guys were Sunbelt types, so they'd fly in young hookers from out West. Swedes from Minnesota. Indian girls from Oregon and Montana. A few blacks. It was damn slick. The girls didn't even know what state they were in, much less who these old geezers were."

"So what went on?" I asked, in the spirit of scientific research.

"The usual stuff. Sometimes they'd have 'em dress up and dance, put on shows. They bought some Girl Scout uniforms for 'em. A lot of 'em couldn't get it up more 'n once a weekend, so they'd wind up having the girls play poker with 'em and cook for 'em."

"Grundy, you didn't pass yourself off as a half-breed whore from Montana to find this out, did you?"

My friend flashed a weasel grin. "Next best thing. There was this one time, ten, twelve years back, that things got rocky. Old ———"—he spoke the name of one of the most odious creatures ever to disgrace public office—"got sloshed, and decided to spank this girl, except he was using the end of the belt with the buckle, and she got cut up pretty bad before the others could stop him.

"Well, the girls were paid decent, usually a thousand for a weekend, and tips on top of that, but this girl, cut up like she was, and real pissed off, they gave her five thousand to calm her down. So that should have been the end of that. Except . . ."

"I see it coming," I said. "Hell hath no fury like."

"Right. This little lady was no dummy. The combination of gettin' whupped with a belt buckle, and having five thousand bucks all at once, it made her rethink her goals in life. She goes to college. Marries a lawyer. Has a kid. And one day she comes to Washington, picks up the paper, and on the front page sees a picture of the son of a bitch who'd beat her up. Until that moment, she didn't have a clue who he was."

"So she calls you."

"This is a woman of fine judgment. I show her some pictures. She gives me positive IDs on six others—four of 'em still in office. A killer of a story!"

Grundy shook his head sadly and spoke the saddest of words: "But . . ."

96

There was always a but. Poor Grundy, he was like a fisherman, telling about the one that got away.

"The bitch wouldn't talk. Not to have her name used, her picture taken. Because that way her husband would know she'd spent a couple of years working on her back. I begged her. I told her we'd write a book and she'd make a million bucks. I told her she owed it to her country, to make a better America for all the little kiddies. I threatened to use her name anyway, but she was tough—she said her husband would kill me.

"I just wanted the names of the other girls, but she didn't remember any. I spent two months touring whorehouses out West, looking for girls who'd been flown east to a cabin. But I couldn't nail it down. Oliver Grundy was defeated. Oh, I stirred up enough shit that The Lodge went out of business, but I never broke the story, never found out who was behind it."

"Behind it?"

"You didn't think those weenies organized The Lodge themselves, did you? Those bozos couldn't organize a circle jerk. This was big-league logistics, finding those girls, flying 'em in, paying 'em, keeping this operation going twenty years that I know of. Somebody slick was in charge.

"Don't you see, that's the story. If the boys did it themselves, that's fun and games. But if somebody else is doing it, that's a different ball game. Who was it? The defense biggies? The oil companies? The AMA? The Arabs? The mob? The Russkies? Because whoever did it, they had those bastards cold. They'd sold their souls for teenage nookie. Who knows how many tax bills got bottled up because of The Lodge? How many environmental laws were shot down? How many wars were fought so those old farts could get their rocks off? Think of it, man, with six or eight whores somebody took control of the U.S. Senate!"

Grundy was rhapsodic, transported by the enormity of the conspiracy.

97

"And you've got no other leads?"

"She said there was this one guy in charge. He met the plane, drove the girls to the cabins, paid them, pretty much ran the show. But she was vague—he was young, average size."

"Somebody's AA, maybe?"

"Naw, AAs don't think that big. I'm telling you, it was somebody on the outside, somebody who's got plenty of bucks and plenty of smarts. Somebody who collected enough IOUs to make the Senate dance like a puppet on a string. One story I heard, it was at The Lodge they rounded up the votes to pass the Civil Rights Bill of '64."

"Are you saying that one alumnus made it to the White House?"

"Maybe two or three."

I pondered Grundy's mind-boggling revisionist view of modern legislative history. "So you think The Lodge is out of business now?"

"I've got sources on the Hill who swear it's over. But, see, the desire of old farts for young flesh is eternal, so I'm wondering if maybe they've regrouped. This Boys' Club, it rings bells. Maybe it's a new version of The Lodge. So what I'm saying is . . ."

The door flew open, throwing a beam of light across his face. Grundy's reaction was that of a cornered rat: his shoulders began twitching, he sank down in his seat. "They're after me," he muttered, and shot out of the booth and past the bar toward the men's room.

I looked over my shoulder and saw nothing more ominous than a man making a beer delivery. In time I made my way back to the men's room. No Grundy. Only one small, barred window above the toilet seat. Above it, someone had scrawled, "If you can read this, you're pissing on your foot."

I stuck my head in the kitchen, where Latins were smoking handmades. "Did a guy in a raincoat go out this way?" I asked.

"Door locked," one of them muttered.

Grundy had vanished, I was stuck with the check, and I wondered if I'd wasted my time. He'd clearly had no interest in Doyle Kane's death. And I didn't know what to think of Grundy's tale about The Lodge; it was my instinct to believe only a fraction of what he said. This is a man who once had cards painted up with a smile face and the inscription "Have a nice day—fuck somebody!"

Yet, over the years, most of what he'd told me had checked out; Grundy hadn't won his Pulitzers for writing fiction.

At the very least, he had me curious about The Boys' Club.

16.

Spring slipped in quietly, like an old friend. Addie asked me over one sweet April evening and we sat on her deck overlooking Rock Creek Park, breathing the scent of lilacs, sipping rum-and-tonics, floating in the cotton-candy haze of sunset. She was just back from a swing through the Midwest with Don Allworth.

"He's getting more thematic," she told me. "More visionary."

"Good," I said. "Issues just piss people off. Rhetoric is what the world wants, pretty words."

"He can't dance around all the issues," she said. "You know what's surfacing now?"

I shrugged.

"AIDS. Farthington's column last week—it was the opening salvo. Why spend three billion dollars on a 'so-called epidemic' that'll only kill ten thousand a year, most of them gays and junkies? If it's not a threat to heterosexuals, big money will be hard to come by."

"You know about Farthington, don't you?"

"I know he's a dreadful bore."

"He's in love with his dog, Martha."

"Tom, this is serious."

"So is Farthington. Martha is the great passion of his life. But, of course, she's a *female* dog. Nothing queer about Farthington."

Addie lightened up and told me about an editor at the *Post* who'd had a fling with a secretary in the office, then dropped her for another woman. As it happened, the secretary had access to the *Post*'s computers, and thus to all the details of her ex-lover's travels; soon, whenever he took a trip, his hotel or plane or car reservation would be mysteriously canceled. He raved and ranted but never suspected his ex-lover might be to blame. The climax came when the editor married and set out for a honeymoon in Acapulco, only to be stranded all night in the Tijuana airport. Defeated, the newlyweds returned home to find their power had been turned off (at the customer's request, the records said), the temperature in the nineties, and all the food in the house spoiled.

"Women terrify me," I admitted, when she finished this chilling tale. I wondered if I should use an item on the episode. Or would it cause anarchy in corporate America?

"All we want is a little respect."

The prize-winning reporter was barefoot, wearing jeans and a MOSTLY MOZART T-shirt, and devoid of makeup. She was thin and had a crooked tooth and silver in her short, dark hair, but she also looked sly and sane and smart as hell. And something else: behind her jaunty smile lurked an air of mystery that left me endlessly intrigued.

"Ed Dement, the president of the network called," she said. "Called as a friend, he said. Ho-ho-ho, like I've met him twice at Christmas parties. Wanted to know if Mike and I might reconcile. For the good of the kiddies and all that."

"For the good of the ratings, he means."

"He said he certainly hoped I'd be careful what I said, because Mike was in a very precarious position. They're scared to death. It's those damn tabloids. ANCHORMAN IN LOVE NEST. My God, it's so degrading."

"He's sending a friendly warning," I said. "If Mike loses his million a year, could you afford to keep this place?"

"Oh, what do I care? This was Mike's dream house, not mine. I'm just a girl from Oklahoma City."

Their house was sensational, and sensationally expensive; Mike once told me they spent thirty thousand a year just to heat and cool it, never mind the small army of gardeners outside. Or his Jag and her BMW. Or all the private schools. Or August in the Hamptons and ski trips to the Alps. He made a million a year, she pulled in a hundred thousand or so, and they were broke.

"You met the girl, didn't you." It wasn't a question; more an accusation. "What did you think of her?"

"She was pretty and bright, nothing special. Women aren't very interesting at her age."

"They're easing her out. Back to school, and dangling a job to keep her quiet."

Addie walked to the railing. Cars whizzed below us on Rock Creek Parkway.

"What do you want, Addie? Do you want him back?"

"It's too late for that. But it hurts, more than I thought it would. I worked on this marriage, we both did. I learned to fish and to pretend to like baseball and to go to the ballet alone. Mike learned to cook and change diapers and to be civil to my family. When he had his little flirtations I looked the other way. And now he does this to me, to us. Why?"

How many women, wronged by some man, have asked that "Why?" And there is never an answer. When there is, you can't tell them.

"I think that at some basic level we men are dogs in heat and not responsible for our actions."

"He knew how much he had to lose."

"Maybe he had a death wish. Maybe he felt guilty about that million a year. Maybe the pressure was too much and this was an easy out. Television makes people crazy, you know that. There's too much money, too much uncertainty, too many half-wits at the top second-guessing you. Or maybe he was making a statement. Maybe he felt overshadowed by you."

"Overshadowed! That's a laugh. He's famous, he makes ten times as much money, he . . ."

"But you were the one people took seriously. That's not easy to live with."

I poured more drinks. Her anger unnerved me.

"I don't like being alone," she said. "I don't like wondering if our friends will chose sides. I don't want to date, to go through all that. I have a friend who was widowed, a wonderful woman, she says dating is like work, they're all so immature, all so deep into role-playing. My life with Mike wasn't perfect, but it was my life." She started to cry. "Dammit, why are men such idiots?"

As if to prove her point, I took her hand. We stood there in the treetops, watching the cars below us, the moon above. She stroked my hand absently.

"Aren't you going with anyone?" she asked.

I shook my head.

"Afraid of AIDS?"

"Afraid of women," I confessed. "I'm disaster prone. You know, lucky at gossip, unlucky at love."

"You have to keep trying."

"I was in analysis for a while. What we figured out was that I was raised by three women who gave me uncritical love— my mother, my grandmother, and my nanny. Ever since, I've been looking for uncritical love, but they've stopped making it. Women wake up in the morning and hand me a list. 'Read this, Tullis, it's fourteen more things you're doing wrong.' "

She squeezed my hand. "Is that what you want, a nanny to tell you what a sweet little babykins you is?"

"Absolutely. That's my kind of love."

She touched my face. "We're alone and lost, Tommy."

I was unprepared for her words, her emotion. Her eyes gave back the moonlight. She looked very like someone who wanted to be kissed, but I hesitated, studied the kaleidoscope of her face, shrewd and vulnerable and lovely.

"Why won't you kiss me?" she whispered, so I did, gently, because I thought we were old friends playing games, moonstruck.

But I was wrong, this was no game. We kissed until we passed the point of turning back. Had I been rational I would have said, "Addie, this is a serious mistake." Instead, when she whispered, "Come on," and led me inside, I followed eagerly.

I hold to an old-fashioned theory that if a woman is kind enough to go to bed with me I should try to make her glad she did.

It is the only one of my theories with which no woman has ever disagreed.

So I did my best to please Addie that night, to ease the pain that Mike left her, to give her the love she wanted and needed. It seemed a miracle, to be so close after so long, to touch and laugh as lovers.

We had her radio turned to a classical-music station. At one the news came that Don Allworth had lost the Wisconsin primary. Addie sat up in bed and listened, until I pulled her back down. When the news began again at two, I turned it off, unwilling to share her with that far-off world.

In the morning we enjoyed a bubble bath in her gigantic sunken tub. After coffee she said I'd have to go because her daughter was due home from school. We nuzzled like teenagers at the door.

Then she said, "Oh, by the way"—and with women like Addie there are no oh-by-the-ways—"the Heart Ball is next

Friday and I have to go—would you like to be my escort?"

The Heart Ball is a big charity do, not my scene at all, but I could refuse her nothing that morning.

"Have tux, will travel," I said cheerfully.

And yet, as I drove home, my cheer faded. The night had been wonderful, but first nights with women are almost always wonderful.

Why me, Addie, a lowly gossip columnist, instead of one of the political lions and media princes who would hasten at your call? I had a feeling that a most formidable woman had me in the palm of her hand. It was a warm, pleasant, interesting place to be, so why did I feel this unease, why did I think myself waltzing on quicksand?

17.

The death of Doyle Kane was not my problem, true; I hardly knew the man.

And yet he had once done me a great service, and I had treated him badly. Perhaps but for my indifference he would be alive today.

What had he known? What sinister "they" had he feared? Was his knowledge tied to the rumors of dirty money that kept cropping up in the campaign? Or to the mysterious Boys' Club that Gloria and Grundy had heard whispers of?

Perhaps there was nothing to it. Perhaps Kane had overreacted to the corner-cutting that goes on in all campaigns. Perhaps his death was entirely the result of his sexual risk-taking.

Perhaps, but I could not escape nagging questions, and one morning a mixture of curiosity and guilt led me back to Capitol Hill to see what I could see.

Only the dead know Brooklyn, Thomas Wolfe said, and the Hill is like that.

Once, between journalistic jobs, I toiled there for four months. The place fascinated me, but I never scratched the surface.

Essentially, the Hill is a sleepy Southern town, population about twenty thousand, ruled by 535 elected barons. At first glance, it seems the best of all possible worlds. It boasts good restaurants and snack bars, subways that run on time, an excellent barbershop, glorious gardens, free mail service, lovely young pages, elegant if overcrowded offices, patriotic paintings on the walls, formidable security, and, for excitement, the distant rumble of legislative drama. People are well and regularly paid, vacations are frequent, and if there is an occasional crisis or all-night session, this little paradise more often moves at the sleepy-stately pace one associates with county seats of the rural South.

And yet, beneath the surface, all is not so stately or serene. In that regard, the Hill recalls the movie *Blue Velvet,* which began with roses and white picket fences, and ended with the monsters and madness that lurk in the shadows of Anytown, U.S.A.

I once put words in the mouth of one of the most powerful men on the Hill. He was one of the queerest ducks I ever hope to meet, a borderline paranoid who was convinced that his staff was out to destroy him. To protect himself from what he saw as overeducated, overly liberal aides, he constantly deceived and belittled them. His main agent of self-defense was a twenty-eight-year-old, gum-popping ex-receptionist named Mattie who was a shrewd judge of character and a natural politician. She understood the Senator far better than his Ivy League advisers, and he insisted that they earn Mattie's approval before submitting any proposal to him. To some young lawyers and Ph.Ds., dealing with Mattie was an intolerable humiliation, and they soon sought work elsewhere. For my part, I knew full well that Mattie was brighter than anyone else there, but that she was also terribly insecure. So I accepted her criticism, flirted a bit, and got along fine with her and the Senator. That's how things work, even if it's not what they teach you in Political Science 101.

The Senator and Mattie are only one of 535 stories on the Hill. There are a few saints there, an abundance of sinners, plenty of mediocrities, a few people who are brilliant, and more who are brilliant but dangerously bent. The cold statistical fact is that if you take 535 Americans who have money and power, you will find in their midst at least one of just about everything, from saints and poets to transvestites and psychopaths.

There was the bizarre case of the gay Congressman who was operating his office along the lines of a San Francisco bathhouse until a disgruntled ex-employee blew the whistle. I knew one Congresswoman who operated like Caligula in skirts, so much so that certain members of her staff were well along in an assassination plot before they came to their senses.

I have known congressional offices that were run not by a mistress, but by the member's iron-willed wife, and I knew one office where a wife and a mistress grudgingly shared power. I knew one case of a senile Congressman who was more or less a prisoner of his top aides for his final year; he was dead for three days before they could bring themselves to tell the world the truth, and thus remove themselves from the gravy train.

Soon after my arrival in Washington I was among those who urged a certain rugged Midwestern Senator to run for President. Alas, our hopes were dashed when his press secretary one day announced, "I have good news and bad news. The good news is that the Senator yesterday had a long and inspiring talk with his brother. The bad news is that his brother has been dead for ten years."

Need I go on, like some crazed Scheherazade, with a Thousand and One Tales from the Hill?

Suffice to say that, by Hill standards, Don Allworth's office was deadly dull. Don was a hardworking, honest heterosexual whose only known character flaw was a lust to be President. His staff was well qualified, and he was not known to sleep with any of them. His wife, until she decried "junk" in American life, was not considered a problem.

When I returned to Don's office that sunny April morning the Capitol grounds were bright with flowers. Lovers picnicked on the lawns, and I envied them.

I was admitted to Mac McKenna's cubbyhole. I found poor Mac was more certain than ever that the "outsiders" in the campaign would destroy Don's quest for the White House and probably his Senate career as well.

I asked him about Doyle Kane's death.

"A perfect example," the AA said. "Doyle was a capable guy, but Ratcliffe hadn't been there a month before he'd run him off."

"Why didn't you take him back on the Senate staff?" I asked.

Mac made a face. "We didn't have a slot. And he was pissed at us. So he hooked up with Craxton."

"The police say Kane was gay, and probably some guy he brought home killed him," I said.

Mac fiddled unhappily with a chain of paper clips.

"Doyle was a sweet guy. A good worker. But I don't know about his private life. I didn't want to know. But I'll tell you this. Twice, in the three years he worked here, he came in beat up bad. Said he'd been mugged. I worried about the guy."

"Do you know who his friends were?"

Mac shook his head.

"Family?"

"He was from Florida; he never talked about it."

"Mac, do you have a file on him, anthing that might give some leads?"

"Sure," he said. "We keep a file on all our people. A report

109

on them, memos they've written, things like that. Sometimes it comes in handy."

He led me down the corridor to another suite of offices; then he pulled out some keys and unlocked the door to the dark, dusty storeroom. One wall was lined with old green filing cabinets.

"Here we go," he said, and started to unlock a cabinet. But it was already open. "That's strange," Mack said, and then he started digging through folders.

"Dammit, where is it?" he roared.

Mac searched for five minutes before he would admit that Kane's file was not there.

"That's impossible," he raged. Mac's vision of the Senate did not include breaking and entering.

I decided to bite the bullet. "He said there was illegal money coming into both the Allworth and Craxton campaigns."

"Goddammit," Mac moaned. "That damn Ratcliffe, I knew he'd pull something like this."

"What should we do?" I asked him.

"Look, however crazy Doyle's personal life was, he played straight at work. If Doyle said there was dirty money, I believe it. I'm going to the mat with that damn Ratcliffe."

"Are you going to tell Don?"

"No, because that creates new problems. Some things it's better for him not to know. But I'll settle with Ratcliffe. What I want you to do is not say a word about this. If there's a problem, we'll handle it internally, so it doesn't blow the campaign all to hell."

"I understand," I said.

"I won't forget this, Tom." He shook my hand gravely.

I was halfway back to my office before I realized I didn't have the slightest idea who'd stolen Doyle Kane's file or why. Once more I'd failed to penetrate the mysteries of Capitol Hill. And back at my office, another jolt awaited me.

Mike Cunningham lay in wait for me outside the *Vindi-*

cator office, as red-faced and unhappy as a lobster in a pot.

It was hard to imagine what Mike was angry about. His "love nest" scandal, to everyone's surprise, had redounded to his benefit, at least professionally. The "respectable" media hadn't done much with his fling with Robin, but the tabloids had gone crazy. For weeks Mike had been up there at the checkout counter with Michael J. Fox, Princess Di, and the latest Elvis reincarnation.

The result of all this gutter journalism?

Superstardom!

Mike's ratings shot up, pulling his evening news show to number one for the first time in six years. This meant his network was raking in extra millions each week, and it also meant Mike's lawyer was renegotiating his contract.

So why is this man angry?

"Damn you, Tom, what do you mean talking to Robin, tricking her like that?"

Mike was bigger than I, and he truly looked near the edge. Still, I doubted that he'd take a swing at me. There was always the chance that I would swing back, and this man's face was his fortune.

"Oh, hell, Mike, come in and calm down."

He followed me to my office but he didn't calm down. "You tricked her!" he repeated.

"Oh, bullshit! She knew who I was. You're a reporter, too, remember?"

"You're damn right I am," Mike raged. "A reporter! Not some damned gossip columnist shoveling out crap and trash and . . . and . . ."

"Garbage," I suggested.

"That's right, garbage!"

"It is true that I write a gossip column," I admitted manfully. "Alas, mine is not such a pretty face that the network moguls will pay me a million bucks a year to read short sentences written by other, more literate men."

"You're jealous," he replied sullenly.

"Mike, has anyone told you that you're the asshole of the year? Potentially of the decade?"

"Damn you . . ."

"You've lost Addie and you're losing Robin. You're stuck with all those perverts who write you fan letters, and I hope you're happy."

"What do you mean, losing Robin? She loves me!"

I stared at him in disbelief. Was she still stringing him along?

"What do you want?" I asked gently, as if of a child.

"I want to know what you plan to write about me."

I wasn't going to write anything now that I was involved with Addie, but I didn't tell him that.

"I've been waiting to see what you'd say."

"I've got nothing to say," he declared.

"Come on, Mike. Did you think Addie would look the other way while you cavorted with a girl Robin's age?"

"You stay away from Addie. You're just taking advantage of her. She's too good for you."

I'd taken Addie to the Heart Ball and to dinner at Paolo's the night before; we had entered the public domain.

"You idiot, nobody's gonna take advantage of Addie. As for her being too good for me, let her decide. She sure as hell thinks she's too good for you."

One of our interns, an impressionable teenager, looked in the door and cried, "Oh, wow!"

The dashing anchorman tossed her a smile, then stood up. "You're real cute, Tom," he said. "You always were. Glib. But you'd better watch out for Addie. She's not like you think. She's ten jumps ahead of you. You could get burned real bad. I fucking hope you do!"

On that enigmatic note, my friend the anchorman signed off. It sounded like sour grapes to me.

Still, his visit left me depressed. I was hurt by Mike's scornful dismissal of me as a gossip, a busybody, a dealer in crap and garbage.

I like to think mine an honorable calling. Gossip, I tell myself, is not a luxury but a necessity for human happiness, right up there with food, shelter, clothing, booze, and sex. And yet the professional gossip is scorned—like the pimp, the bootlegger, the pornographer—for meeting a need that most mortals feel but are too hypocritical to admit.

I was jolted from these dreary musings by a ringing phone and an approaching deadline.

In my last column I'd run an item about "funny money" in the primaries, and reporters had been calling, with more tales of cash flowing. I added an item called "More Funny Money."

To keep my deal with Grundy, I inserted an item that read: "City Hall is abuzz with talk of Hizzoner's amazing prowess at the poker tables, where, as elsewhere, he is forever a winner."

I took a call from a reporter who wanted to tell me about curious doings the night before at a celebrated lobbyist's bachelor party. Some forty media and political notables were wining and dining when a naked lady leapt out of a cake and attacked them. She was armed with a can of whipped cream, which she used to achieve instant intimacy with various guests. Her conquests included one federal judge who gobbled a huge mound of whipped cream off her person, apparently on the theory that amid all that whipped cream there must be a cherry somewhere.

A nice story, but I passed, because so many journalists were involved. One had to respect one's peers. In Lyndon Johnson's inspiring phrase, You don't spit in the soup.

Next came my friend Hightower, a genial ex-admiral who calls every few months to pass on the dirt on some poor bastard. Sometimes I use it, more often I don't, but Hightower doesn't care. A man with a steady supply of top-grade dirt will always find someone to print it.

Hightower is a hatchet man for the Pentagon. It comes down to this: if you mess with the military, they'll get you, sooner or later. Maybe you're a Congessman, or a journalist, or a White House aide, or a Defense Department whistle-blower. You try to serve your country by opposing the bloated Pentagon budget, or exposing some billion-dollar boondog-gle, or revealing some cozy military scam. Fine, you're a pa-triot, but the generals have long memories, thick files, and sharp knives. Someday they'll find that you're cheating on your wife, or you didn't pay your taxes, or your brother was indicted, or *something,* and they won't rest until they've used that fact to cause you maximum pain and suffering.

If the American military is as resolute in war as it is in savaging its critics, World War Three will be a snap.

Hightower's call concerned a former White House aide, now a Washington lawyer, who'd been arrested for possession of cocaine in the Miami airport. I declined the item, for in my circles possession of cocaine is considered a social grace, not a crime, but I had no doubt the story would surface elsewhere.

Mac McKenna called. "Tom, I had it out with Ratcliffe," he announced. "There'll be no more screwing around by him. He did have some sources of cash, but that's over now. But we've got to keep this quiet."

"Mac, at least tell me . . ."

"Can't talk now. Call me later."

Another call, this time a giggling society matron informing me that one of her rivals had undergone her third face-lift. "I don't do face-lifts," I informed her. It's true. I do divorces, sex-change operations, and trips to Betty Ford, but I draw the line at birthdays, charity balls, face-lifts, and senile Sen-ators who wander about the Capitol with their flies open. A man has to maintain some standards, even in Washington, D.C.

When I left the office that evening in the April twilight, a woman fell in beside me.

114

"Surprise," she said.

It was Dinah, in a grungy old raincoat, looking weary.

"You're back," I said.

"Buy me a beer?"

We walked up to Timberlake's, a noisy and goodhearted bar on Connecticut Avenue.

"So where were you?"

"They sent me to see our finance chairmen out West."

"How was it?"

"Oh, people are giving like crazy. Our people, Craxton's people, the money is flowing."

"You know about Doyle Kane?"

"Yes." She lowered her eyes.

"What do you think?"

"What can I think? It stinks. But I can't prove anything. The poor bastard. He knew something and nobody would listen."

"I told Mac McKenna what Kane had been saying about cash. He confronted Ratcliffe, told him it had to stop."

"I'll believe it when I see it," she said. "Things are so crazy. It's like there are two campaigns. The one everyone sees, with rallies and speeches and balloons, and this underground war that's fought with money. We're still getting a lot of checks from people we never heard of, from PACs we never heard of—I'm right in the middle of it, and I don't know what's going on. I don't know what to do."

I sipped my beer. Smokey Robinson's "Shop Around" was playing on the jukebox. "Why not do nothing?" I said. "Do your job. Don't worry about the rest of it."

She looked pained. Inaction was not Dinah's style.

"Tommy, while I was in Oregon, I did some checking on Wally Love."

"He's for real, isn't he?"

"What's real? He was a newspaper editor. He's lived there all his life. But there's more."

"Like what?"

115

"Did he tell you he was an alcoholic?"

"No, but why should he?"

"He's been in and out of treatment for alcoholism and chronic depression. He's had big problems."

I finished my beer. "Dinah, look. You can't expect a fellow who decides to spend millions of dollars on a man he's never met to be perfectly normal."

"It scares me," she said. "The spending in this campaign is out of control. It's like a war, a money war, that nobody can win."

"Look, he's trying to elect our guy President. You want to demand an investigation? He may be a nut, but he's our nut. Relax."

Dinah stared glumly into her beer.

"Who's doing independent stuff for Craxton?" I asked.

"A guy out of Miami named Rojack. He's already running anti-Allworth spots out West."

I looked at my watch. "I'm sorry, I've got to go."

She gave me a look. "Got a hot date?"

"Sort of."

"Anybody I know?"

Dinah could ask me anything; we were past having secrets.

"I've been seeing Addie Hopkins."

She did a double take, then began to laugh. "Mike Cunningham's ex? Tommy, that's wild, that's truly wild."

"She's a fine lady."

"I don't doubt it. But it's still wild."

I stood up and tossed some bills on the table. "Okay, it's wild," I said. "But that's how it is. See you later."

18.

Addie and I quickly became an Item. Not in my column, to be sure, but my brothers-in-gossip Chuck Conconi of the *Post* and Rudy Maxa of the *Washingtonian* were quick to note the New Couple in their respective journals.

New Couple or Odd Couple? I still felt a certain puzzlement about this romance. Granted, I am fairly trim, have all my hair, and look quite presentable in my tuxedo, but there were nonetheless more celebrated men-about-town Addie might have chosen. Her estranged husband was grumbling to anyone who would listen that the only reason she would be seen with me was to humiliate him.

In any event, thanks to Addie's rock-solid A-list status, we were waltzing our way to the Capital's finest parties.

Buzz Makito's seated dinner-dance for two hundred intimate friends that Saturday night was a case in point. It was held at his mansion to honor some visiting Japanese moguls who, it was variously rumored, were here to buy General Motors, make an offer for Hawaii, or kidnap David Rockefeller.

Addie and I arrived late—her many virtues did not include promptness—and found the party spilling out into our host's flowering gardens. The men all wore tuxedos, except for one raffish economist who sported a pinkish dinner jacket. And the women—my God, the money that had gone into that explosion of high fashion could have paid off half the national debt.

Buzz Makito had conjured up a perfect spring evening, complete with a full moon and balmy breezes. We of the Capital elite guzzled champagne, told each other how good we looked, and gossiped about the campaign. Addie was soon huddled with other journalists, endlessly pondering the political tea leaves.

I meanwhile talked to wives, whom I found far more entertaining than the high-muck-a-mucks who were their husbands. One dotty old party confided that she'd poisoned her first husband some forty years before, so she could marry his law partner, now the chairman of a powerful Senate committee. A columnist's wife swore that a former First Lady was having an affair with a certain thuggish TV evangelist. A TV megastar was said to be on the brink of divorcing her wimpish producer/husband to run off with a Washington-based novelist.

The evening was like that. In our demimonde, gossip was the accepted currency, like wampum for the Indians. Unlike sex, you could do it all day long, over the telephone, and without mussing your hair. To be sure, ours was a stunningly vicious little world; people would flatter you to your face, then slander you mercilessly when you turned your back. To be the first to leave a room could be social suicide.

Yet perhaps our mania was inevitable, when you consider how many politicians and journalists were crowded unnaturally into our govermental ghetto, thousands of hungry, angry, snarling dogs fighting over a few scraps of glory. What could we do but gossip? It was that or homicide.

I chatted with Joey Swink, the ex–White House operative who had become Buzz Makito's second-in-command. He was a swarthy little man, a hustler even in his thousand-dollar Calvin Klein tuxedo, but not without a certain rough charm. He almost always favored me with a few choice nuggets of political gossip. Tonight he told the tale of the Senator who the day before had tried the drug Ecstasy in the company of two teenage pages and wound up wandering the corridors of the Dirksen Building in his skivvies, bellowing "Some Enchanted Evening" at the top of his lungs before his staff recaptured him.

As we were parting, Swink leaned close, his safecracker's eyes fixed on mine, and said, "Tommy, what have you heard about The Penner Project?"

"The what?" Penner is the expensive girls' school in Northwest Washington from which both our daughters had graduated.

"Maybe it's nothing," Swink shrugged, and was gone.

Dinner recalled Versailles in its heyday. Food that was to weep, wine that was to die. I slipped a twenty to the comely lass serving me and was rewarded by a magical wineglass—it was never empty, despite my heroic efforts to the contrary.

After brandy and cherries Ferdinand, Buzz Makito did something unprecedented in our Capital's social history. He did not make a speech. Understand, he had us cold. He could have talked for an hour and we couldn't have complained, not after the meal he had laid on us. Instead he welcomed us, introduced his guests of honor, and was back in his chair in under two minutes, to deafening applause.

A clever, clever man.

I watched Buzz, admiring his charm and good sense, and yet troubled by strange mixed feelings. When I was a babe

119

in arms, I lost an uncle at Iwo Jima, and in our family mythology the Japanese were fiends who tossed babies in the air and speared them on their bayonets.

Today, of course, I am a man of the world. I admire Japanese culture, respect Japanese know-how, value Japanese friends.

In my mind, I know they're fine fellows. But in my guts it's still 1945.

These murky broodings were mercifully ended as dinner broke up and dancing began. Don and Polly passed by, and the candidate pulled me aside.

"Dammit, Tom, I see these 'funny money' items of yours, and I talk to our people, and they say we're clean as a whistle."

"Maybe I'm wrong," I said lamely. What else could I say? That Mac and Ratcliffe were keeping the truth from him? Telling him the truth was their job, not mine.

He was gone as quickly as he'd come, and I found Polly in my arms, as the band played "Misty."

"You were great on the 'Today' show," I told her.

She floated on air; it was like dancing with a dream.

"Jane was so sweet. It went by in no time."

"So what's next?"

"More TV, I guess. There are still people denouncing me." She smiled wanly. "It's so crazy."

"Poor Polly. An enemy of the people."

"I'm learning what it does to you," she said. "You can't be yourself, can't be spontaneous. They ask you these trick questions, hoping you'll say something dumb, so you have to be bland. It's dehumanizing."

"But you're going to give it a shot?"

"I guess so. It means so much to Don. Have you found out anything more about Doyle Kane?"

"No," I said. "No, not a thing."

Someone cut in on me; then I was seized by a celebrated hostess who took my arm and poured out a tale of fear and loathing among her circle of rich, idle, some would say dangerous, women.

"Uma is my absolute best friend but she has this absurd crush on Tony and of course he's living with Alexa, and I had invited them both, not knowing about this infatuation, and Alexa told me, 'If I see that slut I'll scratch her eyes out,' and I said, 'Well, darling, maybe you'd best not come to the party, I already have the entertainment planned,' and she became utterly furious and said, 'If you're her friend, you're not my friend anymore!' Well! What can you say? I utterly adore Alexa, but, my God, she *can* be an absolute pluperfect cunt sometimes, can't she?"

My companion was fortyish, and very beautiful; her off-the-shoulder Oscar de la Renta gown was a miracle of pinks and whites. What struck me most were her shoulders; they were as pure as her mouth was foul. I was seized by the insane desire to kiss those perfect white shoulders, and I was saved from my folly by the arrival of a butler who said my host wished to see me. I murmured a goodbye to the lady of the perfect shoulders and followed the butler to the library.

Buzz rose and took my hand.

"Ah, the Gatsby of the Orient," I said gravely.

"Tom, always joking. Do sit down. Something to drink? Name it."

"No, thanks."

"Tom, my colleagues are in this country making certain investments and acquisitions," he said. "I have a list of their purchases, if that interests you."

"Absolutely," I said.

Buzz passed me a sheet of paper. I glanced at it. Fishing fleets on Chesapeake Bay, vineyards in Virginia, a plastics company in Maryland: Buzz was tossing me a few crumbs of local interest, while no doubt saving choicer morsels for the *New York Times* or the *Wall Street Journal*.

A waiter brought him coffee. I relented and asked for a

brandy. Buzz said, "Tell me, Tom, what's your reading of the campaign?"

I had no reading of the campaign. Part of me was pulling for Don Allworth, sure, but another part thought we should choose the President by lottery. I mean, a nation that lurches from Johnson to Nixon to Ford to Carter to Reagan clearly needs a new approach.

"Buzz, it's going to be either a bloodbath or a mudbath. Or both."

Buzz frowned at my frivolity. "I noted the items in your column on the subject of funny money."

"Ah, well, it's just gossip," I said modestly.

"No, I take these reports seriously." He lowered his voice. "I've heard the same reports myself."

I must have cocked a skeptical eyebrow, because he was quick to add, "Of course, Tom, as you know, I never involve myself in American politics. My concerns are purely cultural and economic. Still, as you will understand, I have friends, and they ask my opinion. . . ."

He grinned his most engaging grin. "And, being human, I am curious."

His brandy had me primed to pontificate.

"Our campaign-finance laws are a joke; anybody who wants to give big bucks can, legally, so if you are giving illegally it means you've got a serious problem."

"A problem?" my friend echoed.

"It suggests someone unpopular, someone who can't afford to have it known he's giving money, because it might cause a backlash."

"Who, Tom, for example?"

I shrugged. "I hear that a lot of rich gays are going to give a hundred thousand or more because they want to elect a President who'll move against AIDS in a big way."

"Most understandable," Buzz murmured.

I savored my brandy and my status as an Informed Source.

"Joey has a theory," my host continued. "Perhaps you'd like to hear it."

"You bet," I said.

Buzz spoke into his phone, and moments later Joey Swink joined us. "Yeah, I've heard some talk," he said in his raspy voice.

Now I leaned forward. "Yes?"

"This can't go beyond these four walls."

"Absolutely."

"It's the defense gang," he said. "An alliance of the billion-dollar contractors. They're afraid the next President will cut back the Pentagon pork, and they're trying to buy enough clout to head it off."

"Which contractors, Joey? Can you be specific?"

Swink shrugged. "Maybe you can check it out, pal."

I tried to look crafty. In truth, investigative reporting was not my game, although I could always unleash the intrepid Grundy.

Hooked, I blurted out a question.

"A man who worked on one of the campaigns wanted to tell me about illegal money coming in, and he was killed. Do you think that . . . ?"

Joey Swink's little eyes glistened.

"It wouldn't surprise me, Tommy," he whispered. "We're talking billions. There's people around who'd zap you and me and everybody here tonight for that kind of dough."

Buzz Makito leapt to his feet. "Enough, enough," he cried. "Let's enjoy ourselves, gentlemen."

Clearly the talk of murder had shaken our host. He escorted me back to the party. I found Addie on the dance floor, and took her in my arms.

Despite Addie's charms, my mind was still on Swink's warning. Money might be funny, but murder wasn't. What was a nice boy like me doing in a mess like this?

And yet, as Addie and I twirled under the stars, I was

gripped by a new fantasy. In it, Tom Tullis, Busybody, was reborn as Tom Tullis, Ace Reporter.

Middle Eastern money? Defense money? Mob money? Whatever. If I could get to the bottom of this I could be a star!

GOSSIP WINS PULITZER

From such fantasies, Reader, do rash, sometimes fatal, actions flow.

When I took Addie home she asked me to stay. It didn't strike me as a good idea, but I lacked the strength of character to refuse.

I should have followed my instincts, because when the moment came I was an absolute zero. I groaned and said, "I'm sorry, I think my head is messed up."

She gave me a long look. "What's wrong?"

I hadn't told her of my concern about Doyle Kane's death. I feared she would think me a conspiracy buff, a crazy.

"I don't know. Maybe I'm not comfortable being here. In the marriage bed, so to speak."

"It's just a bed now," she said, ever the pragmatist. "My bed. The marriage is over."

In truth, I loved her bed, the way it floated among the treetops, among the stars.

"I hear Mike's after you to take him back."

"Fat chance."

"Life might be simpler that way."

"If I had wanted a simple life I wouldn't have left Oklahoma City."

"And now you're a famous reporter and life isn't simple at all."

"They've offered me a column," she announced.

"Oh, God. Poor Addie."

"What should I do?"

"It's journalism's Catch-22. No one has ever turned down a column. And no one has ever written a column without exposing himself as a fool and/or a bore. God did not intend for human beings to be clever and/or profound three times a week. Once a week is the absolute limit."

"Broder's good."

"He'd be twice as good if he wrote half as much. The rest of them are twits. Columnists should be shot after five years. A mercy killing."

"You know what I'd like to do?"

"What?"

"Quit this rat race, teach journalism somewhere, and have time to write books. That's been my secret dream ever since my Nieman."

"Another reporter seduced by Harvard."

"One can tire of being lied to by politicians."

"One can tire of being told the truth by politicians." I began to stroke her back.

"That feels so good," she said.

"I'm glad."

She giggled. "Want to hear a perfectly awful story?"

"Sure."

"Charlie and Kevin went to the Knot Inn yesterday and got smashed."

"No news so far."

Kevin and Charlie were two Senators, one divorced and one separated, who'd been playing Butch and Sundance for the past year.

"I mean, the disarmament debate bores them, so they wander over to the Knot and get stinko. And proceed to play catch with their waitress."

"Play catch?"

"They're sitting in a booth. Charlie grabs her. A cute little thing, weighs about ninety-five pounds. Kevin says, 'Hey, I want her!' so bighearted Charlie throws her across the table to Kevin. But now she's yelling, so he throws her back to

Charlie. They decide this is a hell of a sport, like Ping-Pong. Everybody in the place is petrified. Finally it sinks into Kevin's thick skull that maybe this is not good PR, so he gives her a twenty-dollar tip and they stagger back to the disarmament debate."

"Those idiots," I cried. "Those goons."

"The girl is shaken up, the bartender is not stupid, and certain calls are made. Money changes hands."

"How much?"

"A thousand each, I heard, and it should have been more. We got wind of it, but the girl isn't talking, no one's talking, so the question is whether we go with what we have. And we wimped out."

It was a nice slice of life. Your Senator at Work. I could use it without the names; everyone would know who the two rowdies were.

And yet I thought, My God, must gossip follow me even into bed?

"I don't think Kevin wants to be President," Addie said. "I think he's essentially self-destructive."

"Let's don't talk about that fool," I said. "It'll give me a headache. Let's talk about you. Tell me what you were like as a little girl."

I kept stroking her back while she pondered my question. Addie was happier talking about wayward politicians than about herself.

"I wore hand-me-downs and was the smartest girl in the class. My best friend was the prettiest girl in the class. I'd gladly have killed her."

"But now you're older and wiser."

"Did I ever tell you about my father?"

"No."

"He was an interesting man but a violent drunk. I was afraid of him. I think that's one reason I married Mike. I thought I could control him."

Inanely, I said, "Did you see Polly on the 'Today' show?"

126

She muttered into the pillow.

"Didn't you think she was great?"

". . . thought she was vapid."

I kept stroking her back. "Polly is a kind, decent, gentle woman. And talented too."

"Vapid."

"You two aren't the same type."

"I should hope not. I only hope she doesn't destroy Don's campaign."

What she would not quite say was *I fought to create a successful career and that woman has stayed home and played with clay for twenty years.*

"You like Don, don't you?"

"He's a good Senator. Did you ever meet his mother?"

I thought a moment. "I don't think so."

"I'll tell you a story about Don's mother. Never to be repeated. She was shanty Irish, ignorant as dirt, and horribly strict. When he was a little boy, she'd tell him that if he wasn't good, he'd be kidnapped and murdered, like the Lindbergh baby. He still has nightmares about it."

"Jesus," I cried.

"Aren't mothers grand?"

"How do you know this, Addie?"

"He told me, off the record."

As a journalist, an itinerant prober of the political psyche, I recognized the story as one of those rosebud-like gems that you stumble upon once or twice in a career. If true, that story—that specter of his mother—would go far toward explaining the discipline, the drive, the passion that lurked beneath Don's placid surface.

Yet I was surprised that he would let something so revealing drop in an interview, even off the record, even to someone as disarming as Addie.

I applied my fingernail creatively to her knobby spine. "I heard that the defense people are pouring cash into the primaries," I ventured.

"That's crazy. They're all traumatized by the procurement scandals—they're afraid to jaywalk."

She spoke with absolute certitude. And yet Swink had too. I kept stroking her back—was this foreplay or backplay?

"One question."

"Ummmm."

"Why me? Why am I here?"

"Maybe I'm lonely."

"Get a dog."

"Don't be vulgar."

"Addie, I'm flattered but confused."

"You're sweet, Tommy. As men go, you have a low bullshit factor. And you are a veritable Itzhak Perlman of the lower back."

Languidly, she began to kiss me. Kissing, in this era of instant sex, is very nearly a lost art, but not with Addie. Her kisses were subtle and sad and dreamlike, homage to the simpler joys of yesteryear, to backseats and proms and true love; her kisses were not foreplay but a gloriously erotic end in themselves.

We were still kissing when we fell asleep.

19.

The next morning Gloria, just back from her Cuban junket, called in a tizzy and said she had to see me. I hastened to Thirty-first Street, where I was greeted by a distraught woman whom I barely recognized as the Gloria I knew and loved.

"What's wrong?" I asked, as she threw herself into my arms.

"Tommy, I'm in the most awful mess of my life."

That sobered me, for Gloria has survived some spectacular messes.

"Outside," she whispered. "They may have the house bugged."

We went into her garden; work on the new pool had been halted by the contractor's departure for a month in France.

"So what's wrong?"

"It's Castro!" she wailed. "It's that damned Castro!"

A touch of madness has always been central to Gloria's charm, but I feared she had slipped over the edge.

"Start at the beginning," I suggested.

"Horace Moses, this guy I've been seeing—the one I said was at State?—actually he's CIA. He's the one who called me about the trip. It started out so well. They flew us to Havana, four women writers, and we toured the university and talked to intellectual types and soaked up rum and sun. Your basic cultural-exchange junket."

"Sounds fine," I ventured.

"Just wait. The last night, they tell us Castro will see us. See, Castro's a lot like Hugh Hefner—or like Hef used to be, before he had his stroke. He sleeps all day and prowls around all night, meeting with Polish trade delegations and the like. Except here we are, these four American chicks, of whom I am the youngest by a decade, and we meet him in his cabaña by the sea and we talk about Hemingway and Mickey Mantle and Elvis Presley and all this pop-culture stuff. And Fidel is a sweetheart. I mean, he's a bit thick around the middle, and he wears grubby fatigues and smokes vile cigars, and I do think birds nest in that beard, but the man is not without a certain satanic appeal."

In one blinding flash I saw it coming.

"So finally the rosy-fingered dawn tiptoes in, and we start to leave, and then this soldier whispers that El Presidente wants me to stay for breakfast. Just me."

"No, Gloria! No, no, no."

"Yeah. You got it."

I was speechless; Gloria had outdone herself.

"Well, how was it?"

She shrugged. "Oh, you know how Latins are."

I was impatient. "Gloria, this was clearly a great adventure, but what's the problem?"

Her anger flashed. "The problem, dammit, is that now the CIA wants me to kill him!"

"*What?*"

"They set me up. I mean, they figured if they got us together it was a pretty sure thing. And they were right. So, when I get back home, my friend the spook comes to me with a deal. I'll go back to Cuba and see Castro again, but this time they'll give me a ring. And while we are, shall we say, entwined in passion, I'm supposed to scratch his butt. There's poison in the ring, and a few hours later he'll take the big sleep."

"Those idiots!" I cried. "Twenty years ago they tried to kill him with an exploding cigar."

"This time I'm the cigar," she said bitterly.

"Still, it's a great piece for *Reader's Digest*," I mused. " 'I Fucked Fidel for the CIA.' "

"But that's *it*, Tommy: I want to *write* it—what a plot for a novel!—but I don't want to *do* it."

"Well, dammit, just say no!"

She nibbled a hangnail. "It's not that easy."

"Are you saying they've got something on you?"

"Well, Horace—he's the one I've been getting my coke from—he supplies the contras, I think—he hinted that I'd have a lifetime supply if I did the job for them, but I might have a legal problem if I didn't."

"Gloria, this only makes sense if they think you're a junkie and/or crazy. But since you're not, just tell those madman to go to blazes."

I was silenced by the roar of a plane on its approach to National. Low-flying planes are one of the charms of Georgetown, along with traffic, crime, and drunken undergraduates who race about howling and throwing beer bottles all night.

When we could hear again, Gloria said wistfully, "Do you think I should do it?"

"*What?*"

"You know, the ring bit. What a book it'd make."

"You *are* insane, damn you!" I raged.

"I'd go down in history. Like Mata Hari."

This encounter with Gloria was even more surreal than

most. I might have left in frustration, except that I had my own agenda.

"You still seeing Sammy Shiner?"

Her eyes cut to mine. "Why?"

"You remember when you told me about him and The Boys' Club, told me to check it out?"

She looked away.

"Well, I have checked. And run into a stone wall. I need help."

"I don't know anything," she said sullenly.

"Ask him about it. Or maybe you'll hear something."

"You're just like the lousy CIA," she grumbled, "wanting me to do your dirty work."

"Gloria, this is Tommy," I pleaded. "It's important."

"Go away," she said. "I need to think."

I left, angry and unsatisfied. This was not like Gloria. She owed me one, owed me a dozen. Had a deadly dose of Castro, cocaine, and the CIA driven her round the bend?

Or was I the crazy one, for sticking my nose where it didn't belong?

20.

A few mornings later my daughter appeared on my doorstep, tanned and lovely, as if her ordeal on the Mexican border had agreed with her. We embraced, I gave her coffee, and she gazed dreamily around my modest townhouse.

"Haven't you noticed?" she said abruptly.

"Noticed?" I was accustomed to her nonlinear thinking.

She waved her hands. "I've quit smoking."

"Great," I said.

"I've quit red meat too. But I still eat fish."

"How's Vern?" I asked, remembering her partner in crime, last heard of in a Laredo jail.

"Oh, he's back at Stanford."

"Who was he?"

"Just a guy I met in Acapulco. We were staying at the Princess Hotel, and one morning we were walking on the beach, and this guy who looked like Pancho Villa comes up and points a gun at us. Vern said, '*Gracias, amigo,* but I don't want to buy a gun,' but the thing is he was holding us up. He took all Vern's money; that was why Vern got talked into smuggling dope back, to make up the loss."

"So are you going back to school?"

Holly was on what her college quaintly called "academic leave," which in simpler times was known as flunking out.

"They won't take me till September. They're such jerks. I thought I might work in one of the campaigns, Senator All-worth's maybe."

I stirred my coffee, stalling. A campaign is no place for an innocent girl, but, let's face it, Holly isn't all that innocent.

"Campaigns don't pay much," I cautioned.

"Oh, I wouldn't need much," my daughter said with a bright smile. "I can live here with you."

I did not cry aloud in horror. Could I turn away my beloved daughter, fresh from the indignities of a Mexican jail?

"I'm on my way to the office," I said.

"That's okay. I'm going to crash for a while; then I'll call Deakie." Deakie was a Penner classmate of Holly's, the cool-eyed daughter of a Spanish diplomat.

I had a thought. "Have you heard of something called The Penner Project?"

"Give me a hint."

"I don't know. Somebody asked me about it the other night."

"I'll ask Deakie. If it's kinky, she'll know."

At my office I called Grundy, who shared Addie's view that the defense industry could not be the source of illegal campaign money on any large scale because they were too shaken by their recent scandals. I was puzzled. Joey Swink, one of the best-informed men in town, had floated the defense-industry theory, yet two astute reporters said it was crazy.

I left at noon to meet Forrest for lunch at Duke's. I arrived first and was quickly escorted to my usual choice table. But then I noticed a man named Elliot Surry at the table by the kitchen door, and I went back to speak to him. When I was first in town, there were giants in the Senate, men like Kefauver, Douglas, and Fulbright, and Elliot Surry was among them. He'd been the first establishment figure to break with Johnson over the war, and millions of us had rallied around him, but for his trouble he'd been defeated in the next election. He hung on in the Capital, of course, practicing public-interest law; they never go back to Pocatello.

Elliot was having a drink with a sportswriter named Hurst who'd been another big man in town until he lost his column. Ghosts, I call them, men who had power once and lost it and don't get the invitations or the good tables anymore.

I chatted with Elliot Surry for a few minutes. It was the least I could do for a man who'd once spoken for sanity in a time of madness. But in truth it wasn't any fun; ghosts tend to tell stories that are twenty or thirty years old. When I saw my friend Forrest arrive, I left Siberia and returned to my choice table, reminding myself once more that if Harriet fired me tomorrow and hired a baboon to write the column, the baboon would rate the choice table and I'd be back with the ghosts by the kitchen door.

Forrest looked like hell. My burly, handsome friend had deep circles beneath his eyes, and his hands shook.

He ordered a scotch, then told me, "I'm leaving town. I wanted to see you before I left."

"Leaving? Why?"

"A close friend of Chuck's and mine died last week," he said.

Chuck, as I guess I've mentioned, is Forrest's lover, a very decent guy.

"We'd both been nursing him in the evenings," he continued. "We're both exhausted. He was the third close friend we've lost this year. We need to get away."

"Is there anything I can do?"

"Not really, Tom. But thanks."

I thought how little I really knew Forrest. We were political friends, Washington friends, but we'd never gone beneath the surface. Few people did, in this polished, many-mirrored, ever-changing world we moved in.

"We've never really talked about it," I said. "I guess I've tried not to think about it."

"What is there to say?" he asked bitterly. "A generation is being cut off in its prime. By the most slow and insidious of deaths. And no one on the outside gives a damn."

Our second round of drinks arrived and we downed them greedily.

"I think people care," I said cautiously.

"Oh, individuals care," he said. "I'm talking about the body politic. I've seen polls—I've *done* polls. The ignorance, the indifference, the hostility, they're horrifying. There is a consensus in straight America that we've brought it on ourselves and we deserve what we're getting."

"A lot of us think it's a tragedy," I told him. "But we don't know what to do."

"Ultimately it's a political problem," he said. "We need popular support to get the money to carry out the research to save the lives that still can be saved."

Our club sandwiches arrived. I nibbled mine; Forrest's remained untouched.

"Dammit, Tom," he said with sudden anger, "whatever our sins or mistakes, they're dwarfed by those of this government, this society. If this disease struck straight middle-class whites, there'd be a fifty-billion-dollar program underway. This inaction is criminal, it's monstrous!"

There was nothing I could say.

"To be honest, there's another reason we're going to Florida. This campaign disgusts me. It's bad and getting worse. Before it's over, it'll be the dirtiest campaign in history. The really dirty, nasty negative spots that people have been running in state campaigns are going to surface nationally. I don't want any part of it."

"Won't the negative stuff backfire?" I asked.

136

"The experience at the state level is that negative spots work the first time out. It takes a few years for people to get fed up with them."

"I saw Don Allworth at Buzz Makito's party the other night. He acted confident as hell. Do you think he has a chance?"

"Craxton is pulling away from him," Forrest said. "Allworth never reached people at a gut level. Joe Six-Pack never had a reason to give a damn about him."

"He's starting to hit the get-tough-on-trade button pretty hard. Can it help?"

"Help with workers, hurt with the big-money people. Don better watch out or he won't be invited back to Makito's parties."

"Buzz claims he's apolitical."

Forrest looked amused. "The Japanese culture does not encourage loose cannons. Everyone is part of the team."

"I had an interesting talk with Buzz and Joey Swink, about the dirty-money reports. Swink says it may be the defense contractors."

"That's rather far off your beat, isn't it?"

"A guy I know was killed, and it may have been connected. If you hear anything, let me know."

He looked at me sharply. "My advice is stay out of it."

"Why?"

"Why? Number one, the *Post* and the *Times* are on it, and you can't compete with them."

"Maybe I can," I said stubbornly.

"Number two, you've got to draw a line between gossip and serious business, and this may be serious."

I was annoyed. It wasn't like him to try to scare me off a story. "What do you know about something called The Boys' Club?" I demanded.

He looked at me a long time, long enough that I knew he knew plenty.

"It's some prominent gays," he said finally. "They have parties from time to time."

"Like who?" I pressed.

Another long look. "Tom, what do we have now? Two openly gay Representatives? Okay, the true figures are probably more like fifteen to twenty Representatives and four or five Senators. These people are still in the closet, living under terrible pressures, and they like to socialize once in a while. But they and their guests are consenting adults. It's no story."

"I know a lot that I don't print," I told him. "But I like to know it. These people wouldn't be raising money for the campaign, would they?"

"It's a social group," he replied. "And I can't in good conscience say anything more."

We turned down coffee and ordered brandy instead. Duke's is not a place where people normally get sloshed in the afternoon, but the practice is not prohibited.

"Tell me about Joey Swink," I said.

"What about him?"

"I keep hearing stories."

"Joey's a hustler who came out of nowhere and made it big in politics. He didn't get where he is because he's an expert on foreign policy."

"Meaning?"

"When Japanese businessmen come to town, they're like visiting firemen everywhere, except they have more money. They want quality entertainment, tall blondes, preferably, and Joey understands."

"And Buzz Makito knows about this?"

Forrest sighed. "You have a most romantic view of Mr. Makito. Giving money to widows and orphans isn't his entire agenda."

The waiter brought our check, and we parted on Connecticut Avenue.

"Tom, this thing about the campaign money," he began. "As a friend, I say stay out of it."

At that, Forrest went his way and I went mine.

At my office, Cassie buzzed from the switchboard.

138

"No calls," I told her.

"It's Gloria," she said firmly. Gloria was her favorite writer.

"Please, no bad news," I whispered.

"You asked for it," Gloria replied. "It's about Sammy. I was at his place last night. He invited me to a dinner at the French Embassy on Sunday—he gave money for the war orphans, or something—then he took a call. Took it in the other room. When he came back he said he had a conflict, he couldn't go. He wouldn't explain and was nervous as a bug. I thought, My God, what would he turn down the French Embassy for? And my guess is this damned Boys' Club, whatever it is."

"Your guess, Gloria? That's a big leap."

"I listened in," she admitted. "That's what some man said, 'the monthly meeting of The Boys' Club,' very proud of himself."

I put down the phone and stared at the wall. I was a gossip columnist, deluged every day with enough raw material to fertilize Iowa. I had a daughter to contend with. I was involved in an interesting affair with Addie. My life was full, and my talents as a Junior Crimestopper were next to nil.

Forrest was right. Whatever was happening was NMP, not my problem. Let Grundy and the *Post* and the cops and the U.S. Attorney worry about Doyle Kane and whatever funny money was floating around. There was not one good reason in the world for me to be involved.

I give myself such excellent advice.

Why do I never follow it?

21.

I once had a drink with a very unhappy writer who was struggling with a biography of the Duchess of Windsor. The problem, he explained, was finding anyone with anything good to say about the woman.

If this were fiction, not the unabashed truth, I would, in the interests of "balance," seek to invest Sammy Shiner with redeeming qualities. I would reveal that he doted on his mother, took in stray cats, collected Chuck Berry 45s, or *something* positive. But the sad truth is that I have never heard a good word about Sammy, not even from the writers whose salaries he doubled at the magazine he bought. Sammy has inspired a rare consensus: a rat, through and through.

This beady-eyed blob made his fortune robbing widows and orphans in New England, then came to the Capital to claim his rightful place among those who lead our nation.

There are several ways that the newly rich seek prominence in our Capital. Some raise money for politicians, but that requires a certain level of charm and integrity. Some identify themselves with the Big Issues, bankrolling a Council on This or a Committee on That, but this demands at least minimal intelligence.

But there is a third way to buy a seat at the great poker game of politics, one that attracts the worst scoundrels, for its requires neither charm nor brains nor morality, and that is the one Sammy chose: he became a publisher.

As such, he conducted himself like many tycoons turned media moguls—that is, with the subtlety of a drunken Turk, hiring and firing editors at random, embracing bizarre causes, butchering the work of better men, cuddling up to the most loathsome political vermin at home and despots abroad, all the while dashing off incoherent editorials to be emblazoned across the cover of the once-proud *National Beacon*.

He had, needless to say, achieved his goal: Sammy Shiner was now a power broker whose calls were returned by everyone from Ted Kennedy to Jesse Helms. Moreover, by hosting a series of lavish receptions in his Georgetown mansion, he had achieved social notoriety. Divorced, and a certified Big Spender, he squired various of the Capital's more eligible belles, including my pal Gloria.

Gloria's suggestion that Sammy's yen for gals was only a cover for a more basic yen for guys was interesting but could not lower my opinion of him, which was already at rock bottom. He was the poor man's Rupert Murdoch, a moronic sleazebag who had hacked his way into the temple of journalism, and I would gladly have seen him drawn and quartered.

Still, to be fair, Sammy had good taste in cars. He was driving a gorgeous Lamborghini Countach when he set off from his home that Sunday evening with me in cool pursuit.

I'd been parked up the street for hours, in a borrowed Ford sedan, wearing Ray-Bans and a gimme cap as my disguise.

My expedition started on a light note, as porcine Sammy, swaddled in tweed, struggled to enter his $140,000 toy. The Countach's doors swing up like a gull's wings, and Sammy had to crawl in, then slide into the more or less horizontal driver's position. It looked uncomfortable as hell, but the machine was capable of going 180 mph (at eight miles per gallon), which meant I was in trouble if Sammy put his foot to the floor.

Happily, Sammy was in no hurry. He floated down to M Street, shot across Key Bridge, and hooked a right onto the George Washington Parkway, that most green and serene of byways. I could easily stay a car or two behind him, and my pursuit was made easier by the fact that the Countach has almost no rear visibility; its driver is supposed to focus on the car ahead, which he's about to pass, not the guy behind, who's already eating his dust.

When Sammy pulled onto the Beltway, headed into Virginia, my heart skipped a beat, for life is cheap there, but sensible Sammy took the first exit, right on Route 193 toward Great Falls. It was a narrow, twisting, two-lane road, built for the horse-drawn wagons of a century ago, not the tens of thousands of commuters who now clog it each weekday, but on this weekend evening we whizzed along, with me still two cars back and confident that I'd not been spotted.

We passsed the Madeira School, where girls on horseback were loping about a green field (a lovely sight, if you're not paying for it), and came to the hamlet of Great Falls, where Sammy stopped at a gourmet ice cream store. I veered into the 7-Eleven next door, ordered a grape Slurpee, and kept my eyes peeled.

My quarry flapped open the wings of his car and, apparently unable to exit unassisted, handed a teenager some bills. The boy went inside and returned shortly with a triple-dip chocolate ice-cream cone with sprinkles. A hint of humanity for Sammy: Can any man who pigs out on chocolate ice cream be all bad?

Soon we were off again, shooting through the countryside along Route 193, past the turnoff for L'Auberge Chez François, then west on Route 7, into the pink riot of the sunset.

I was caught up in my adventure, yet troubled, too, wondering if this was idiotic, a wild-goose chase. What did I truly know? Only that coked-up Gloria and crazed Grundy both suspected that Shiner might be tied in with something called The Boys' Club, which might or might not combine political fund-raising with sexual pleasures. I'd have laughed them off, except for Doyle Kane's death. *Something* was happening, and I was caught up in my fantasy of solving the mystery.

We entered Loudoun County, passed endless new subdivisions, each one uglier and more expensive than the last, crossed over Goose Creek, crested a hill, and could see the lights of Leesburg ahead. Little Leesburg had only one traffic light when I first visited there twenty years ago, but it had exploded into a jungle of cheap townhouses and fast-food joints. It even boasted a bypass, which Sammy took for a mile, then curled onto Route 15, headed south.

I knew this road well—the Carolina Trail it was, two centuries ago—for one year I courted a lady who trained horses in this green valley, courted her until it became clear that she preferred the company of horses to that of men. We passed Oatlands, site of riotous point-to-point races each spring, and then, as I daydreamed, Sammy Shiner abruptly turned off the highway onto a dirt road and vanished into the wooded darkness.

What to do? If I barreled after him he would almost certainly see me. If I didn't I might lose him. But I spotted one of those state signs that said "Road Ends 0.9 Miles." This must be Sammy's destination. I therefore pulled onto the shoulder, locked my car, and plunged into the woods.

Branches tore my hands and face until I came to the dirt

road Sammy had taken. I jogged along it in the darkness. A dog howled in the distance. Suddenly headlights swept the road from behind me. I leapt for cover, all the while straining for a glimpse of the driver. But I saw only the dark, blurred silhouette of a powerful car shooting past.

I followed its lights until I reached a clearing, and saw in the distance a cabin that faced a small pond. Sammy's car and the one that had passed me were parked in the shadows beside the cabin, and two men stood on the porch. One I took to be Sammy; the other was somehow familiar.

The men went inside and a dim light went on, a candle perhaps. I inched closer, intending to peer in the window. This, I thought proudly, was gossip collection at its most fearless, an adventure that even Grundy might have admired.

I was still smiling when I heard a twig snap behind me and, an instant later, felt the blow that crashed against my skull.

When I awoke, a light was shining in my face. My head throbbed and I was in some kind of box, curled into a fetal position. I was disoriented, confused, helpless.

Behind the blinding light, a man spoke.

"God, he looks awful. Lookit all that blood. You reckon he's daid?"

Another voice answered, "Naw, see him breathin'?"

I groaned and reached toward the light.

"Okay, buddy, just get up slow and easy."

Hands helped me from my prison—the trunk of my borrowed Ford—and I found myself in the custody of two sturdy Virginia troopers.

I learned that it was three in the morning, that my car was just where I'd left it, and that my billfold was still in my pocket. There remained the problem of answering the troopers' polite but persistent questions. I identified myself—both lawmen were among my readers—and mingled fact with fiction. In my new account, I had been following a prominent politician to his love nest; the rest of my story was fact, right down to the thump on my head.

The troopers nodded sagely; the handsome buffoon I mentioned was famous for making love, not laws.

"Fellows, maybe I shouldn't have been following the gentleman, and maybe I was on private property, but I still don't think they had to dent my skull like that. Could we just check out that cabin?"

The troopers, lured by the prospect of hot gossip, quickly agreed, and we set off toward the cabin I'd never reached.

"This here's Miz Neville's place," one trooper declared.

"Who's she?" I asked.

"A real nice lady lives over the hill. She sure didn't bang you on the head. The thing is, kids come down here and swim and use the place. She never locks it—they'd just break in."

The troopers drew their guns as we advanced upon the dark and silent cabin. Its door was open, as promised, but the cabin was empty. We found few signs of life: a can of soup in the cupboard, a half-used candle, a cold fireplace, dust on the mantel.

"You sure you saw somebody here?"

"Two men on the porch, plus the one that beaned me."

"Funny they'd haul you back to your car."

"Funny as a crutch," I amended.

"Mr. Tullis, I don't see what else we can do. The truth is, it ain't smart to go followin' folks around, particularly when they're out for some lovin'."

I could not disagree, so I thanked them and started the long drive back to the Capital.

I staggered to my office the next morning, my poor battered head still throbbing, and was greeted by a call from Polly. "Tommy, I'm at Harris Ratcliffe's office. Can you come over right away?"

"What's wrong?"

"I . . . I can't talk. There's a problem. Please come."

"I'm on my way," I said.

As I cabbed to the Hill, my thoughts were less on Polly's problem than on my fiasco the night before. Clearly, at some point Sammy Shiner had known he was being followed. Maybe he'd called for help on his car phone. Maybe the stop for ice cream was to allow time for a trap to be laid. With brilliant hindsight, I decided that a deserted cabin was no place for a group of powerful men to meet, but a fine place to dispatch some fool who tried to follow one of their members.

Forrest had insisted The Boys' Club was social, not political. Even if that was true, a group of powerful gays wouldn't take kindly to a gossip columnist poking into their secret lives. With a shudder, I realized I was lucky to be alive.

At Allworth headquarters, I found Harris Ratcliffe scowling at his desk like some rancid Buddha, Mac McKenna perched nervously on a chair, and Polly huddled on the sofa. I went over and took her hand.

"What is it?" I asked her.

She shook her head and looked at Ratcliffe. "He'll show you," she whispered. "I'm sorry, Tommy."

Ratcliffe heaved himself up and popped a cassette into the VCR. "Take a look at this, Tullis," he growled.

A black-and-white picture of Don filled the screen. But not the handsome, commanding Don I knew; here the photographer had captured an oafish grin on his face.

"Senator Allworth says he's a friend of working Americans," a seductive voice said.

Suddenly a picture of Polly, also in black and white, a picture that somehow made this infinitely kind woman look like a pinched, cold-eyed shrew.

The real Polly flinched and turned away.

"But Senator Allworth's wife says American workers produce junk," the voice declared angrily.

The evil Senator again.

"Senator Allworth says he's a friend of America's teachers."

The hag again.

"His wife says our public schools are a mess."

The oaf again.

"The Senator says he can lead America to greatness."

Polly again.

"His wife doubts if America's problems can ever be solved."

Then the two of them together.

"Instead of running for President, shouldn't Senator Allworth get his own house in order?"

The picture held for a ten-count, the two of them recalling

the evil king and queen in a Disney film. Even knowing them, I shuddered.

Polly was sobbing. I held tight to her hand.

"Who did it?" I asked Ratcliffe.

"Some so-called 'independent' outfit, probably tied in with Craxton. We're checking."

"Has it run yet?"

"It starts tomorrow in California and New Jersey. A network guy slipped us a print."

"It'll backfire," I said. "It'll create sympathy for Polly and Don."

"Maybe. But we can't count on it."

"Why not?" I was too mad to think straight, but I remembered what Forrest had said, that negative spots usually work the first time out.

"In the first place, there's a germ of truth. Everything in it, she was quoted as saying in the *Post*."

"But it's distorted, twisted out of context."

"So what else is new? The other thing is, Americans love to have a Dragon Lady to hate. Eleanor Roosevelt. Jane Fonda. Once a broad gets on the shit list, she never gets off."

"It's poison if the idea gets out that a politican can't control his wife," Mac McKenna added.

"Don has to denounce this crap," I said. "Defend his wife. Demand that the rats come out of the sewer and show their faces. A news conference, with him and Polly and the kids together."

"All that's gonna happen," Ratcliffe grunted.

A question arose in the slow-motion of my mind: If they've made their plans, why am I here?

Mac McKenna, reading my thoughts, said, "Tom, we all agree that Don has to meet this head-on, defend Polly, show outrage, and so on. But that's not enough. We have to retaliate in kind."

"In kind," I said blankly.

"Someone is trying to sink Don. Let's face it, we're running second now. This spot isn't just to beat Don this year, it's to bloody Don so he never has a shot, four or eight or twelve years from now."

"We're not even sure it's Craxton," Ratcliffe growled. "Maybe somebody's trying to stir up a fight where they both get bloodied. All we know for sure is this is hardball: you fuck us, we fuck you. And that's how we're gonna play."

"How?" I asked.

"Craxton was a judge for a while. We can paint him as the best friend the rapists and heroin dealers of America ever had."

"Go to it," I said. I was worried about Polly. I was holding her hand but she wasn't there.

"We're looking for a kayo punch," Ratcliffe said. "We're looking real hard at that wife of his."

I began to catch on. Ava Craxton was a big, brassy blonde. A lot of ugly stories were circulating about her and the governor. That she'd had an affair with a state police captain. That they were childless because he was impotent. Lovely stories.

"We're hoping you can help us, Tom."

I stared at him dumbly.

"We were talking one time," Mac continued. "Didn't you tell me about her having an illegitimate child?"

I groaned inwardly. A couple of months before I'd shot my mouth off at a party, mentioning to Mac an anonymous letter I'd received that claimed to identify Ava Craxton's illegitimate son.

It was nothing I'd print—junk like that came in every day— but it was juicy enough that I'd repeated it.

And now they were desperate, counting on me to give them the dirt to demolish Craxton's oft-proclaimed facade of "family values."

And they had poor, tearful, beat-up Polly there to put even more pressure on me.

I didn't need this. Moral decisions aren't my game. They went out years ago, with fuzzy sideburns and bell-bottom pants.

I didn't give a damn for Craxton, and the attack on Polly was beneath contempt. But was it my job to put the knife to Ava Craxton? Was I still some kind of journalist, however depraved, or just a hired gun doing hits for my political pals?

I was tempted. Part of me thought, Okay, play the game, and if these oafs blunder into the White House they'll owe you a big one.

But they had made a mistake, hotboxing me with Polly there. I couldn't do it, not with her watching. I'd rather she thought me a coward, an enemy even, than a sleazebag.

"I got a letter, Mac," I said. "But it was junk and I threw it away."

"You don't remember the names?" Ratcliffe bellowed.

I shook my head. I was lying, of course. I had the letter on file. I have everything on file.

"Sorry, fellows." I looked at my watch. "So if there's nothing else . . ."

Mac McKenna looked ninety years old. "Well, there is one thing. Polly was hoping . . ."

Polly turned her sad eyes on me. "I was hoping you could help me with a speech," she said.

"You've got it," I said, and hurried us to a little Mexican restaurant on Eighth Street.

Polly wanted to do a speech on the homeless. Some political consultant had produced a draft. She showed it to me and I could see that she had been right to reject it. It was illiterate, statistic-laden drivel.

"Just tell me what you want to say," I told her.

Polly's daughter Christie, a student at Sidwell Friends, had been volunteering in a homeless shelter on weekends, it seemed. Polly had gone to pick her up in the evenings, and been shocked by what she'd seen. "All winter, Tommy, I'd think about us at home, so warm and secure, and those people out there in the cold. It's so awful. We talked to Don, and he told us how little the government was doing—that was the first time I thought he should run for President. And if they want me to make appearances, that's what I want to talk about, how shameful it is that our country would let people live like that. But I don't know how to say it."

I was taking notes. "All you have to do is say what you just told me," I said. "Just what you feel. No bullshit—leave the bullshit to the candidate—just a personal, factual statement."

"That's exactly what I want," she said. I promised to rough out a draft overnight, then walked her out to her car.

"I'm sorry I couldn't be more help back there."

"You had that letter, didn't you? About Mrs. Craxton."

I must have looked stunned. She took my hand. "You're a lousy liar, Tommy."

"I couldn't let them use me like that."

"Of course not," she said. "Don shouldn't lower himself to dirt like that. No matter what they do to me, it's no excuse to hurt someone else."

Her eyes glistened. I held her close and prayed she was strong enough for whatever lay ahead.

When I reached home my daughter was there. Instead of joining the Allworth campaign, she'd taken a job as a waitress in a trendy Georgetown restaurant. "It's really neat," she declared. "Everybody in the place is wired."

"Except you," I reminded her.

"Or course," she said primly. "Daddy, you remember you asked me about something called The Penner Project?"

"I remember."

"Who told you about it?"

"Just a guy."

"How much did he know about what's going on?"

"Dammit, Holly, let me ask the questions. Did you find out something or not?"

"You'd better believe I found out something."

I waited.

"Daddy, it's gross and unbelievable."

I could only laugh; what else would it be?

She settled on the floor across from my chair. My daughter has long blond hair, milk-white skin, and an angelic face. But an angel she is not.

"When I was a senior at Penner, let's face it, we were pretty wild, but there was this freshman class coming along that was *really* messed up. Well, they're seniors now. That's what this is all about."

"The younger generation."

"You remember the Friday intern program? Girls work one day a week in a congressional office? Well, this year things are absolutely out of control. I got all this from Deakie— she's psyched, she couldn't *believe* it!

"This one girl started having an affair with the press secretary in her office, and the others started saying, hey, why mess with a press secretary, why not go for it? I mean, it got to be a competition, to see who could seduce their Congressman or Senator. And you know what?"

I groaned. I knew what.

"It wasn't hard. I mean, a few were too old, or too noble, or gay, or whatever, but at last count six girls have scored."

"Oh, God," I sighed.

"It gets worse," Holly warned. "This one girl's father has a house on Third Street, right behind the Supreme Court, but he's in China, so everybody takes the guys there, and they've rigged up a tape recorder under the bed. They try to get the guys to talk, you know, about politics and what they believe and all. They've got really wild stuff on tape. That's why they call it The Penner Project—like it was a sociological study. Everybody's arguing about what to do with the tapes, send them to reporters, or publish them, or what."

My head hurt worse than ever. "Holly, listen to me. Tell

those girls to burn the damn tapes and shut up about this, or a lot of people could get hurt. This isn't a joke—they're playing around with people's lives."

She touched my hand. "Look, I absolutely agree. I don't know what's wrong with these kids today."

My daughter, the reasonable woman.

Addie called that evening, just back from a campaign swing, and asked me by. We ate cold chicken and sat on her deck and talked.

"I think I'm going crazy," she declared.

"Me too."

"No, really, it's just too much. The house was broken into. The carpenter showed up drunk. I dropped the car off for a routine checkup, they did two thousand dollars' worth of work. My maid quit. My car was booted. Sarah has decided she hates me. Mike's lawyer has been giving my lawyer a lot of crap. The dog has worms, my shrink is out of town, and now my editor wants a *series* on the campaign. I can't *deal* with all this."

"You need a wife."

"Ha ha."

What can you tell Superwoman when the going gets tough? That if you drive a sixty-thousand-dollar car you are going to have two-thousand-dollar checkups? That divorces are messy, that big empty houses are broken into, that kids are tough, that editors want output from their star reporters?

"I haven't told you the worst of it."

I braced myself.

"I keep running into Mike. Yesterday, at the Press Club, he marched up and kissed me on the cheek. I wanted to scratch his eyes out."

"Make the sign of the cross with your fingers. Like he was Count Dracula."

"I despise him so. Why can't he understand?"

I did not consider this a healthy topic. "I talked to Polly today. She sends her best."

Addie made a face. "How is she?"

"Surviving. She's been campaigning some."

"I thought campaigning was beneath her dignity."

"She wants to help Don."

"It's a bit late for that, isn't it? She's done too much damage already." Her sharpness startled me. What reason did she have to be so angry with Polly?

In time we went to bed. Everything was simpler there. She could quit being the brass-knuckles journalist and be a little girl again. "Tell me I'm pretty," she said, and I did. I loved the way she smiled after we made love, the way her eyes sparkled, her face softened in the moonlight. I didn't understand Addie, but I was crazy about her.

And yet, as close as we were, I felt a distance between us; I thought something was going on in her mind that was beyond me. I puzzled over what it could be. Sometimes I suspected that in time she would take Mike back and she was using me to keep him jealous. Does that sound unkind, unfair, cynical? Perhaps it is, but in my experience women like Addie are exceedingly tough; they've been screwed over by men for decades, and by the time they reach forty they don't miss many tricks.

My father was a handsome alcoholic who devoted his life to serious study of the opposite sex. Ah, the tales that man could tell. There was the time his second wife, the Montana cattle queen, chased him off the ranch and stalked him in the mountains with a deer rifle for two days and nights.

Once, when I was a teenager and he was coming off a binge with a Houston oil heiress who he claimed had murdered three husbands, he said something I've never forgotten: "Son, always remember this—any woman, given the opportunity, is capable of anything."

Perhaps his words sound sexist today, or oversimple, or otherwise objectionable, but I have found them a useful guide to life's misadventures. I love women, fear them, and do not often let myself be surprised by them.

And what does this have to do with Addie?

Only this.

I was glad to seize all the warmth and comfort I could, amid the madness of that long election-year spring; I savored my nights with Addie, the sweet yielding anger of her body, the starlight in her eyes, but I remembered my father's advice and I assumed nothing.

23.

I did some checking on Joey Swink once, when I was in Los Angeles on a pilgrimage to the Playboy Mansion. As best I could discover, Joey turned up in L.A. at age twenty and quickly progressed from bartender to manager of a go-go joint to producer of stag movies.

From there it was not a great leap to politics. His film company eased out of porn and into making political spots. One of his candidates was elected to Congress, whereupon Joey arrived on the Washington scene and in time talked his way into the White House media office. He left the White House to start a one-man "media consulting" office. Business was good, particularly after Buzz Makito hit town and became his number-one client.

Joey's was an unusual career, perhaps, but hardly unprecedented. Each new administration sweeps people up from obscurity in California or Texas or Georgia or wherever; the

156

magic carpet of politics carries them to 1600 Pennsylvania Avenue, where they sniff that dangerous drug called power. Soon, if they are even halfway bright, they carve out a place for themselves in the loose-knit alliance of law firms and corporations and media empires that rules America.

You hear mostly about the charmers: Clark Clifford, the Golden Boy of the Truman administration, who went on to be the ultimate Superlawyer; Ted Sorensen, Kennedy's "alter ego" and later Keeper of the Flame; Bill Moyers, LBJ's Boy Wonder and later so relentlessly high-minded a journalist that he seemed hardly human.

What you don't hear so much about are the rogues, hustlers, and con men who also ride the magic carpet to power. Now and then they surface in some scandal, but mostly they operate in the shadows, making big bucks off their White House connections, and Joey Swink is a prime example.

To some, the swarthy, somewhat disreputable Joey seemed an odd partner for the subtle, cultured Buzz Makito, but I found their union natural enough. Swink was schooled in modern, state-of-the-art image-making, and Makito's goal was to project a shining image for his native land.

Buzz was doing a good job of that, with his lavish parties and his millions for charity and culture, but I was starting to wonder if there was more going on. Forrest Keel claimed that Joey supplied women to visiting Japanese businessmen. If that was true, you wondered what other games they might be playing.

I called Joey's office the next morning.

Joey wasn't in, but his secretary confided that he was at home. I knew where that was: a mansion on Foxhall Road previously inhabited by one of the lesser Rockefellers.

I drove there, found the gate open, pulled into the driveway, and discovered Joey, in a bathing suit and sneakers, washing a classic cherry-red '57 Corvette.

As I approached he grinned broadly. "Tom, what a pleasant surprise!" he declared, extending a soapy hand.

"I didn't know you washed your own," I said, all charm.

"Who else would I trust with this baby?"

"She's a beauty."

"To drive her is to be young again!"

"I'm sorry to bother you at home . . ."

"No bother!"

"But something important came up."

"Then come in, have a beer. Stay for lunch."

Joey led me to the patio behind his house. He slipped on a shirt and we sat in canvas-backed director's chairs. A screenplay lay on the table; he saw me glance at it.

"I'm moving into film production, Tom," he said gravely. "It's always been my dream."

I nodded respectfully and got to the point.

"The other night you asked me if I'd heard about something called The Penner Project."

Joey's eyes were as frozen as his smile.

"I did some checking," I continued. "Something very unfortunate has been going on. I've sent word that it should stop, that all the evidence should be destroyed. These girls don't understand the implications of what they're doing. It's important that neither you nor I say a word about this to anyone."

For the longest moment, his face was cold as a lizard's; then Joey broke into his winningest smile.

"Tom, you've got my curiosity aroused," he declared. "But I honestly don't know a thing. Somebody said something about The Penner Project, but no details. I took it as a joke. I knew your daughter had gone there, so I mentioned it. I won't breathe another word."

I didn't know whether to believe him or not, but if he was lying, at least I'd warned him.

"Who told you about it?" I asked him.

Joey looked perplexed. "Thomas, I'm searching my memory, but I'm damned if I can remember."

I doubted if Joey had ever forgotten anything in his life, but I couldn't argue.

The door opened and a pretty, dark-haired girl, about Holly's age, looked out. "Oh, excuse me," she said, and retreated into the kitchen.

"Your daughter?" I said.

He nodded. "It's amazing the things they get into, isn't it?"

"I've quit being amazed," I admitted.

He walked me to my car, which looked dowdy alongside his sleek Corvette.

"You still after the campaign-finance story?"

"Yeah. I don't think it's the defense people."

"Maybe not," he agreed. "I've been hearing a new angle."

"What's that?"

Joey had dark, curly hair and a narrow, cunning face. "I probably shouldn't say. I've got no proof."

"I could check it out."

"Let me think about it."

He wouldn't budge, so I left, unsatisfied. I didn't know what game he was playing, and not knowing angered me.

I hadn't learned a thing from Joey—or had I?

All the way home, I had a maddening sense that I had seen or heard something important at his house, but it would not come into focus. I thought and thought until I wanted to cry out in frustration, but whatever it was remained just beyond my mind's reach. I was as confused, as lost, as ever.

24.

Grundy was crazy drunk, raving, sweeping me along into the sulphurous swamp of his soul.

"Who rules this fucking country?" he raged. "You think it's whatever clown we elect every four years? Bullshit! He's the front man. He makes pretty speeches and when the crunch comes he does what the boys in uniform tell him."

He paused to slosh more Southern Comfort into his glass. Grundy wore only torn jeans, an EAT IT RAW T-shirt from a Key West oyster bar, and an expression of radiant, beatific madness.

In desperation, I had come to his rathole of an apartment, above a massage parlor on Fourteenth Street, and told him of my ill-fated pursuit of Sammy Shiner. Grundy cursed my stupidity but otherwise was indifferent to my fiasco. His mind was aflame with larger issues.

He began raving again, a conspiracy theory, the Kennedy

assassination, a Pentagon-CIA-FBI plot, a secret memo he claimed to have stolen from J. Edgar Hoover's office. He had details, dates, documents, the fruits of a quarter-century's investigation.

I could not bring myself to ask the obvious question: Why haven't you printed the story? Where is your proof? Poor Grundy believed in his conspiracy theory as other men believed in God. The Kennedy assassination was his Moby Dick, and he would pursue it to the death.

I slowly tuned him out. My concerns were less cosmic. Who killed Doyle Kane? What about the stories of money in the campaign? What I had seen or heard at Joey Swink's house that day that would not quite come into focus?

Grundy's monologue was interrupted by the phone. He listened a moment, then howled, "Get out of my life, bitch!" People called Grundy constantly with tips, theories, grudges, fantasies; I wondered when he slept.

There was gunfire outside, the sound of a woman screaming.

"The Kennedys were gonna get out of Vietnam," Grundy continued. "They were gonna make up with Castro, make an arms deal with Khrushchev. Well, no way the generals are gonna sit still for that, so they zapped JFK, them and the CIA, and set up that moron Oswald."

"Grundy, all this is interesting," I said, "but it doesn't help me with my problem. I keep hearing that somebody is feeding illegal money into the primaries, and maybe they killed Doyle Kane, because he was about to blow the whistle. The question is, could this military-intelligence cabal of yours be involved?"

He squinted at me, as if noticing me for the first time. "Not a bloody chance. Those bozos running this year—Allworth, Craxton, the rest of 'em—are all the same. Tweedledum and Tweedledee. It don't matter which one wins, so why would they spend money, much less zap somebody?"

I was ready to leave. Grundy's conspiracy theories couldn't answer my questions. But as I started to rise, the phone rang.

Grundy waved me back into my chair and tossed me a set of earphones.

"Mr. Grundy? It's me."

The voice was breathless, frightened.

"Who are you? Tell me your damn name."

"No, I can't. Not yet."

"Then come over and we'll talk."

"I'm afraid."

"You're gutless, is what you are."

"Call it that if you must. I only know I don't want to die the way Doyle did."

"Was he your good buddy?"

"We were very close, for a time. Oh, we drifted apart, but I always thought of us as brothers."

"Well, if these bastards killed your brother, you ought to do something about it."

"I want to, Mr. Grundy. But I'm afraid. They have so much money, so much power."

"What money? What kind of money?"

"Isn't it obvious?"

"Dammit, man, this government is a goddamn corpse with a thousand vultures circling over it. Which ones're you talking about?"

"Drugs, Mr. Grundy, drugs. They're what I'm talking about. They've got billions in cash and they desperately want to change the laws."

"Yeah, but who are they? Give me names," Grundy demanded.

"No. I've said enough already."

"Level with me and I'll nail the bastards. Oliver Grundy ain't afraid of nobody. But I can't wait forever."

"Please, I need time to think. Goodbye for now."

Grundy slammed down the phone. "That's the third time he's called," he growled. "He'll probably get himself killed before he tells me his damn story."

On that enigmatic note, Grundy lit a joint and seemed to

lose interest in me. As I left he was starting a Chuck Norris movie on his VCR.

Out on Fourteenth Street, police were fighting with young black men. Whites were being pulled from their cars and handcuffed, for buying crack, I guessed.

I found my car miraculously untouched and drove away, depressed by Grundy's lurid tales, yet excited that the caller might know something about Doyle's death.

Then, out of my confusion, something strange happened. The workings of my mind are a mystery to me. All I know is that I was driving out Sixteenth Street, listening to a Mel Torme tape, when in the depths of my mind I made a connection. Something that had not been there before was suddenly as clear as the road ahead of me. One moment I was lost in Grundy's horrific theories, and the next I knew what I had seen on the dark road in Loudoun County.

But what was I to do with my knowledge? Take it to the police, who would surely scoff? Or to Grundy, who in his madness might spoil everything?

Abruptly, I made my decision. I would grasp the nettle, seize the moment, act boldly.

And immediately, the very next morning.

25.

I started calling Buzz Makito's office at eight the next morning, but no one answered that early. While I waited I watched the news.

The hot political story was the TV spot attacking Don and Polly. The news showed part of it, followed by Don denouncing it.

Meanwhile, Governor Craxton protested his innocence, and the spot itself had been withdrawn by whoever aired it in the first place.

To me, at least, Don came off as forceful and Polly as an innocent victim. But who knows how those things cut? For a few thousand dollars, whoever made the spot had implanted in the national subconscious a picture of a wimpish Don and a shrewish Polly. Maybe that was all that mattered.

I tried Makito again, still got no response, and started

reading the *Times,* which carried a friendly "Woman in the News" profile of Polly.

I was so pleased that I called Polly to congratulate her. To my surprise, the candidate answered.

"Don? Hey, you looked great on the tube this morning. And that was a good piece on Polly."

"Yeah, things are looking up. I'll blow Craxton away in the next couple of weeks."

"Can you tie him to that dirty ad?"

"We're working on it. Listen, I want to talk to you."

"Same here."

"I'm leaving for a week. Why don't you hook up with me somewhere? Talk to Mac, he's got the schedule. How about it? Go play reporter for a couple of days."

Did I want to plunge into that madness, even as an honored guest?

"I'll try to."

"Great, Tom. We'll have a ball."

Finally I reached Buzz Makito's secretary, made an appointment, and at ten was ushered into the big, bright office where the enigmatic Japanese held court.

Buzz rose and took my hand. His cream linen suit, handmade in Hong Kong, fit like a second skin. Buzz always dressed beautifully, unusual for men in the Capital. He made the rest of us, in our lookalike Brooks Brothers suits and Britches sport coats, look like drones.

"Thomas, what a pleasure," Buzz declared. "Do sit down. Will you be comfortable there?"

A young man appeared, unbidden, with coffee.

My host inquired gravely about my health, my offspring, and my view of the election.

I smiled and made small talk and reflected that I no more understood this man than if he'd just stepped off a flying saucer.

He came from a land I've never seen, spoke a language I

don't speak, and embodied a culture utterly foreign to me. Moreover, he and his countrymen were in the process of buying up my country's real estate, hotels, office buildings, factories, and financial institutions at an unprecedented rate. A few American politicians had protested, and as a result Japanese corporations were now spending $50 million a year to hire American lobbyists to protect themselves from the American Congress.

I'd even read that someone had opened a piano bar in Manhattan exclusively for Japanese businessmen, who paid fifty dollars for a drink plus music and agreeable young women.

Maybe it was poetic justice, after a century of American economic imperalism, but I thought it stank.

"I appreciate your seeing me on such short notice."

"A pleasure, always. By the way, that was a fine item you carried on the golf-course purchase."

I wondered if Buzz's hospitality had made me too anxious to please him. When people start liking what a gossip writes about them, he's losing it.

He was leaning back in his chair now, legs crossed, fingers steepled, clearly engrossed in my tale, clearly anxious to enlist in my cause.

"Buzz, I told you I'm investigating illegal money in the primaries. I'm afraid a friend of mine was killed for trying to find out what was happening."

My host nodded gravely.

"The other night I followed someone I thought might be involved. He led me out to Loudoun County, to a dirt road off Route 15. I followed on foot and got banged on the head for my trouble. But before that happened, a second car drove down the road."

My hands were trembling. Was I right to have come here? Should I be telling this man what I knew? That had been my instinct, seized upon the night before—be bold, take the initiative.

"It was dark. I only had a glimpse of the car as it shot past me. I wasn't sure what it was. But then, two days ago, I saw it again."

Buzz Makito waited, inscrutable.

"It was Joey Swink's '57 Corvette. Those lines, even in the dark, stuck in my subconscious, and when I saw his car the other day I recognized it."

My host's boyish face registered alarm.

"I want answers. What was Swink doing there? Who knocked me out? Who's putting money into the campaign? I don't trust Swink. But he works for you. And I know you're concerned about this. So I hoped that . . ."

What was that sound roaring in my ears? Was it my fear that I had made a terrible mistake? To confront Makito, to make him my ally, had seemed a master stroke the night before.

My host was looking above and beyond me as he replied. "Joey of course is not my employee," he began, "although it is true he has worked closely with me. I came to this country, on behalf of a number of my countrymen, to see if it might be possible to combine good deeds with the business of making money. There was much I did not know, and many decisions I had to make. To trust this person or that one. To support this project or another. To avoid the pitfalls that beset a foreigner in your Capital. I sought advice from many successful men. Time after time, Joey was the one who gave me the most shrewd advice.

"I am aware that Joey has a shadowy past. But he is a valuable man. The fact that he has served in your White House suggests that fact."

"I don't doubt that he's useful," I said. "But I want to know who banged me on the head."

Buzz looked pained. "Joey is a free agent, with involvements that are unknown to me. He can be hotheaded and impulsive. But I have faith in his basic honesty. Let's be candid, Joey is a wealthy man. Why would someone who's

167

worked so hard to get where he is risk it by illegal involvement in a political campaign? He does very well, no matter who's in the White House."

"Buzz, I still want to know what he was doing following me that night."

Makito nodded sagely. "I will ask him, of course. If he has been involved in anything improper, naturally I will sever our relationship."

I nodded.

"Let me be sure I have the facts straight. You saw the outline of a car in the darkness, and later became convinced it was Joey's Corvette."

"Yes, more or less."

"Did you actually see Joey?"

"I saw someone in the shadows I took for him."

"There are of course a good many Corvettes of that vintage in the Washington area. They form clubs, I understand, and hold rallies."

I was taken aback. Once I had fixed on Joey and his Corvette I had not thought about other possibilities.

"That's true," I said. "But I'm sure it was he."

My host fiddled with his cuff link. "What day was this?"

"Sunday," I said. "About eight in the evening."

Buzz leaned forward dramatically. "Then Joey couldn't have been following you, because he was having dinner at my home, along with several other guests."

Zap! His testimony hit me like a hammer. Either Buzz Makito was lying, or Tom Tullis was an idiot.

Or both.

I mumbled that perhaps I'd been mistaken. I only wanted to get out of there as fast as I could. My bold strategy had blown up in my face.

"There must be five hundred Corvettes in this city," I said miserably.

"And we must find the right one," Buzz declared.

"Thomas, have you spoken to the authorities about your concern over this young man's death?"

"The police think he was murdered by . . . by someone he met socially, unrelated to politics."

Buzz lit a cigar. "May I speak in absolute confidence?"

"Of course." I was grateful, after I'd made such a fool of myself, for the way he soothed my battered ego.

"As you know, I never involve myself in politics. But I heard a most alarming story the other day."

"Out with it," I said.

"I was told, in the strictest confidence, that several of the television evangelists have been making large secret donations to various campaigns."

"Which ones? Which of the preachers, I mean."

"I don't know."

"But why would they give illegally?"

"My source said they want both respectability and certain changes in the tax code. Friends in the White House could help them achieve both ends. But they are afraid to operate in public, for fear of offending their unsophisticated followers, and also for fear of media criticism. So they give in secret and keep their purity."

"Interesting. I talked to Joey yesterday, and he had a theory, but wouldn't tell me about it."

"No doubt he would not repeat it without my approval."

TV evangelists pumping illegal millions into the campaign? A great story, if I could prove it. The trouble was, this was the second story the Makito-Swink team had floated with me. The defense-contractors theory hadn't flown, so now it was the Falwell-Swaggart crowd. Maybe it was true, but it was also possible that my Japanese friend was jerking me around.

I thanked him profusely and left.

26.

The next day I ran off and joined the circus.

Don gave me only a brief handshake as I boarded his campaign plane; he was about to be briefed by his foreign-policy team, three Dr. Strangeloves who kept muttering in German.

Once we were aloft, I grabbed a beer and worked the aisle, besieged by reporters who were bursting with gossip they could not print but felt an overwhelming urge to communicate. Six affairs were reported, innumerable one-nighters, several entries into the Mile High Club, plus a general consensus that Don Allworth, despite his high IQ and manly profile, was full of crap. But of course reporters think all candidates are full of crap; it is a question of degree.

I was embraced by a half-mad photographer called Flash Barnaby, who began bellowing out the story of his long-lost son. "You never knew my second wife, nobody knew her, she just got pregnant, got pissed, and got her ass to California. Never heard from her again, her or the kid either. I figured, hell, he'll turn up if he's worth a damn. And damned if I didn't get this letter, right before Christmas. 'Dear Dad. We've never met, but I've always wanted to know you, even though my mom doesn't approve, blah-blah-blah, so if you'll send me a round-trip ticket from L.A. to D.C. I'll come see you.' Sounded cool to me, the kid's twenty, might as well meet him. So I send the ticket. And when the day comes I go out to Dulles to meet the plane. Took a bottle of champagne, some dope, ready to wlecome my boy with open arms. And you know what? *He fucking doesn't show!* You know why? The little bastard *cashed in the ticket*!"

Red-bearded, bearlike Barnaby was ablaze with fatherly pride. *"He's a chip off the old block!"*

I pushed on, hearing about poker games, dinner plans, nervous breakdowns, girls who might and girls who would; then, to my surprise, I came face to face with Addie.

"What are *you* doing here?" she demanded.

"Hey, lighten up," I said. "The candidate invited me, so I came."

She shrugged. "You may be too late. If he can't win West Virginia and Oregon, his money will dry up, he'll never get to California."

We found seats together. "Denouncing that dumb attack on his wife helped," she said. "But now he's betting a lot on this gay thing."

Gay rights had become an important, if muted, issue in the final weeks of the primaries.

It was a no-win issue, the kind candidates usually run from. On the one hand fearful parents, on the other hand impassioned gays; no one could be sure how it might cut, when it might backfire. Since the campaign began, both Don and Craxton had paid lip service to "a war against AIDS"—but refused to talk numbers—and had cautiously endorsed most of the gay-rights agenda.

Then several things happened. Don started falling behind. He was outraged by the TV spot that attacked Polly. Finally, a member of Governor Craxton's staff died of AIDS, and the evening news showed him attending the man's funeral. It was no doubt a noble act of friendship but politically it put the governor closer to gay rights than he needed to be.

It was only a few days later, in West Virginia, that Don announced himself "deeply troubled" by gay teachers in the public schools. The issue was big locally, Addie told me, and overnight polls showed that Don's popularity had shot up dramatically.

Two days later, in Chicago, he was asked if gay couples should be permitted to adopt children. Don declared it "a terrible idea." Once again, his overnights went through the roof.

"He's pigheaded and crazy," Addie declared. "For short-term blue-collar support he's committing long-term suicide. You can't be elected President by gay-baiting."

"The polls show a hell of a lot of homophobia out there," I said.

"Don's seen those polls," Addie said. "This thing was calculated. He talked to Ratcliffe and McKenna about it. They told him not to do it. They said, if you lose you lose, but go out with class and try again later. This way he can ruin himself forever."

I found the subject profoundly depressing, and I was glad when we landed somewhere—anywhere—for an airport rally.

Over behind a chain-link fence, kept there by the Secret Service, six or seven young men were chanting and waving signs about AIDS.

Don ignored the protestors and delivered his stump speech. The media knew it by heart; some of them recited along with him. "Mush, mush, mush," one TV reporter kept chanting.

Yet the crowd cheered wildly, and I thought they understood more than the reporters, for reporters deal in fact while voters have an eye for magic. The point was not what Don said but what he was: the jut of his jaw, the glint in his eye, his vigor, his aura. I watched this man I'd known for a quarter-century and realized I'd never known him at all. He was different up there, a star, sending off sparks, perhaps presidential.

I don't pay much attention to campaign speeches, but I always study the faces of the people. If you're on the plane, you're cynical; you can't help it. But people out there in the real world aren't cynical. Life is tough for most of them, and they're looking for a leader who'll make it a little better. They ought to be cynical after all these turkeys we've elected, but they keep believing someone decent will come along. So I watch their faces to see if a candidate can soften them, make their eyes shine, make them feel good about themselves and our beleaguered country.

Don did. People were nodding imperceptibly—they saw the star quality the reporters missed, and I thought that somehow he was on the right track.

After the speech, an earnest young reporter said, "Senator, on the question of gay rights, aren't you concerned about individual civil liberties?"

"Of course I am," Don declared gravely. "And the challenge is to balance individual rights against the right of law-abiding citizens to health and safety."

Law-abiding citizens? Were gays criminals?

Reporters were scribbling, film was rolling. Don was dealing in code words, sending out signals, and to my mind it was no better than the old wink-and-nod racism of a few decades back.

Then we were running to the plane, crowding the aisles,

opening beers. Reporters huddled together, replaying their tapes, making sure they had the quotes right, debating what the lead should be. A stewardess, new to the campaign, was shouting that we had to sit down and buckle up during take-off. Some photographers spewed beer on her, and she fled in tears.

For the next forty-eight hours we were endlessly winging toward the Tri-Cities Airport. There are dozens of Tri-Cities Airports in the American heartland, magical places where with one speech a candidate can make news in three "media markets," even in three states.

The campaign plane was a little world of its own, filled with passion and intrigue. Even my arrival had raised eyebrows, because my affair with Addie was not unknown; I was greeted with winks and nudges. But many dramas were in progress. A columnist's wife had turned up unexpectedly one night, their baby in her arms, kicking on the door of his hotel room, as his campaign girlfriend fled down the fire escape.

When we arrived in Portland that first evening, Addie went to file her story. A local reporter named Fergus O'Higgins and I decided to take a walk. He was a portly, bearded fellow who was at work on a novel about a Christlike Martian who comes to earth, campaigns for universal peace, and is assassinated by the CIA.

"Come on, there's somebody I want you to meet," O'Higgins said.

He led us to a fringe neighborhood of warehouses, pawnshops, and discount stores. We entered a storefront office where two dozen young people were busy on telephones and computers. A woman looked up. "The boss in?" O'Higgins asked.

The woman nodded toward a back room, and my friend led us back.

To my amazement, we were greeted by my old friend Wally Love. The pear-shaped money man leaped up from his desk and shook our hands. "Fergie! And Tom! What a fine surprise!"

174

"We flew in with Allworth," O'Higgins explained.

Love's smile faded. "Is it true what they reported on the radio this afternoon? About gay rights?"

O'Higgins took out his notes. "I've got the quotes right here." He read off what Don had said.

Wally Love was stunned. "I just can't believe Senator Allworth would do this." He seemed near tears. He had spent untold hundreds of thousands of dollars on Allworth's cause, and now his candidate had let him down. As candidates are wont to do.

"He probably considers this a tactical move," I said helpfully.

Wally's blue eyes flashed. "This is a moral issue."

"Are you reconsidering your commitment to Allworth?" I asked.

Wally said he didn't know, but his face said he did.

Later, while Don spoke to the party faithful, Addie and I joined some media types for dinner in our hotel's overpriced French restaurant.

We were a typically motley campaign crew. A couple of reporters I was glad to see. A toothsome woman publisher who had dragged along a good-looking young reporter from her staff and couldn't keep her hands off him. A *New York Times* grandee, famous for his loud and unyielding views on all things under the sun, and a former bartender turned novelist who was on assignment from *Esquire* and very drunk. He and the *Times* man kept trying to shout each other down, and the woman publisher howled her views too when she wasn't fondling her star reporter.

She did, however, keep ordering an '86 Pommard at eighty-five dollars the bottle, so we humored her.

For a time, everyone was denouncing the *Washington Post* about the episode when one of its reporters invented a story about a drug-crazed six-year-old.

I shocked the group by saying, "I don't see what's wrong with that."

I was ordered to explain myself. Even Addie seemed scandalized.

"When I had my first reporting job in Tennessee," I said, "we had a feature writer named Orville Neff. Every year Orville went out to the state fair and got drunk and came back and wrote a story about Melody Mae McFee, the little blind girl from Muleskin Gap, who won the blue ribbon for her plum preserves. Or some years for her squirrel pie. Over the years, Orville created an entire Faulknerian saga of the McFees—Grandpa Fudd, who was gassed in the Great War, and Cousin Ida, who wrestled bears, and Mama Mattie, who kissed Jesus in a cave on her birthday every year. That family brought untold joy to our readers; there were thousands of people who only bought the paper once a year, to read about the McFees. If American newspapers are going to survive, we need more creative journalism."

I was hooted down, but I meant every word of it.

Mostly, however, I concentrated on the wine and on whispering endearments to Addie and stroking her hand under the table.

Just as we finished our lobster bisque, Don's press secretary appeared with an unexpected summons: the Senator wished to see Addie and me in his suite.

Our companions were properly impressed, but to my profound embarrassment, Addie protested my inclusion.

"He owes me a half hour for being bumped yesterday," she told the startled flack. "So what the hell is *he* included for?"

My love had reverted to her tough-reporter persona. The others at our table howled with delight.

"Oh, bullshit, Addie," I muttered, and stormed out of the restaurant. Despite my affection for Addie, I couldn't let her push me around. If Don wanted to see us both, that was his call.

She fumed all the way up in the elevator, but seemed happier as Don welcomed us to a big suite filled with neon art, pastel sofas, and a cornucopia of flowers, fruit, and champagne. He greeted Addie with a hug, me with a manly slap on the back, and poured bubbly for all.

Don and Addie settled at either end of a long sofa. I took a chair across from them. Don still had his tux on, but with the coat off and the tie hanging loose.

"You guys want food sent up?" he asked. "Or try the fruit, it's good."

Addie helped herself to a handful of strawberries. "That was an okay speech tonight," she said.

"Just the usual jazz," he said, and to our amazement broke into a few bars of scat singing. I'd never seen Don so loose.

"Whatta you think, Tom? Am I on a roll or what?"

I had to smile at his boyishness, his exuberance, and yet I knew I must tell him what I thought.

"I'm upset, Don."

His eyes were suddenly hooded. "About what?"

"This gay thing. The code words. You're playing to homophobia. It's not what your friends expect from you."

Don's face turned cold. "You may not have noticed, but I'm running for President."

"I've noticed. But . . ."

"Then maybe you've also noticed that I've been getting my ass whipped, mainly because I spent too long worrying about what my high-minded friends in Washington might think."

"Those friends worked for you, gave money. Reporters like Addie, because they admired you, got your campaign off the ground. People expect a lot of you. But not this demagoguery."

"Tom, unlike you, I've talked to thousands of voters. You can't run a serious campaign if you ignore what people want."

"People used to want segregation, maybe still do, but that doesn't make it right."

Don's face flushed. "Do you doubt that as President I'd do everything in my power to find a cure for AIDS and protect civil rights for gays?"

"I imagine a lot of gays doubt it."

"First I have to win the nomination. Then I can get them back in the fall."

I was surprised he was speaking so candidly in front of Addie; I guessed they had an understanding about what was off the record.

"Look at the whole picture. I'm way out front on health care and military cuts. I need balance. What I've said is legitimate, and it's working."

"It's working so far," Addie injected. "But you're going to start taking heat in the major media. Pretty soon, it won't be just gay votes you'll lose but liberal votes too."

Don turned on her. "Screw the liberals. I'm the one whose ass is on the line. Does anyone doubt that Craxton was behind that ad that used Polly to make me look like a fool? Okay, if he wants hardball, hardball it is. If he wants to go to gay funerals, he can damn well accept the consequences. I'm in this to win, and if some people can't understand a tactical move for what it is, they'd better find another candidate!"

The ringing telephone broke the tension. Don answered and was all smiles again.

"Hey, honey," he said. "I've had a great day, how about you? Hey, that's swell. No, I'm just shooting the breeze with Tom Tullis. Want to say hello?"

He handed me the phone.

"Tommy," Polly cried. "I'm in Los Angeles and I delivered our homeless speech and they loved it. I made the evening news."

"That's great," I told her. Even Polly was into news bites now.

When Don was off the phone, he grinned. "Anyway, guys, trust me. If I make it to the Oval Office, I won't disgrace you."

"I worry about you, that you'll hurt yourself," I said.

He smiled with what might have been appreciation, even affection. "Tom, this is a tough business. Sometimes you have to take chances. But I have instincts. About tactics, about timing. I know what I'm doing."

"I hope so, Don."

"Hey, let's cut the gloom and doom. Win or lose, this campaign has been the greatest experience of my life. To travel this country. To meet thousands of people. To learn from them. I don't think I ever realized what a big, diverse country this is. We all get stuck in our own little world. Then you do this, and you meet blacks and Poles and Latinos and stockbrokers and gays and feminists and loggers and computer freaks and coal miners—you move in a hundred worlds you barely knew existed."

He spread his arms. "My God, what a big, strong, vital country! And yet what strains it has, what tensions, hate and greed and ignorance, trying to tear it apart. It's a miracle it's held together all these years—it's a miracle we haven't had anarchy—and the credit goes to this brilliant damn system of government we have. It works, Tom and Addie, I swear to God it works."

I was amazed by what he was saying. It was so vastly different from that anti-gay crap he'd been dishing up.

As if reading my mind, Don said, "We need civility, Tom. I don't enjoy this gay issue. And I don't enjoy having my wife attacked. We've got to put this garbage behind us. Jesus, suppose I'd walked with some woman on the beach last spring, what would it have mattered? That's not the issue. If I get the nomination, in my acceptance speech I'm going to pledge a clean campaign, and try to shame the other side into doing the same."

He yawned and took another call. Addie and I exchanged a look; the visit had been fascinating, but it was time to go.

"I need some time alone with him," she said. "I'm desperate for quotes for Sunday."

She handed me her key. "Wait in my room."

When Don rejoined us, she told him she needed a few more minutes. He and I shook hands. I had never liked him more.

I went to her room two floors below. Later, I awoke as she entered, listened groggily as her dress rustled in the darkness, felt the bed sway as she crawled in beside me.

I laughed and drew her warmth close to mine. This was what campaigns were all about.

27.

Back in Washington, I called Jamie Atwood and asked to see him. We'd met only once, at a dinner party a couple of years before, but now I wanted some information about the drug world, and Jamie seemed a good place to start.

He asked me to meet him at four that Sunday afternoon at a marina on the Southwest waterfront. I arrived at the appointed hour and waited only briefly before Jamie appeared. He was a dark-haired man in his late thirties, wearing sunglasses, red swimming trunks, and a faded polo shirt.

"Tom?' he said, in a soft Carolina accent. "Good to see you again."

He led me aboard a forty-foot cabin cruiser and opened two beers.

"Do you live here?" I asked.

"Part of the time. It's convenient to the courts. I keep an apartment at the Watergate too."

"How's the lawyer business?" I asked.

Jamie Atwood shrugged. "The juries here are mostly middle-class, middle-aged, churchgoing black people who don't have the slightest sympathy for people who sell drugs. The U.S. Attorney knows that, so it's hard to make deals."

He smiled. "But it's a living."

"Let's make sure we understand each other," I said. "I want information about possible drug money going into the campaign, and it's possible that you're the man to talk to."

We settled under a canopy at the back of the boat; a breeze was blowing and sailboats dotted the Potomac.

"It's possible that I am," he said. "I represent a good many people in the drug trade. Mostly marijuana growers. But let me make *myself* clear. If I talk to you it's because, one, my clients and I are concerned about what you might write, and, two, mutual friends tell me that you will respect confidentiality."

"I will."

"No quotes, no mention of me whatsoever, by name or inference."

"Agreed."

"Good. What do you want to know?"

"I've been told that large amounts of money have been going into the Allworth and Craxton campaigns, some in cash, some in other ways, and it might be drug money."

My host waved to a passing speedboat.

"Speaking of the marijuana industry, I can't tell you that no major grower, importer, or distributor somewhere hasn't sent a contribution to a candidate, but I can tell you that there is no organized effort to assist any of them. I'd hate to see you print such a suggestion; my clients have enough problems without being accused of corrupting the political process."

"Are you saying the marijuana growers don't care who's President?"

"Essentially, yes. Probably some of them gave to McGovern

in '72, because they disliked Nixon. Some gave to Carter in
'76, because he seemed to be a friend. He had people around
him who smoked, he cultivated rock stars, so our people were
sucked in. Once in office, he was just another gutless politician. Our people felt burned by Carter, and haven't focused
on presidential politics since then. In national politics, both
sides beat up on us, and neither side does us any good."

"Are you saying your people are interested in local, rather
than national, politics?"

"Of course. It matters a lot who's mayor or sheriff, what
his law-enforcement priorities are. Locally, our people will
support the more friendly candidate, or just wait and deal
with whoever wins."

"How do they operate in local politics?"

"Through lawyers. It's not that you hire a lawyer who deals
with politicians. You hire a lawyer who hires another lawyer
who deals with them."

"All for healthy fees."

"Very healthy."

"You've been talking about marijuana growers and dealers.
What about the people who deal in cocaine?"

"I don't represent them."

"You must know about them."

"I try not to know about them. A lot of them are Mexican
and Colombian, dangerous, violent people, people who re-
flect an entirely different culture. To me, there's a clear line
between grass and coke, and I observe it in my work."

"Do you think it's possible they'd put big money into the
campaign?"

He gave me a long look. "Offhand, I'd say they aren't that
sophisticated. Plus, any candidate who took their money
would be crazy."

The man obviously didn't understand, as I did, that all
candidates *are* crazy, and that money ranks with sex as the
root of their madness.

"Let me ask you this. If you had a great deal of money,

and wanted to inject it into the campaign secretly, how would you go about it?"

Jamie laughed. "There are so many ways. It depends, for one thing, on how much money you're talking about. If there's a thousand-dollar limit, and I want to give you fifty thousand, I might put somebody in a car with a suitcase full of money, and send him from here to Miami. In towns along the way, he'd stop and give fifty friends cash, and each of them would mail you a thousand-dollar check. That would work, unless someone found a pattern to the checks you were receiving."

A pattern. Hadn't Doyle Kane spoken to Dinah of patterns?

"But if you're talking big money, a thousand a shot is too slow. I understand that both parties are hitting fat cats for one-hundred-thousand-dollar donations for so-called 'soft money' in the fall. Money to state operations, supposedly legal. That's the best way to go."

"But your people won't contribute on that scale?"

"Only rarely. A man in the whiskey business or the oil business considers his donation an investment. He expects something in return from the White House, policies that will benefit him. But our people won't get anything in return."

He went into the cabin and returned with an unmarked bottle of clear liquid. "Perhaps you'd like a taste of something rather rare," he said.

"What is it?"

"Coca-wine. Wine made from coca leaves. It gives a coke high, but with the afterglow of the best wine."

"I've never heard of it."

"It's been around for centuries. You can buy a bottle in New York for three hundred dollars. Would you like a glass?"

I laughed and laughed, until my host must have thought me quite mad. "I'm sorry," I said. "It's just that I have enough problems without becoming fond of three-hundred-dollar-a-bottle cocaine-based wine."

He laughed too, and brought me another beer, and mixed a Cutty and water for himself.

"Let me make a suggestion. My clients have an informal intelligence network around the country. I could see if they can pick up anything on the campaigns."

"I don't want my name used in any way."

"Of course. In return, I ask that you write nothing about our people without giving me a chance to rebut the facts."

"Fair enough," I said. "You might check a man named Wally Love who operates out of Parker County, Oregon. And a political consultant named Rojack, out of Miami."

He wrote down the names. "And I had a report that the TV preachers are making contributions," I added.

He cocked an eyebrow. "They certainly have the money."

I didn't have any more business. But I had questions. The best thing about reporting is that people tolerate your snooping; they even like it.

"How'd you get into this business, Jamie?" He looked like a man who could do anything he chose.

He sipped his drink. "I had an older brother. I worshiped him. When I was twelve, and he was eighteen, he was arrested for growing marijuana. In the sixties, this was a very big thing in rural North Carolina. My family had no money or influence, and a judge decided to make an example of my brother. He sentenced him to five years in the state prison. For growing ten marijuana plants.

"I won't bore you with the details, but my brother didn't survive. We buried him when I was fifteen. I took an oath to avenge him. I suppose I could have become a revolutionary. But I became a lawyer instead."

"Do you think your clients today are as innocent as your brother was?" I asked.

"Obviously not. But they're people who meet a need in our

society. They're not violent. I don't think they're any more criminal than the people who sell alcohol or cigarettes."

"Drug dealers aren't violent?"

"Some are. I don't represent them."

"Do you have a plan, Jamie? A timetable?"

"I'm just trying to keep people out of jail."

"Come on."

"All right. I think marijuana should be legal. If it were freely available, fewer people would use the more dangerous drugs. Tax legal marijuana and provide more treatment for people with cocaine or heroin problems. But let's quit putting people in jail because their drug of choice isn't our drug of choice."

"Jamie, I have a feeling that if you wanted to, you could pick up the phone and raise millions of dollars for a political-action fund. And I think you know which candidate you'd like to see President. But you're asking me to believe that you don't want to play that game, that you don't want to make a deal with the next President, that you're happy just to watch from afar and hope for the best. Is that correct?"

My host poured himself another Cutty and water. "Forgive me," he said. "I work eighteen-hour days, and on Sundays I tend to unwind."

"I understand."

"Obviously, all over the country, our people have bribed law-enforcement officials. They consider that a normal operating expense. But I don't see that *modus operandi* at the national level. Maybe I'm naive, but I believe that someday we'll elect a President who's honest enough to admit that our drug policies are a failure, and who wants policies that work. Until then, I'll keep beating my brains out in court."

At that moment, a petite, pretty young woman in white shorts came down the gangplank, carrying a picnic basket. Jamie hugged her and introduced us. Her name was Olivia and she was Puerto Rican and a doctor.

"I love your column," she said, and quickly won my heart.

Jamie gazed at the shimmering Potomac. "What a glorious day!" he exclaimed. "Shall we go for a spin?"

I pondered my host. This might not be the safest spin of my life. But he seemed a man you could trust, even with a little Cutty under his belt.

"Sure," I said. "Why not?"

28.

The primary campaign was blazing toward the final shootout in California in early June.

Passions soared higher with each hot, angry day. Gays picketed Don's campaign stops in California and clashed with pro-Allworth hardhats in San Francisco.

Don had beat a tactical retreat and started talking about compassion and civil rights, but he'd scored his point.

If part of me loathed Don's gambit, part of me was cynic enough to admire it as high-risk, no-net politics. No one knew exactly how it cut politically. The polls showed him losing gay votes, and picking up blue-collar votes, but no one knew how accurate the polls were, because people don't always admit their prejudice to pollsters.

You never find out how many bigots there are until Election Day.

Historically, there are usually more than anyone thought.

. . .

I had lunch that week with Frank Hovater. I'd met the TV evangelist a few years back, when someone at police headquarters called with a tip that his eighteen-year-old daughter had been arrested for buying crack.

I called Hovater's headquarters outside Richmond. I had spoken first with his PR man, who sputtered but did not speak, then within minutes had received a call from the man himself.

"Mr. Tullis, you don't know me and I don't know you," he began. "But I'm calling as the father of a troubled child. I take the blame. I've spent too much time preaching, and not enough time parenting. Ruth is crying out for a father's love. She's been receiving treatment, we thought we were making progress. But now we've had this setback."

He had an amazing voice; even over the phone it was hypnotic.

"Mr. Tullis, I don't question what anyone writes about me. I'm fair game. If you catch me off-base, nail my hide to the wall. But publicity might destroy this fragile child. I understand that you have a job to do, and that this incident is a matter of record. But perhaps you're a parent yourself, and I ask you to show mercy to this child!"

Maybe I wouldn't have printed anything even if I hadn't talked to him. Maybe I just called to rattle his cage. But he made an impression. He spoke with force and dignity, and had the good sense to spare me any Bible-thumping. And of course when he appealed to me as a father, he grabbed me where it hurt. Believers or agnostics, we all have to deal with our daughters.

So I didn't print anything; I even called my source and told him to lay off. Hovater got lucky and no one printed the story. After that, his PR man called a few times with showbiz items—a new TV deal, a Get-with-God rock video—and I used some of them. Then one day the man himself called again and asked me to lunch.

We met at Morton's steak house in Georgetown. Hovater was a fleshy, powerful man with thinning red hair and fiery blue eyes. He ordered an excellent Burgundy and a sixteen-ounce sirloin, extra rare. When the food arrived, his eyes fixed mine, and he lowered his head. I felt myself doing the same, as he murmured, "Lord, we thank thee for all our many blessings."

Raising his head, he grinned and added, "Mr. Tullis, the Lord has blessed us with two of the best steaks east of Kansas City."

It developed that a publisher had offered him a million-dollar advance for his memoirs. He'd learned that I'd ghosted a couple of books for politicians, and he wanted my advice. Should he use a collaborator? Should he hire an agent? Should he talk to other publishers?

He asked good questions and made shrewd comments. I guessed he was eyeing me as a possible ghost, but I didn't encourage him; we would have been too odd a couple for either his friends or mine to stomach. But I enjoyed him. We talked books, and he spared me his religious views. He invoked the Almighty once or twice, but only in passing, the way I might mention my publisher, although he clearly had a higher opinion of God than I did of Harriet.

The fascinating question about the TV preachers, of course, is simply this: Do they sincerely believe in a literal Heaven and Hell, in which case a good deal of passion is justified, or is salvation just their scam?

I decided Frank Hovater probably did believe in the product he was selling. Either that or he's the best actor I've ever seen.

Now, after Buzz Makito had floated the idea that evangelicals were making big campaign contributions, I decided to have another chat with my fundamentalist friend.

We met at the same steak house. He ordered the same sirloin and a better Burgundy, said grace, and then eyed me: "Now, Doubting Thomas, what can I do for you?"

That was his nickname for me. We'd never discussed religion *per se,* but he could spot a lost soul a mile away.

I decided to bluff. "Frank, I've been told that you and some of your peers have been making illegal cash contributions to the campaign."

He was raising his wineglass as I spoke. He put it back down untouched.

His eyes shone with perfect fury.

"That is rubbish, Tom, absolute rubbish. Whoever told you that is either a liar or a fool."

"Why is it rubbish?" I pressed.

"Because every time one of us has entered the political arena he has been badly burned. Look at poor Jerry, who is not a stupid man at all. He was riding high; then he decided to be a kingmaker. What happened? He became the most unpopular public man in America, literally—the polls prove it. His ministry virtually collapsed. Fund-raising dried up. He finally had to disband the Moral Majority. And for all his misery, did he get what he wanted from the Reagan gang? Of course not. They used him for their own selfish ends and didn't give a damn about him. Lie down with dogs, get up with fleas."

A well-dressed woman came to our table and shyly asked Hovater to autograph her napkin. He scribbled his initials and flashed a by-the-numbers smile. "God bless, sister, God bless."

His eyes returned to mine. "Take my word for it, we've learned our lesson. Render under Caesar, et cetera. I might give a thousand dollars to a candidate or two, but that's the end of it, and there isn't a doubt in my mind that my leading colleagues in Christ feel the same way."

When we parted, I was left wondering who to believe.

What Hovater said made sense. Morever, if he'd known that one of his rivals was bending the law, I think he'd have said so, competition being what it is.

But if Hovater was right, then Buzz Makito and Joey

Swink were wrong about the evangelists, just as they'd been wrong before about the defense people. Which suggested that either they were pretty damn dumb, or they were trying to steer me in the wrong direction. I didn't think they were dumb.

Jamie Atwood called the next week. He didn't want to talk over the phone, so I met him at a coffee shop near the federal courthouse. He looked like a legal gunslinger with his mustache, dark blue suit, and black cowboy boots.

"I sent an associate of mine to the FEC to study the reports," he told me over coffee. "We found an unusually high number of thousand-dollar checks to Allworth from single men living in big cities. These checks seemed to come in clusters, from one city one week, another city the next. It reminded me of the operation I suggested to you, putting someone in a car with a suitcase full of cash, except done by plane."

"Are you saying these were gay men?"

"All those we checked were."

"So you're suggesting an organized effort to inject gay money into the Allworth campaign."

"The evidence suggests it."

"Yet he's campaigning against them."

A smile split the lawyer's craggy face. "He wouldn't be the first politician to bite the hand that fed him, would he?"

"It's very strange," I said.

"It gets stranger. We found a similar pattern in the Craxton campaign."

I shook my head in dismay.

"What do you think that means?"

The lawyer shrugged. "It suggests people with enough money to hedge their bets."

The waitress brought us more coffee, clearly smitten by the dashing lawyer.

"You also asked about possible cash infusions by TV evangelists."

"Yes."

"I can't pin it down, but some of my people have heard the same thing."

"But nothing as specific as the checks from the gays?" I asked.

"Not yet." He smiled. "It may be that gays are launching the sort of national operation that I think would be unwise for drug people to undertake. I suppose the threat of AIDS creates more urgency than the threat of prison. So long, Tom."

His cowboy boots went click-clack on the tile floor as he made his exit.

I took the Metro back to my office.

Many, many questions faced me, but it came down to this: What the hell was going on and what the hell was I doing in the middle of it?

What did I really know?

That Doyle Kane was dead, that was all. Everything else was speculation, charge and countercharge.

Maybe his death had nothing to do with money or politics.

Or maybe, as Dinah was convinced, he had uncovered a pattern of illegal contributions to the campaigns, and someone had killed him to keep him quiet.

But who?

I had some scuttlebutt about The Boys' Club, but my friend Forrest Keel insisted it was a social club, not at all political.

The odd couple, Buzz Makito and Joey Swink, had first fingered the defense gang, and when that didn't fly had said it was the TV preachers.

My new lawyer friend, Jamie Atwood, blamed the gays, and also pushed the TV-preachers theory, which I was convinced wasn't true.

And there was Grundy's anonymous caller, who blamed a mysterious "they" in the drug world for killing Doyle—but

Jamie Atwood insisted that the drug kingpins weren't interested in presidential politics.

The whole tangled mess reminded me of the tax-increase
jingle they sing on Capitol Hill: "Don't tax you, don't tax me,
tax that fellow behind the tree!"

Everyone thought there was funny money going into the
campaign, but everyone blamed the fellow behind the tree.

But whoever was behind the tree, if they were killing people, what was I doing sniffing after them?

My guilt about Doyle Kane, who'd once befriended me;
that was part of it.

And stubbornness; that's basic.

And my old friend pride, convinced that I could find the
truth where lesser mortals would fail.

Little questions nagged at me. Like, if Jamie Atwood really
hated the cocaine culture so much, why did he offer coca-
wine to his guests? Petty questions that could keep you twisting till dawn.

I needed help. I tried to call Forrest, to ask him about the
gay contributions. He'd given me a number in Naples, Florida, where he and Chuck had gone, but the operator said it
wasn't in service.

Another mystery.

Near the end of the day, Joey Swink called.

"Tom," he began, "Buzz and I were wondering if you'd
had any luck checking out that report we heard."

"About the TV evangelists?"

"Right."

I was sick of Joey Swink. My supply of tact, never vast, was
exhausted. "Joey, I talked to a well-informed source who said
that was absurd, because they've all been burned too badly."

Swink grumbled but didn't speak.

What I said next popped out, out of sheer perversity. "You
know what I think it is?"

"What?"

"Big drug money. Cocaine lords from Colombia, trying to buy into the system."

"Who says that?" Joey snapped.

"It figures," I declared. "They've got millions in cash, and they need friends in high places to keep the heat off them."

"Are you going to print that?"

Joey was losing his cool; I wondered why. "I'm still checking."

"Why don't you come see me and Buzz tomorrow morning?" he said. "Maybe we can come up with some angles. Ten o'clock?"

"Sure, Joey, ten o'clock," I said, and put down the phone, puzzled by his agitation.

Then the phone again, a summons from Grundy.

I was to come to his apartment at ten that night.

There was someone it was urgent that I meet.

Naturally, he would not say who.

A nervous young man was perched on Grundy's tattered sofa.

"Tom Tullis, Greg Farabee," Grundy said.

Farabee put out his hand. He was painfully thin, with a widow's peak and sad brown eyes.

"Pleased, I'm sure," he said, and we settled around Grundy's kitchen table. Sirens wailed down on Fourteenth Street. A cockroach skittered across the floor.

"Tullis here knew Kane," Grundy said. "You better start at the beginning."

Greg Farabee sighed dramatically. "I hardly know what the beginning is anymore."

"How about the White House?" Grundy grunted.

The young man nodded. "Yes, you're right, Oliver. That's the true beginning. You see, Mr. Tullis, I'm an accountant, a rather good one, not that it matters. And a few years ago

I found myself working in the White House, which sounds more exciting than it was."

"I know what you mean," I said.

"Well, my office, naturally, was across the street in that ghastly old Executive Office Building, but my boss had an office in the White House basement, and so did Joey Swink, so I'd see him sometimes. This was before he left and started his own business."

His eyes darted between me and Grundy.

"So you and Swink were friends?" I asked.

"Oh, no, no, he never knew my name! It was because of Chandell that I knew about him."

"Chandell?"

"My boss's secretary. A truly stunning girl. But very sensitive, very vulnerable. Chandell was like a sister to me."

"And Swink started banging her," Grundy injected.

Farabee looked as if he'd been hit. "Please. He took advantage of her, made her all kinds of promises. But when she got pregnant he made her have an abortion. And even after that he did this horrible thing—I'm not even sure I can discuss it."

I was rapidly losing interest in Chandell's star-crossed romance. Grundy, reading my mind, growled, "Tell him about the coke."

"You see, Mr. Tullis—and I'm an avid reader of your column, let me say—in her darkest hour, Chandell came to me for love and understanding. And one night she told me everything."

I smiled my encouragement.

"Joey Swink, as I'm sure you know, just shot up like a rocket in Washington. He worked on the Hill, he advanced to the White House, and then he opened his own firm and made an absolute fortune. And I won't deny that he's a clever man. But the real secret of his success was drugs. Cocaine."

Grundy had a tight little smile on his face, and I was listening closely now.

"He always had the best cocaine, which he supplied to political people at cost—or for free—and with absolute discretion. And, don't you see, once someone takes cocaine from you, you've got something on him. It's like blackmail pretending to be friendship."

"What do you mean political people?" I asked.

"Congressmen and Senators. White House staff. They want to get high as much as anybody else, but they can't buy it on the street corner. They could always depend on Joey Swink. He used to take Chandell to parties at his house. She made me a list of dozens of Congressmen and Senators she'd seen him give coke to. A lot of doors are always open to Joey Swink, day or night!"

I said, "Greg, I agree that Swink is a rat, but I thought we were going to talk about who killed Doyle Kane."

He looked hurt. "I'm getting to that. You must understand, it's all interrelated."

"Of course," I said.

"There was a group of men who met every month or two to socialize."

"The Boys' Club," Grundy grunted.

"Some called it that, yes. Very prominent men and their younger friends. A way to get acquainted. All very elegant and understated. The best food and wines, the finest classical music, the most stimulating conversation. This was where Doyle met Joey Swink."

"Wait a minute," I said. "These were gay men, right?"

"Yes, of course."

"Are you saying Swink was gay?"

"No, no, no. Didn't I just tell you? He was there to supply the *cocaine*."

"Ah."

"Swink was at The Boys' Club only twice that I know of. The other time he was there was when an ugly incident occurred."

198

"Tell him about it," Grundy said.

"These bikers appeared one night. Three of them. Just barged in and helped themselves to food and whiskey and acted in a very menacing way. It was at the home of a prominent judge, and he couldn't very well call the police. Instead, he called Joey Swink. And just *minutes* later these two *warriors* arrived, one this huge black man with the most amazing biceps, and the other a truly fierce Latin who dressed all in black. They threw those bikers out in about twenty seconds. When one of them tried to get smart, the black man broke his jaw, just like that. After it was over, Swink came by, like a conquering hero. He called the black man with the biceps Bobby; the Latin was Rudy."

"But what about Doyle's death?" I pressed.

"I'm *getting* to it. He called me. He said there was a pattern of illegal money coming into the campaign. He was convinced it was drug money and Joey Swink was behind it."

"What kind of a pattern?" I asked.

"The checks, where they were from, who sent them, things like that."

"But how did he know Swink was involved?"

"I . . . I don't know. He just *knew*. He said he knew how much I despised Swink, and we should meet and develop a plan of action."

"Did you?"

"I was leaving on vacation. He was killed the day I returned."

"So you have no proof about Swink, just Doyle's charges and your own guesses?"

"Well, he *is* dead," Farabee said. "And I suppose he had reason to be afraid of Swink. And when he wanted to, Swink could produce those two *killers* in a matter of minutes. So it's rather a strong case, in my opinion."

"You've done a hell of a job, Greg," Grundy declared. "We're gonna nail the bastards."

"Who supplied the coke?" I demanded.

The young man looked confused. "I told you . . . Swink did."

"No. Who supplied him? Where did he get it?"

"I . . . I don't know."

I looked at Grundy. "The girl should know."

He shook his head. "She claims she doesn't. She says Joey never used his name. Just called him Mr. Big and The Man and My Friend, crap like that."

"Wherever the coke came from, the money comes from," I said. "Swink damn sure didn't spend his own money or give away his own coke."

Farabee stood up. "I've got to go now," he said. "But I think I should tell you the other part about Chandell. The thing Swink did to her."

"Sure, go ahead," Grundy said.

"After she had the abortion, one day he called and wanted her to have a date with some Japanese businessman. At first she didn't understand. But then he started talking about how much money she could make. Imagine. She truly loved him and he could do that to her."

"Some guys got no taste," Grundy said.

Grundy called a cab and walked Farabee down to meet it.

When he returned, he said, "I've been checking. The action now is out in the states. This 'soft money.' Usually a hundred thousand a pop, to the state parties, and there's no regulation worth a damn."

"So what've you got?"

"I have pals in a couple of states. So I got lists of people who'd given their hundred thou. Mostly the same old crowd who give big every time—bozos who figure someday they'll make ambassador. But there were some new names on the lists. People nobody'd ever heard of before. I checked 'em out. Some of these guys, they're young lawyers, flashy types, gold chains and BMWs, never political before. But now they cough up."

"Drug lawyers."

"Yeah. So there was one bank where a guy owed me a big one. I got a look at this one lawyer's records. Two days before he wrote his check for a hundred thousand dollars to the state party, he deposited a check for a hundred thousand dollars. You follow?"

"Yeah, I follow. Who was his check from?"

"From Joey Swink's lawyer's secretary's roommate."

"Then Swink's a middleman for drugs and money too."

Grundy nodded. "Listen, pal, and listen good. Swink's a rat, dangerous when cornered, and the boys behind him are dangerous all the time. We've got to keep cool, keep our mouths shut. In a couple more days I'll take what I know to the U.S. Attorney and break the story. Until then, keep your head down."

"Oh, hell," I groaned.

"Oh, hell what?"

"I talked to Joey today. He'd been saying it was right-wing preachers giving the money, and I told him that was crap and I thought it was drug money. I was just wising off. I'm supposed to see him in the morning."

"You better stay away from Swink," Grundy said.

"I think you're right," I said, and started unhappily for home.

30.

When I left Grundy's place I was weighing my Pulitzer fantasy against the unpleasant realities that were starting to surface.

So befuddled was I that I hardly noticed the fire trucks shooting past me. I didn't pay attention until I rounded my corner, and saw flames shooting high into the night sky.

A moment later, I realized that the house ablaze was mine.

I leapt from my car and ran forward, disbelieving. Fire-hoses crisscrossed the yard, and firemen were shooting jets of water through my broken windows.

I saw Holly's car at the curb and with a cry realized she must be inside. I started running toward the front door. Two firemen tackled me and I was fighting with them when a soft hand touched my face.

"Get a grip, Daddy. I'm okay."

The firemen released me. I embraced Holly and led her toward the street.

"Your cute little house is gone," she said.

I asked her what had happened.

"I was in the kitchen, eating ice cream. Something crashed through the front window; then there was fire everywhere. I got out the back. If we'd been asleep it would have been a real downer."

Some cops wanted to talk to us. One of them was my friend Briley. Holly and I climbed into the back of his cruiser.

"Anybody want to kill you, Tullis?" he asked.

For once, no quip passed my lips. "I don't know."

They questioned Holly, and it was clear that someone had thrown a firebomb through the window.

"Tullis, if it'll make you feel better, it may not have been meant for you."

"What?"

"They might have been gunning for the guy next door, and hit the wrong house. These hoods aren't real good at numbers."

"Van Dyke? He's a stockbroker."

"He sells more than just stocks. You got a place to go?"

"To a hotel, I guess."

"I can go to Deakie's," Holly said.

"You stay with me," I told her.

One of my neighbors was on his porch, enjoying the excitement. He kindly let me use his phone.

My new friend answered on the second ring.

"It's Tom Tullis. Sorry to wake you, but something crazy just happened. Somebody firebombed my house. It may have been a mistake, but . . ."

"Where are you?" Jamie Atwood demanded.

"I'm still there."

"What's the address?"

I told him.

"I'll be right there," he said. "Don't leave."

I hadn't been trying to summon him, only to suggest that we talk the next day. But he arrived within minutes, in a Mercedes sedan. Dark-eyed Olivia was with him, looking sleepy.

The fire was out now, the cops had gone, and firemen were mopping up inside. Jamie looked in the window and shook his head.

I introduced him to Holly.

"You can give us a ride to a hotel," I said.

"No, come stay with us at the Watergate."

"But you were at the marina."

"Not after this I'm not," Jamie said.

I was confused. "The detectives said they may have been after the guy next door and hit my house by mistake."

Jamie pulled me aside. "This was no mistake. You've been looking into illegal campaign contributions. Somebody doesn't like that, and they've sent you a message."

"You don't know that," I said stubbornly.

"No, I don't. But I'm sufficiently convinced that I'm not going to spend the rest of the night on a boat that could be blown to hell by one Molotov cocktail. I'm taking Olivia to the Watergate, and I suggest you and your daughter come with me."

His message slowly sank in. I'd been playing at investigative reporting, but maybe the other side wasn't playing.

"Have you got room for us?"

"We each have an apartment. You and your daughter can use mine."

As it turned out, Jamie and I sat up until dawn. He drank coffee and I drank brandy. I told him about the campaigns, about Wally Love and Doyle Kane and Dinah's concern about cash, about The Boys' Club, and my conversations with Buzz and Joey.

"You have to get out of this," Jamie said. "Just back off. It's not . . ."

"Not my problem," I said. "I know. People keep telling me that."

"Get some sleep. I'll check on that guy next door to you. But my guess is he hasn't got half as many enemies as you do."

"I'm such a nice person," I said. "Oh, did I tell you I have an appointment with Makito today?"

"Forget it," the lawyer advised.

I did forget it. I slept until afternoon. By then Holly was gone. She left a note saying she and Deakie were going to visit Deakie's grandmother in Newport. A good plan.

I went by my house. The inside was wet and black and unspeakably sad. Books I loved were soggy lumps now. Not much had survived, upstairs or down. What the fire hadn't gotten, the smoke and water had.

I poked around for a while, looking for the odd survivor: a cuff link here, a tennis racket there. It was like attending my own funeral.

I didn't care about the clothing and furniture, I could replace those. But some things were gone that were as irreplaceable as an arm or a leg. Things I'd hung on to, from house to house, marriage to marriage, decade to decade. Just about every record that Jerry Lee Lewis and the Everly Brothers and Billie Holiday and Louis Armstrong ever made, globs of wax now. Signed first editions of *Horseman, Pass By* and *The Noblest Roman* and *Heads* and *The Tears of Autumn* and *The Wanting of Levine*. Battered copies of *Main Street* and *The Summing Up* and *Gatsby* and Flannery O'Connor's stories ("I want to make a good case for distortion," she said, "because it is the only way to make people see") and *Candide* and *Garp* and *Riddley Walker* and *Portnoy's Complaint*. My Cocteau watercolors. Pictures of me and Holly, both younger and more innocent.

My talismen, my life, up in smoke.

I wanted to cry out in rage. It hurt so much to admit that, as everyone kept reminding me, I was way over my head.

I went back to the Watergate, intending to leave for a hotel, but Olivia insisted that I use her apartment. That was hard to argue with. The Watergate felt secure, a fine and private place.

I had a few drinks, watched the news on TV—Allworth and Craxton, each proclaiming his deathless devotion to Family Values—whose family? what values?—and then went to sleep again. I slept about fifteen hours that night.

And a good thing, too. Because I needed all my strength to survive the next day's madness.

31.

I have a theory that presidential politics no longer has much to do with how we are governed, and much more to do with providing what is at best a national mythology, and at worst (which is to say most of the time) a national soap opera.

We don't expect good government anymore, only a good show.

And that, at least, we get: an endless procession of saints and sinners, heroes and clowns, who aspire to lead us. Start with the dying Roosevelt elected for a fourth term. Flash to gutsy Harry Truman threatening to zap some critic who didn't like his daughter's singing. Proceed to Camelot, to Dallas, to LBJ showing us his scars, to Bobby's brief moment of glory, to Teddy at the bridge, to the spectacle of Watergate, to the peanut farmer with lust in his heart, and finally, inevitably, to the incomparable Gipper.

It is too much, Reader. The mind boggles. They say if a million monkeys banged at a million typewriters for a million years, eventually one of them would produce *Hamlet.* I say a million Shakespeares writing for a million years couldn't concoct a drama so comic, so tragic, so improbable as that which has graced our national stage in our lifetime. And there is no relief in sight.

I offer these thoughts as a preface to the events of June 2, events that involved both my friend Don Allworth and his rival, Governor Craxton. If they seem bizarre or improbable I can only say that, in the context of our national soap opera, they were minor blips, mere footnotes to our national mythology.

I was in my office that morning, finishing a column on the Allworth campaign, when Cassie yelled, "Turn on your TV."

I did, and found Governor Craxton and his wife, Ava, standing with a young man before a microphone in his state capitol building. The young man was a puzzlement, because the Craxtons had no children.

Craxton was a craggy, ferocious-looking ex-Marine. His wife was a brassy blonde who looked like she enjoyed a good time but wasn't having one now.

"My wife and I have an announcement to make," the governor said grimly. "I think it's best if she speaks for herself."

Could they be splitting? But who's the kid?

Ava Craxton blinked into the cameras like a frightened doe.

"I . . . I want to introduce my son, Steve Hubbard," she said. The boy, who looked about twenty, stepped forward. He was a chunky, clean-cut, unexceptional kid.

"Steve was born when I was sixteen," she continued. "I wasn't married. My parents insisted that I put him up for adoption. Steve was raised by the Hubbard family in Toledo. He never knew about me. But since my husband has been a candidate for President, he found out I was his mother and made contact with me. He's a wonderful young man, and I love him very much, and my husband has been very supportive in this."

She looked warily at the governor, who leaned into the mike and said, "I just want to add that I'm proud of Ava and I'm glad to meet this fine young man. That's about all. This is a personal matter."

He whispered to his wife and she inched back to the mike. "I want to add," she said in a tiny voice, "that when Steve was born . . . my parents . . . we took steps . . . so I wouldn't have more children."

Zap!

The network reporters came on the air, chewing over this unexpected revelation, and eventually arrived at a profound OTIC:

One Thing Is Certain, Dan, this will focus a lot more attention on Ava Craxton as the campaign rolls on.

Not much else was certain. Sitting there in my office, I tried to figure out what I'd just seen.

The obvious question that any civilized person would ask is, "Why are these people telling us this?"

Clearly, the boy's adoptive parents had known who Steve's mother was. And when she seemed headed for the White House, someone had told the boy and he'd had a natural desire to meet his mother.

And he had.

And she'd told her husband.

And the good governor, like any candidate for high office, had cried, "What the hell are you trying to do to me?"

And called in his media advisers.

And they said, "Governor, if this leaks, you're dogmeat!"

They conjured up the headlines in the supermarket press:

AVA'S LOVE CHILD HAUNTS CAMPAIGN

So they agreed upon Preemptive Disclosure, which means you tell the bad news about yourself before your enemies tell it for you, and thereby at least get credit for being honest.

We've seen it before, at one of the national conventions,

for example, when a certain Senator, an aspiring Vice President, started blabbing about his wife's alcoholism, while she looked on in horror.

If the question that decent people ask is, "Why are they telling us this?" the question that we in the Capital ask is, "How will it play?"

For an answer to that question I strolled out to the switchboard to see Cassie.

I didn't even have to ask. Tears glistened on her withered old cheeks.

"That poor woman," she sobbed. "Her own Mama and Daddy forced her to give up that beautiful baby. Even tied up her tubes. And then she married that awful man. It ain't easy being a woman, Tom."

"Don't you like him at all?" I asked.

Cassie mopped her face with a wad of Kleenex. "Well, he stuck by her, I'll give him that. I guess he ain't all bad."

I returned to my office, convinced the Preemptive Disclosure had worked, by humanizing Craxton and winning new friends for his wife.

I had another theory about this event, too, one that had escaped Cassie's sentimental eye.

Because the Craxtons had no children, unkind rumors had circulated that the governor was impotent—or worse. But Ava's revelation that she'd had her tubes tied had redeemed the governor, proved he wasn't shooting blanks, never mind how much humiliation the public admission cost her.

Watching them, there'd been no doubt in my mind that he'd pressured her into adding that unnecessary detail for precisely that reason.

"How come you didn't have that story?"

My publisher loomed in the doorway.

"I screwed up again."

Harriet's latest lover had fled, and she tended to take out her frustrations on the help.

"I read your column on the Allworth campaign."

I awaited the royal verdict.

"Pure tapioca," Harriet announced. "I hear he's having an affair."

In truth, I had heard a few gossamer wisps of rumor—that bit about his walking on the beach with a lovely young thing, for example—but nothing you could pin down, only the usual inventions of bored reporters with dirty minds.

"Did you happen to hear who he was having this affair with?" I asked politely.

"That's your job, buddy boy," my employer growled, and lurched on down the corridor.

"Sit on it, Harriet," I muttered, not loud enough for her to hear.

The phone. A reporter calling about another reporter's suicide, insisting that a certain warped, power-mad editor had driven her to her death.

The phone. An editor in New York. Had I ever thought about writing a book? I babbled incoherently and asked him to call another time.

The phone. Dinah. "I just heard about your house. I'm afraid."

I got rid of her.

The phone again. Jamie Atwood.

"The stockbroker next door to you, he's a very minor player. Have you thought of leaving town?"

"I don't want to run away."

"Somebody sent you a message. You could send one back, that you're out of the game, no threat anymore."

"I could go to the police," I said.

"And tell them what? That you have vague suspicions about Joey Swink, who's a prominent, powerful man? Tom, the police don't even think the firebomb was aimed at you."

"I guess I could use a vacation," I said.

I drove back to my borrowed apartment in the Watergate. Jamie met me there.

"Are you going away?" he asked.

"I don't know."

"You can have this if you want it." He put a small revolver on the table. "Do you know how to use it?"

"More or less. What's the deal on it?"

"It's unregistered and untraceable. If you're found with it, it's illegal."

"Thanks. I guess."

He left. I turned on the evening news and confronted more chaos.

"What do we know about the Senator's condition, Fred?"

"Dan, he's at the hospital, I understand he was conscious when he arrived, but . . ."

What the hell is happening?

I switched madly from network to network.

Slowly the facts emerged, fragments, images.

Don Allworth arrives at a rally in San Francisco. Gays and police clash outside.

Don's speech. Strong defense. Family values. He's in a groove, confident, forceful, a winner.

Then the pop-pop-pop that witnesses always say sounded like firecrackers or a car backfiring, unless they'd known combat; then they say they hit the ground fast.

Don doubles over. Screams. Don on his hands and knees, sinking to the floor as the Secret Service surrounds him, guns drawn. The camera jerking madly, a mob scene, people pushing, running, falling.

A phrase throbs in my mind: Sow the wind, reap the whirlwind.

And he might have been great. He might have. But he went for a shortcut.

I called Polly. She'd left for the airport.

I thought and thought and thought, pushed my poor tormented brain to its outer limits, and finally I decided it was time for me to leave too, time to be moving on.

I travel light. That's one of my virtues, along with quick exits and short goodbyes.

I packed my bag the next morning and would have headed straight for the airport, but I had to stop by the office to announce my sudden vacation.

My house had been firebombed, my nerves were shot, the world was mad, and I was fleeing to Florida. Even my sex-starved publisher could understand that.

The morning news said Don Allworth was not badly hurt, and that over his doctor's objections he planned to leave the hospital and address a rally later in the day. Big drama by the Bay.

The phone. A reporter for one of the tabloids asking me about the firebombing. I hung up. A great headline for the bastards: GOSSIP GETS HIS.

The phone. Dinah.

"I'm leaving for Florida," I told her.

"I want to go," she said.

I groaned.

"I'm serious. I quit my job. The whole thing is too crazy. I have some money."

"Oh, God, Dinah." I wanted to be alone, a rolling stone.

"We don't have to *do* anything, Tommy."

She was so sad, how could I refuse?

"Meet me at the Eastern counter at National in an hour."

I would fly to Miami, rent a car, drive to Key West, and take refuge in the sprawling, glorious Casa Marina. I was taking Jamie Atwood's advice, waving a white flag to whoever burned down my house: I surrender, you win.

Writing a gossip column is a bad enough way to live; it's sure nothing to die for.

Harriet appeared. I told her my plan.

"The conventions are coming up!" she raged.

"A pox on the conventions," I said.

My sanity was at issue. Had anyone ever been driven mad by too much gossip? Might I be the first? The Tullis Syndrome?

What about that editor who called me about a book? Did his plan include a healthy advance? I wanted to lie in the sun and make sense of my life.

I tried to call Addie, but she was out covering the campaign. I didn't know what to do about Addie. Every week or two she hit town, and we'd stay up late and drink wine and make love, then she'd drift back to the make-believe world of the campaign. I saw more of her plants than I did of her; she'd entrusted me with a key to the house, so I could water them and confuse burglars.

Dinah hugged me at the airport. Dinah in a straw hat and peasant blouse was real, solid, tangible.

"Just before I left, I played *Abbey Road*," she said. "Side Two, I mean. Do you ever play *Abbey Road* and wonder how many other people are playing it at the same time all over the world?"

We boarded a flight for Miami.

We had a window and aisle seat up front, and an empty between us. Dinah squeezed my hand. "I can't believe it about your house," she said.

"Believe it," I said.

"Who do you think did it?"

"I don't know, but I'm going to Florida so they won't do it again."

I looked out the window. You could see across the Potomac to the monuments. Such a pretty city. From the proper distance.

"Tommy!"

I groaned. I wanted to sleep, perchance to dream, not have this addled ex-hippie tormenting me.

"Those guys who just came aboard. They were staring at you. See them?"

A few rows ahead of us, two Latins in leather jackets and gold chains were patting their hair and flexing their muscles.

I groaned.

Quick exits demand quick decisions.

"Let's go," I said.

The ground crew was closing the door.

We ran up the aisle.

A stewardess blocked my path.

"Sir, you can't . . ."

"My wife's in labor," I said.

The stewardess's eyes grew large, Dinah puffed out her belly, and we made our escape.

No one followed.

Another miracle: I gave a cargo guy twenty, and he retrieved my bag. I needed that bag. It had my toothbrush, my bathing suit, and Jamie's gun.

"Now what?"

"We take the next flight to anywhere in Florida."

"Are we paranoid?" she asked.

"Paranoids live longer."

We caught a flight to Sarasota, this time with no dangerous characters aboard.

At the Sarasota airport I rented a red Thunderbird, studied a map, and decided that we should drive south, spend the night somewhere on the Gulf Coast, then the next day take the Alligator Alley across the Everglades to Miami. Maybe a day there, then down to the Keys. Soon we'd be on that pier in Key West, with hundreds of tourists and freaks, cheering that glorious end-of-the-world sunset over the Gulf.

I'd driven south a hundred miles before a highway sign jogged my memory: I was headed for Naples, the resort town where my friend Forrest Keel was living.

It was odd. I hadn't thought of Forrest at all. I didn't have his number or address. But fate had steered me to Naples, and I wanted to talk to him. Maybe he could make some sense out of this mess I was fleeing.

Dinah was sleeping as we pulled into Naples. I liked what I saw: swaying palms, pastel homes, a sparkling marina, plush bars built over the water. A lot different from the funk of Key West. I thought Dinah and I could pass an agreeable day or two here, so I pulled into the Sea Spray Motel.

In our room, as I unpacked, Dinah saw me take Jamie's revolver out of my bag.

"Tommy, what in the world?"

"People have been throwing bombs at me, remember?"

"I hate guns. Guns never solve anything. They *kill* people. Is it loaded?"

I nodded.

"Oh, Jesus, Tommy." She was truly terrified.

In truth, I didn't feel so in need of a weapon as I had in the Capital. "Look, I'm putting it in the bottom of my bag," I told her. "It won't go off by itself. Maybe later I'll toss it in the Everglades."

We found a quiet restaurant overlooking the Gulf, where we watched the sun burn down into the sea, the long plum afterglow, the coming of the stars. We dined by candlelight on fresh crabs and grouper and two bottles of chilled Meursault. The waitress made good suggestions and left us alone, and I didn't mind the bill. Good evenings are worth what they cost.

Back at the motel, we had twin beds, but Dinah slipped into mine. I'd forgotten how sweet she could be.

When I awoke at ten, Dinah was still zonked. I lay by the pool till noon, then showered and dressed.

Dinah groaned.

"I'm going to see if I can reach a friend of mine," I told her. "I'll be back after a while and we'll have lunch."

She groaned again.

I hadn't told her about Forrest. I thought he and Chuck wouldn't mind an unexpected visit from me, but I wasn't sure they'd welcome a woman they didn't know.

Not far down the highway I noticed an inviting-looking place called the Cove Inn Club. I went inside and found the phone booth, but I couldn't find a listing for either Forrest or Chuck—not in the telephone book nor from information.

Cursing my luck, I sought inspiration at the bar. The Cove Inn Club was quiet, shadowy, spread out over a series of rooms.

As I sipped my chilled Bass Ale and looked around, my eyes fell on three men at a table in the next room.

I did a double-take.

One of them was Wally Love, a long way from Oregon.

One of them, laughing and waving his hands as he told a story, was Forrest's friend Chuck.

I didn't know the third man, who was burly, balding, and tanned.

I tried to make sense of the scene. Wally had no reason to know Forrest or Chuck.

Chuck was a stockbroker and, according to Forrest, utterly apolitical.

I passed the bartender a twenty and asked him if he knew the third man at the table.

He glanced at the bill, at the man, and back at me. "His name's Rojack. He's in politics."

Now I was totally befuddled. I knew Rojack had been working for Craxton, just as Wally had for Allworth.

What to do?

I quickly devised alternate plans.

Plan A was to take advantage of this happy coincidence and go say hello to Wally and Chuck.

Plan B was to leave quietly, head for Key West, and not look back.

I was inclining toward Plan B when a hand touched my arm.

I turned and was face to unsmiling face with my friend Forrest Keel.

"We owe you an explanation," he said.

33.

orrest and I shook hands.

"Let's join the others," he said.

Wally Love jumped up and greeted me like a long-lost brother. Chuck was cordial but wary.

"I've got to go or I'll miss my flight," Rojack announced. "You want a ride to the airport, Wally?"

"That'd be great," Wally Love said.

"Heading back to God's country?" I asked.

Wally looked mournful. "I had a crazy call from my boy Charlie, my editor. He thinks he's in love."

"I heard you quit Allworth."

"I'm sick about the whole thing," Wally admitted.

When they were gone, Forrest, Chuck, and I looked at each other uneasily.

"I'm on my way to the Keys," I said. "Thought I'd surprise you."

"And indeed you did," Forrest said.

I nodded.

"Let's go back to our place," Forrest said. "This may take a while to sort out."

I offered to drive my Thunderbird, but Forrest said to come in his El Dorado. We drove south out of town.

"Seen the morning news?"

I shook my head. "In Florida I tune out the outer world."

"Don Allworth spoke on the hospital steps, on crutches, his loving wife beside him, and vowed that an unnamed 'they' would never stop his crusade for a family-loving, God-fearing America. Great stuff. He'll win California."

"Then what?"

"Then an interesting convention."

We turned through high iron gates, onto a long finger of land that jutted into the Gulf. We passed palms and fiery tropical flowers, and stopped at a red-roofed, Spanish-style mansion perched at the water's edge.

"You mentioned a condo," I said.

"A friend made me a better offer," Forrest said.

I thought about Dinah at the motel. Would she think I'd ditched her? I'd call if I could. But I didn't tell Forrest and Chuck she was waiting for me.

Inside, a long living room opened onto the Gulf, which glittered so brightly you looked away. A tile floor, heavy Spanish furniture, flags fluttering in the sea breeze, a blue-and-white speedboat down at the dock.

"Nice," I said. "Whose is it?"

Forrest seemed not to hear my question.

"Let's take the boat out," he said.

Surreality loomed. "We came to talk."

"I'm expecting two . . . associates soon," Forrest said. "Let's wait for them."

"Associates?"

Again, he seemed not to have heard. We followed a flagstone path down to the dock. A muscular young Latin in a

220

bathing suit was gassing the boat. A tangle of gold chains set off his tan.

As we pulled away from the dock, Forrest called, "Back in an hour or so, Rudy."

Rudy.

Rudy was the name of one of the toughs Joey Swink had sent to oust the bikers who crashed a Boys' Club party.

Forrest and Chuck were all smiles. They popped three beers and gave me a gossipy tour of the Naples coast, pointing out the homes of famous Florida politicians, heiresses, and drug dealers.

My thoughts were elsewhere. Like: What the hell am I doing here?

Yet, these were my friends.

Rudy met us at the dock. A huge black man was with him. He'd been in Farabee's tale, too.

What had been the black guy's name?

Up at the house he brought us a pitcher of daiquiris. "Thanks, Bobby," Chuck said.

Bobby had been his name.

"I do need to be getting on," I said.

"Relax," Forrest said. "My friends will be here soon."

I tasted my daiquiri. The magic had drained out of Florida's rum and sun. It tasted like battery fluid.

Chuck excused himself to take a nap.

Forrest and I looked at each other.

"You didn't see the news?" Forrest asked.

"No."

He smiled. "Craxton's gang says Allworth staged his own shooting and your friend Ratcliffe hints that Craxton trotted out his wife's long-lost son so he could talk about family values too."

"The mud flies."

"Lyndon's Law."

"Call your opponent a pig-fucker. Make him deny it."

We laughed, then we stopped laughing.

221

"I kept looking into those campaign donations," I said.

"I know."

"I've heard some strange things about Joey Swink."

Forrest gave me so cold a look that I did not continue. We heard a car outside. "That's my friends."

The front door banged, and a moment later Joey Swink and Jamie Atwood walked into the room.

I was floored. I had no idea that Atwood knew either of them, or that Forrest and Swink were more than acquaintances.

Jamie looked at me and shook his head sadly. "You were going on vacation."

"This is it. I dropped by to see Forrest."

Jamie sighed. "You have the most amazing luck."

Swink muttered something and left the room. A moment later I saw him walking across the lawn with Bobby and Rudy.

Forrest poured daiquiris all around. We settled in chairs that faced the Gulf.

"Tom talked to Greg Farabee the other night," he said. "About Doyle Kane and the money. And he's learned things about Joey."

Jamie nodded wearily. "We have a problem," he said.

"You know, none of this is really any of my business," I said.

"On the contrary," the lawyer said. "You've been so persistent. We owe you a full explanation."

"Not really," I said.

"The problem is Joey, you see," Jamie said, stretching out his long legs. "His infinite greed."

"It's the money," Forrest said. "So damn much money floating around. Everybody wants in the game. And Joey was a player."

I looked at Jamie, my new Washington friend. He still wore his boots, with pale blue slacks and a Hawaiian shirt.

"You were his source, weren't you?" I said. "Mr. Big, the

man who supplied the cocaine that he used to seduce politicians."

"You figured that out, did you?"

"And it *was* drug money, cocaine money, going into the campaign."

Jamie rubbed his eyes wearily. "The pressures are unendurable. You have these violent, impulsive Latins with tens of millions in cash. They have the American government hounding them. The solution seems quite obvious to them: buy off the American government. You tell them it doesn't work that way and they won't believe you. You're about to lose important clients because you won't take their money. So you take their money. And what can you do with it that's legal or else can't be traced back to you? Nothing. You can't even keep it, because they want an accounting. What the hell can you do?"

"You can give it to Joey Swink," Forrest said bitterly.

"Yes, you can give it to Joey," Jamie said. "Joey, who's got a million schemes for spending it. The Colombians love Joey—he promises them action, big deals, miracles. And of course takes his cut off the top. Wonderful, clever Joey blasts off. And the whole crazy merry-go-round spins out of control."

"I can see it would be difficult," I said.

"Oh, Joey thinks big. His strategy was to be flexible, to try out all the avenues of investment, to contribute to all the major candidates, so that no matter who won we would have a line to him. A full-court press, he called it."

Jamie walked to the bar and poured some rum.

"We had people sending in thousand-dollar checks, but that was too slow and involved too many people. We were fascinated by the loophole that permits unlimited expenditures by independent operators. But who should such a person be? How would he explain himself? Who could spend several hundred thousand dollars in the primaries and not be traced back to us?"

"And you came up with Wally Love," I said.

"Love used to be a drinker. He got in some scrape when he was in Los Angeles for a publishers' convention, years ago, and Joey knew about it. Joey never forgets anything. So Joey went to see him. Probably Love sees him and thinks blackmail, but instead Joey talks politics, and it turns out that Love loves Don Allworth, thinks he ought to be President, so Joey tells him there's a way he can help. Joey's very clever that way. Love was totally sincere. The only trouble was, he got disillusioned with the candidate. But it was a nice exercise while it lasted. For a while, Joey had Love and Rojack and three others spending all they could."

Seagulls squawked outside. The Gulf shimmered, silver-blue. Rudy and Bobby lingered in the doorways.

"Finally he fastened on the soft money as the best way to spend big. But it's hard to make one-hundred-thousand-dollar donations that can't be traced. You work through two or three layers of lawyers, but who knows who might be checking? The FEC? The IRS? The other party? If they reach Joey they might reach me, and if they reach me there are serious problems. The whole damn thing was a nightmare. But Joey was having the time of his life. And my colleagues south of the border were mightily impressed."

"What are you doing in this, Forrest?" I couldn't overcome my curiosity, despite the mess it had me in.

My friend shrugged. "Greed. Joey needed help. I took polls, produced media spots. I tried to stay on the legal end of things, but once you're in you're in all the way."

"What went wrong?" I asked.

"Doyle Kane was the first thing," Jamie said. "He saw a pattern to some of the checks and he put two and two together. He had a grudge against Swink, so he began talking to people. To you, to Farabee, to the O'Shea woman, and God knows who else."

"He tried to talk to me," I said bitterly. "I didn't listen."

"In time we sent someone to talk to him."

"Jamie, should we go into that?"

The lawyer shrugged. "Let's just say that persuasion was called for, but force was used, too much force. Those damn fools. It made me understand how Nixon must have felt during Watergate. You employ people, you assume they're competent, then they botch things on an unbelievable scale. They bring you down with them."

Forrest spoke up. "And you, Tom, you were a problem. You kept asking questions. Printing those items about funny money. Stirring up that damn Grundy. Asking about Wally Love. You thought it was a game, but it wasn't a game."

"I had this fantasy about a Pulitzer," I sighed.

I felt like the biggest fool on earth. All I could do was keep talking. "Forrest, did you come to Florida because of Doyle's death?"

"More or less. Things were out of control in Washington. I didn't want to be close to it. We could work from here. I could pretend I was distancing myself."

I forced a smile, as if I glimpsed some spark of hope in this disaster. "Look, I came down to get away from this mess. It's none of my business. The best thing is for me to leave now, drive down to the Keys, and forget the whole thing."

I stood up. No one else moved. Rudy and Bobby lurked in the doorways. All eyes were on me. Waves lapped against the dock. After a moment I sat back down.

"You know so very much," Atwood said. "It truly is a dreadful problem."

"I don't see it," I protested. "I don't know who killed Doyle Kane. The police think it was somebody he picked up."

Jamie Atwood gave me a disdainful look. "It's not that simple," he said. "The police, thanks to you, have sent FEC lawyers to examine the Craxton finances. Quite possibly they'll see what Kane saw and one thing will lead to another."

"You mean, lead to this group."

"It could."

I decided to take my shot. As far as I could see, Jamie was the brains of this operation. "Then it's clear what you should do. If Doyle was killed by accident, or whatever, that's not your problem. You didn't do it. All you've done is play money games. Remember, in Watergate, it wasn't the original break-in that brought Nixon down, it was trying to cover it up. If the police come around, give them the ones who did it. Maybe they've got a case, maybe not. But don't risk yourselves to protect Swink and a couple of thugs."

"You son of a bitch," Swink muttered from the doorway.

I ignored him. "Be smart. Cut your losses. Give them whoever did it and save yourselves."

Rudy spat an obscenity from across the room.

"Let's all keep cool," Atwood said. "The Watergate analogy doesn't apply. Our group is tighter-knit than Nixon's. I'm afraid we sink or swim together."

"Why are you wasting time with this fool?" Swink demanded.

"Be patient, Joey," Atwood said.

"You see, Tom, there's another problem," Atwood continued. "Some of Buzz Makito's associates decided to invest in the campaign. As insurance against the trade bill. It was idiotic, but Joey encouraged them. He has this whole other operation—we didn't even know until a few weeks ago. Any serious investigation of Joey might lead not only to me and my clients, but to some Japanese nationals who have no business at all meddling in American politics. It would create a terrible scandal, particularly if, as I suspect, Buzz has ties to Japanese intelligence."

"Look, none of this has anything to do with me," I protested.

"That's what we kept trying to tell you," he said. "But you wouldn't listen. And now we face these unacceptable risks. Damn you, you brought it on yourself."

226

Jamie Atwood abruptly left the room. Through the doorway, I saw him talking to Swink; then they moved out of view. Soon a car roared away outside.

That left me and Forrest. The late-afternoon sun, slanting off the water, filled the room with melancholy orange light.

"The time I followed Shiner," I said. "The time I got banged on the head. Were you there?"

He nodded. "He called me. I probably saved your life. Dammit, why didn't you take the hint?"

"The first time I met Jamie, he talked about his brother dying in prison, about how marijuana was okay but cocaine was bad, about how he didn't represent the bad guys. Was there any truth at all in that?"

"It's how he started out. Idealistic. Defending college boys busted for a joint. But if you're good, the big boys want you to defend them. The money sucks you in, a step at a time. There's so damn much money. You want a Porsche? Hey, how about twenty of them? Boats, planes, sex, drugs, all yours, if you please the big boys. Later on, you figure out that they use the carrot and the stick too. The stick is, they kill people."

"The other day I told Swink I thought there was drug money going into the campaign. That night my house was firebombed."

Forrest lowered his voice. "Joey's half-crazy at this point. He's not safe, nobody's safe. The whole thing is impossible. We have this stupid, senseless murder. And you, blundering around, knowing just enough to make a nuisance of yourself. We tried to throw you off. Distract you. Swink gave you that Penner story—and instead of printing it you tried to hush it up."

"People kept tossing out theories. Gay money. Defense money. TV preachers."

"We wanted you to go off on a tangent. But you kept on coming."

"I keep telling you, I don't know anything."

"You know that Swink and Rudy and Bobby went to see Doyle Kane, to scare him, and wound up killing him."

"Nobody knows that. The police have no evidence."

"They may have a witness who saw them entering the apartment house. That's why we have them out of Washington. The whole thing is falling apart. You picked a lovely time to visit."

"Look, I want out."

"This is a bad situation, Tom. A terrible situation."

"This is insane."

"I'm part of a group. We've made a lot of money. But we've also made a serious mistake. We could all go down. The group has to protect itself."

"Forrest, we're friends."

"Friends?" He seemed to weigh the word. "Washington friends. Political friends. Lunch at Duke's friends. I was your gay friend, you were my gossip-columnist friend. It only goes so far. Not far at all when survival is the issue."

Forrest was crazy, they all were, and sweet reason wasn't getting me anywhere. Bobby and Rudy were nowhere to be seen. I leapt to my feet and made a break for it, out the French doors.

I flew like the wind for about thirty feet and then Bobby shot out of nowhere and tackled me. I went down hard, with his bulk atop me. I twisted my knee and it hurt like hell. Bobby dragged me back inside.

"Sit down, Tom," Forrest said wearily. "Have a drink. Let's be calm, please."

Reality was sinking in. These people might kill me. But, if that was true, why were we sitting here guzzling daiquiris?

I figured that out soon enough. We were giving the kingpin, Jamie Atwood, time to distance himself from the unpleasantries.

Then what would it be?

The Gulf? Or the Everglades?

228

The sharks? Or the alligators?

Long shadows crept across the room. I kept searching for an escape route. Or a weapon. There was a candelabra on the piano. If I could reach it, maybe I could crack Bobby's thick skull.

I was studying Bobby, measuring the distances, summoning my courage, when a voice rang out.

"Don't anybody move! Move and I'll blow you away!"

34.

We looked toward the terrace and saw a figure easing
through the French doors, a shadow against the sun, a gun
clutched before her.

It was Dinah, and the gun was mine.

Forrest and Bobby froze. They didn't know, as I did, that
my savior was terrified of guns. That "blow you away" line
must have come from a Clint Eastwood movie.

"Come on, Tommy," she said. "This place sucks."

I leapt up, greedy to feel the weapon in my hands. Then
my banged-up knee buckled.

I sank to the other knee, and then a strange thing happened.

Bobby, with a dreamy smile on his face, began to move
toward Dinah.

She was holding the gun before her, in both hands, pointed

at his chest, but he moved ahead, grinning now, wagging one finger at her, as if she were a naughty child.

"Stop!" she said fiercely, but he kept shuffling forward.

"Hey, missy, you wouldn't shoot ole Bob, wouldja?"

"I will," she said. "If you don't stop, I will!"

He kept on coming. He was ten feet from her.

I tried to rise, but my knee wouldn't hold me.

Six feet.

"Dinah, shoot the son of a bitch!" I roared helplessly.

Her face was a mask of frustration. Poor Dinah, the pacifist, the vegetarian, the anti-nuker—in her whole life Dinah had never hurt a fly, and now she had to blow this fucker away.

The madman was wagging his finger inches from the muzzle of the gun. "Don't shoot ole Bob," he whispered.

"Do it, Dinah, do it!" I cried.

It looked as if it might kill her, but she did it: she pulled the trigger.

And nothing happened.

Bobby did a little soft-shoe shuffle and lifted the gun from her grasp.

Suddenly I understood.

Jamie Atwood had given me that gun. And it was filled with blanks. They'd known it, they'd been way ahead of me.

"You sons of bitches," I groaned.

"Enough of this crap," Rudy yelled. "Lock these clowns up."

They threw Dinah and me into a small storeroom. The door slammed, a bolt turned, and we lay tangled on the floor in darkness.

"Tommy, are you okay?"

I didn't know whether to laugh or cry.

"Sure," I said. "I'm great."

"The gun," she said. "What happened? I pulled the trigger."

I explained it to her. "It was all my fault," I said. "My stupid fault. You were great."

"Who *are* these people?"

"Joey Swink and a lawyer named Atwood have been pumping drug money into the campaign. They killed Doyle when he figured it out."

"But wasn't that Forrest in there?"

"The son of a bitch is part of it. My pal." I gave her a summary of what had happened.

When I finished, Dinah said, "We've got to get out of here."

"I figured that out. Do you have any matches?"

She had a fresh book from the Cove Inn Club, and lit one after another as I explored our prison, inch by inch. It was about eight by twelve, with cinder-block walls and a concrete floor. Ventilation came from a duct near the ceiling. Dinah climbed on my shoulders but she could not remove the cover or find any weaknesses in the wooden ceiling. I examined the door carefully but it was solid oak and solidly bolted.

There was no way out. I sat down again to think.

"How'd you find me?" I asked.

"When you didn't come back, I got scared. I called a cab and drove around until I saw the Thunderbird at that Cove Inn Club. The bartender told me who you left with and where you'd probably be. But he talked like it was bad vibes here, like they didn't want visitors, so I drove back to the motel and got all upset and finally I put the gun in my purse and drove here and pulled off my great rescue. Tommy, I've been screwing up all my life, but this was monumental."

I squeezed her hand. "I'm the one who screwed up," I said. "You were brave."

She huddled against me in the darkness. "What are we going to do?"

"I think these people plan to take us for a one-way boat ride tomorrow. Either we talk them out of it, which isn't likely, or we escape."

"Have you got any ideas?"

"It would help if we had a weapon."

"I've got a couple of joints. In the hem of my skirt."

I couldn't help laughing. "I don't think dope is the answer, Dinah. A knife, a file, a bomb maybe, but not dope."

She shrugged. "It might, you know, relax us."

"I don't want to relax," I told her. In my frustration I beat on the door and yelled at our captors, called them the worst names I knew; it was my fantasy that one of them would open the door and I would miraculously overpower him.

But no one came. I threw myself down beside Dinah. She smoked one of her joints.

"It's so crazy for anybody to kill you and me," she told me. "We never hurt anybody."

I reflected that probably I'd hurt a lot of people in my life, although not with guns.

"What looks crazy to us may look damn convenient to them," I said, ever the philosopher.

"What are we going to do, Tommy?"

"Let's get some sleep. Be as rested as we can in the morning. At some point, maybe out on the lawn, I'm going to tackle one of them. When I do, you make a break for it. I'm sorry, that's the best plan I have."

I lay down on the floor with Dinah's head on my shoulder. My knee hurt like hell. I thought about my daughter, my sometime lover Addie, the women I'd married, the mistakes I'd made, the moving finger that writes and keeps moving on.

"Tommy?"

"Huh?"

"You want to make love?"

I did not reject the idea out of hand. There was a certain perverse logic to it, affirming life in the face of the void, and all that.

But I kissed her instead. "Dinah, you're wonderful. But I don't think I'm up to it. Let's just dream sweet dreams if we can."

"Okay, Tommy."

"G'night."

"Tommy?"

"Yeah?"

"I love you. I've loved you since the night of the Michigan primary, twelve years ago."

"I love you too, Dinah."

I wasn't sure who or what I loved, who or what I'd ever loved; probably I'd never loved anything as much as I should have, except for myself and my fantasies and self-delusions, and I'd loved them far too much. But it was the right thing to say.

Voices woke us in the morning. A faint light shone under the door.

"I dreamed of snow," Dinah said. "Skiing in the mountains with Randy, my little boy. It was so lovely."

"Good."

"You know what I'm gonna do, if we get out of this?"

"What?"

"Go straight to Portland. Find a job and get Randy back."

"What about the campaign?"

"I'll make a separate peace. Whoever wins, it doesn't matter unless I get myself together."

I didn't know what to say. She was such an incredible optimist.

"What about you, Tommy?"

"What about me?"

"What'll you do, if we get out of here?"

"Get the hell out of the gossip business, for starters."

The door flew open. The light blinded me at first; then I saw Rudy with a gun in his hand.

"Get up, you two!"

My knee was stiff, but I was able to hobble.

"Hey, I've gotta use the bathroom," Dinah protested.

Rudy scowled, but let us go across the hall. Dinah first, then me.

As I crossed the hallway, I could see Bobby lounging at the kitchen table. Out the barred bathroom window I saw

234

the boat at the dock, the Gulf, gulls, a glorious Florida morning.

I took my time in the bathroom, trying to come up with a plan for overcoming two armed thugs. None emerged.

"Let's go," Rudy said.

He herded us into the kitchen. Bobby stood up and grinned. "Well, how's the honeymooners?"

Dinah glared at him. His face possessed the strength and subtlety of a bowling ball.

"Ain't she cute?" he said to Rudy with a wink.

Rudy jabbed the gun in my ribs. "Hands behind your back."

Suddenly, unexpectedly, the moment of truth arrived. Once I was bound the game was over. I hoped they didn't want to bloody up their sleek new kitchen. So I whirled, swinging wildly.

Before my fist found Rudy's face, the gun barrel crashed against my ear and I crumpled to the floor. Dinah tried to run, but Bobby flung her down beside me.

In an instant our arms were handcuffed behind us.

"You two are crazy," I said. "People know I came here. They'll nail you for this."

"Won't he'p you none," Bobby said. "You be feeding the fishies."

They pushed us onto the terrace. Swink was having coffee at a glass-topped table, reading a movie script.

"Lookie what we found," Bobby said. "Intruders."

Joey studied us from under hooded eyes. All these years, in the Capital, his charm and political status had kept me from realizing what a cold, reptilian little man he was.

"Where's Forrest?" I demanded. I had a wild idea that my friend would save us yet.

"He departed," Swink said. "He asked me to see to your needs."

"You're insane," I said. "They'll turn on you. They'll blame you for everything."

He studied me for a long moment. "No, Mr. Busybody,

you're the one who's insane. You couldn't keep your nose out of other people's business. So now you pay."

"They can trace me here."

"Fine. You dropped by to say hello, you left, and that was that. Your car will be found in the Everglades."

A gossip to the end, I asked him one more question. "You were the one who ran The Lodge, weren't you? The one who flew the girls in from the West?"

Before Swink could answer, Bobby howled behind us. Dinah had kicked him. He rubbed his shin, then grabbed her.

"Rudy, how 'bout you gassing up the boat and taking care of Junior? I'm gonna take missy here inside and teach her a big lesson."

Dinah fought and screamed as he dragged her away.

I had nothing left to lose, nothing except my pride. I kicked over the breakfast table and started hobbling after Bobby. Swink screamed as hot coffee splashed into his lap.

Rudy tripped me and I crashed to the terrace, face first. Rudy started toward me but Swink barked at him.

"Go help Bobby. I'll handle this one."

He kicked me in the kidneys, expertly.

"You fool!" he muttered.

He kicked again, my temple, and the world became a golden haze.

"I'm sick of you, Tullis," he raged.

I dimly heard a shot; then I felt Swink's body crumple onto mine. The gunshot echoed in my ears without meaning. Rudy and Bobby ran from the house, shirtless, guns in their hands.

I lay still. One glance told them all they needed to know about Swink.

"Let's go," Rudy yelled. "The boat."

What happened next happened very fast, a model of efficiency, like a scalpel cutting through flesh or a guillotine at work.

One moment Rudy and Bobby were two dangerous characters making a getaway. The next moment they threw down their guns and threw up their hands.

I struggled to a sitting position and looked around, until I saw what they had seen.

Six men were advancing on them from every direction. They wore combat fatigues and black masks, like terrorists, and they carried automatic weapons, the kind that all decent citizens want to ban.

I had never seen more admirable weapons; I would have joined the NRA on the spot.

One of our rescuers brought Dinah out of the house. Another frisked Rudy and found the key that freed me and Dinah. He quickly used the handcuffs to secure Rudy and Bobby, back to back.

When Rudy cursed, the biggest of the men, the one who seemed to be in charge, stuck his gun in his face. "One more word and you're gone, *amigo*," he said, sounding blessedly sincere.

"Are you people okay?" he asked.

We nodded mutely. Alive was okay. Alive was the blue-ribbon best this planet had to offer.

"Then let's get out of here before the police come."

"The police? Who are you?"

"Don't ask."

He pointed his weapon at Rudy and Bobby. "You vermin start moving. Slow down and we'll blow your legs off."

They scuttled crablike down the beach, moving well for two men handcuffed back to back.

"What about . . . him?" Dinah asked, nodding back at Joey Swink's body on the terrace.

"I shoot 'em, lady, I don't bury 'em," our masked friend said, reasonably enough. "Come on."

He led us down to the dock. I thought at first we were going to get into Swink's speedboat, but one of them yanked some wires to disable it.

They scanned the horizon, and in a moment we saw another boat, a cabin cruiser, headed toward us.

"We meant to take them alive," the leader of the team told us. "But that one kicking you, it looked like he might hurt you bad, so we decided to take him out."

"A wise decision," I told him.

The cruiser shot closer, slicing through the water until it stopped at our dock.

I saw the man commanding it and cried out in amazement. "Forrest!"

"You were expecting maybe Ollie North?" my friend said. "Get in."

Moments later we were racing across the Gulf. I had my arm around Dinah, who sobbed softly into my shirt.

"Where are we going?" I yelled at Forrest.

"First to drop these fellows off," he told me. "Then I have a plane waiting. Florida's not the best place for us, not after they find Swink."

I looked at him with concern. "Forrest, where the hell are you taking us?"

"To Washington," my friend said. "Isn't that where you want to go?"

35.

"You'd be a hell of a lot better off with me dead," I said, ever the realist.

"No doubt about it," Forrest said. "It's not like you didn't deserve it. For sheer monumental stupidity."

He shrugged. "But Dinah, she hadn't done anything."

We were in his office, with the door locked, and a bottle of J&B between us. We'd tried to check Dinah into a hotel, but she insisted on returning to her apartment in Adams-Morgan.

"What more can happen?" she had asked, still the optimist.

But as Forrest saw it, a lot more could happen, most of it bad. "To start, there's the investigation of Kane's death," he said.

"Blame Bobby and Rudy. And Swink."

"Sure, but the prosecutors will pressure them to serve up their bosses. With Swink dead, either they blame Jamie—in which case he starts blaming me—or they just offer me up, figuring Jamie is a good friend to have. And you're a witness."

"I'd tell all I know about Atwood, and I'd say I don't know anything at all about you. Which is more or less true."

"Perjury is a slippery slope, pal. It turns a star witness into a co-conspirator. Not that I don't appreciate the sentiment."

He poured more J&B.

"I'd say I made some media spots for Swink, and didn't know what else was going on. Maybe it'd hold up and maybe it wouldn't. And, of course, there's another problem."

"Which one?"

"Florida. Bobby and Rudy have been charged with Swink's death. Which means they're already talking. They'll put us there, and maybe they'll figure out that the fellows in masks were my friends. And a lot of people are going to be asking who those fellows are. The state of Florida doesn't exactly encourage private armies. We'll both be hearing about that one."

"Two thugs' word against ours."

"Two thugs and Atwood. He's a smart man and he'll do his damnedest to blame everything on us. Jamie's the key. He can make life very complicated for us."

"Dammit, I'm an innocent citizen!" I raged. "He's the crook."

Forrest shrugged and filled his glass.

"The first time I met Jamie, he was so damn charming," I said. "Utterly believable."

"He's an attractive guy. But he got in over his head. Lawyers do it all the time. They think they're invulnerable, because they know how to manipulate our legal system. But they can't manipulate an illegal system, can't outtalk a bullet between the eyes."

"What do you think he'll do?"

"I don't know. The Colombians wanted to play politics, but they didn't want a scandal to blow up in their faces. Jamie's on the spot."

"Forrest, what are you going to do?"

"Probably get out of town for a while."

I looked at this man who had saved my life, at considerable risk to his own, and realized how little I knew him.

Of course, the longer I live the less I think I know anyone. We wear masks, play roles, waltz on, serene in our ignorance.

"Tom, I'm going to tell you something I shouldn't tell you. If you ever repeat it I'll deny it, and you might find yourself in a lot of trouble. But it's probably better that you know."

What now? I thought.

"I have an informal relationship with an American intelligence agency. Which one doesn't matter. It goes back to Vietnam. My political work puts me all over the map. Sometimes I pick up things that are useful to them."

I was trying to take all this in, but my computer was overloaded. "Is that why you were involved with Swink?"

"Sure. He thought he seduced me, but I'd been giving him the come-on for months. It's been clear for years that Joey was pushing cocaine, was in a position to blackmail a number of government officials, and was potentially a threat to national security. The question was who was behind him. I cultivated Joey and figured out that his supplier was Atwood. Then the question was who was behind *him*. We're pretty sure we know that now. I hoped to lure his two Colombian bosses to Miami, where they could be arrested."

He sighed and finished his drink. "This mess in Florida probably killed that. But we've still got Atwood."

I struggled to keep up. "Won't your agency protect you? Legally?"

He laughed. "And blow my cover? It's a one-way loyalty. If I went to jail, they'd probably ease me out in a few months. And they won't do beans for you. It's you I'm worried about now."

"Dammit, how can I have legal problems? I'm an innocent man."

"I'm not talking about legal problems. The ideal solution

to Atwood's problems is for the two witnesses against him, you and me, to square the circle."

"To do what?"

"To wake up dead. Rudy and Bobby are behind bars, but there are others like them out there. You might think about leaving town for a while."

"The last time I did that, it didn't work out so well."

"Don't visit any friends," he said.

"What about Buzz Makito?" I asked. "Was what Atwood said about him true?"

"More or less. Buzz thought he was using Joey, but more often Joey was using him. He went too far when he sucked Japanese money into the campaign. If that gets out, a lot of people will be running for cover."

I threw up my hands. There were boxes within boxes within boxes, and I didn't want to open any more of them.

I left him there and went to Dinah's to sleep on it.

By the next morning I decided I didn't want to flee, not from the U.S. Attorney, not from Atwood, not from anything. I resolved to live my life as if absolutely nothing were wrong. Nothing except the things that are always wrong.

I went to my office, where a mountain of calls awaited me. I returned a few and batted out a column.

In the afternoon I tried calling Addie. I had the idea that seeing her might calm me, that her tough-mindedness could help make sense of the mess I was in. Also, I wanted to see if she'd picked up any scuttlebutt at the *Post* about Swink's death, any inside dope they hadn't printed. But I couldn't find her at home or her office.

I called Don Allworth's office, wanting the latest on the campaign. They said he was at home, so I called there and Polly answered. She said Don wasn't in, and we talked awhile. She was upset. Don had gotten over his wound but she hadn't gotten over the shock of his being shot. I told her I'd try to come by later.

I drove to Georgetown—drawn by the relentless lure of gossip—to see if Gloria was home.

I found her in her yard talking to the contractor, who was still at work on her new pool.

She led me into the kitchen, where I guzzled a beer while she filled me in on the past week's dirt.

"What about Castro?" I said. "He's still alive."

"They wouldn't let me back in," she said. "We think there was a double agent who blew the operation."

"Probably just as well."

"Tommy, you look awful," she declared. "What's wrong?"

"I was in Florida when Joey Swink was killed."

"A rat of the first order," she said. "Who killed him?"

"I don't know," I said. "Terrorists, maybe."

Her glance said she didn't believe me and that she would not forgive my untruth.

"You've had a hard year," she said. I tensed, because sympathy is not Gloria's style.

"I guess it could have been worse."

"You never even found the woman on the beach, did you?"

I shrugged. That was ancient history now. "Don said it was some girl looking for shells."

"And you believed him." So much scorn in four little words. I have long since learned not to seek logic in Gloria's deeds; the woman, I think, is motivated by pure malice.

I was sorry I had come. Gloria is strong medicine, too strong for a man in my delicate condition.

"I'm looking for Addie," I said. What I was really looking for was an excuse to leave. "She's not answering at home, and she's not at the office."

Gloria's eyes gleamed, catlike and cold; I knew that look. She knew something I didn't know.

"Why don't you go by her house?" she asked.

"I called."

"Maybe she's not taking calls, but would want to see you."

"Maybe so," I agreed.

It was around six on a warm, still evening when I reached Addie's house, perched high in the trees above Rock Creek. I parked down the street and walked back, hearing laughter from the deck. I went around to the back of the house and saw Addie's BMW and another car I didn't recognize.

I stood for a long time, trying to think; I felt like such a fool.

Enough is enough is enough. I had Addie's key, from my plant-watering days. I let myself in and crossed to the door that opened onto the deck.

They were having drinks, close together on the love seat. Addie had a dressing gown wrapped around her; Don wore only a blue bath towel; his hair was wet, his chest tanned and powerful.

I stood transfixed, until she saw me.

"Damn you!" she cried.

Don stood up, untroubled as always. "You could have knocked. Want a drink?"

"No, I don't want a drink."

"What *do* you want?" Addie demanded.

"I want to know what's going on. How long has . . . how long have you two . . . ?"

"Quite a while, Tom," Don said. "Quite a while. You sure about that drink?"

I turned to Addie.

"You were the Woman in the Dunes, weren't you?"

"The what?"

"The woman on the beach with him at Rehoboth, last March."

She shrugged, but I had no doubt about it. Gloria must have known all along. She'd given me hints, played her games, waiting for me to wake up. How she must have delighted in my blindness, my idiocy.

"Addie and I care a lot for each other," Don said. "But this is a delicate time. We've had to be careful."

244

"Yeah, you were careful, weren't you." I turned to Addie. She sat with her thin legs curled under her, anger burning in her pale, proud face. "You played me like a fiddle."

"I liked you well enough, Tom," she said. "We had good times."

"Good times!" I raged. "You made me the fall guy, the beard, the biggest jerk in America. Blind Boy Tom, with his cane and his tin cup, a sucker for any cute little trick who . . ."

"Calm down, Tom," Don said evenly. "We're all friends here. Your feelings are hurt but you'll get over it. I wasn't exactly overjoyed about Addie's fling with you, but we can't always control these liberated women, can we?"

"People were getting on to you," I said. "Starting to guess. So you sucked me in, into the campaign and made them forget the gossip about the candidate."

"It was convenient," he agreed. "You were our early-warning system. If you didn't know, no one would."

I sighed and poured myself a drink. Don was right. We were friends. That was the hell of it.

It's difficult to explain what I was thinking at that moment. Did I say once that I loved ambiguity? Well, this was too much, even for me. All over America, at that moment, expensive television spots, designed by some of the most sophisticated mind-manipulators on earth, were convincing people that Don Allworth was Superman, a wise and benign hero who could lead us into the twenty-first century.

Meanwhile, here was the real Don Allworth, with a towel around his middle and a drink in his hand, calmly explaining how he'd suckered me and Addie's husband and the rest of the world to carry out this highly duplicitous and somewhat sordid affair.

The crazy part was, I liked this Don better. He was human. And he knew that. I saw it in his smile.

"What are you two going to do?"

"Maybe nothing," he said. "It's a difficult situation. If I win, that's one thing; if I don't, that's another. But Addie is important to me. It means a lot to have someone who understands what I'm doing, the pressures, the stakes, the way the game is played. It's no fun out there, Tom. She's kept me going."

"Don't you realize what you're risking? Both of you? The *Post* would fire her in a minute for this."

"Of course we do," he told me. "And we're careful."

"I could blow the whistle, you know."

Don shook his head. "You wouldn't do that."

He was so damn confident I wanted to hit him. But he was right. I wouldn't blow the whistle because he was my friend, because despite everything I wanted him to win.

"Gloria knows," I said. "She kept giving me hints. You can't trust her."

Don looked amused. "She has her price," he said, and I did not dare ask him to explain.

I looked at Addie. I thought of what she had done to me, to poor dumb Mike before me, and I found myself laughing.

"What's so funny?" she demanded.

"You," I said. "You've proved my father's rule about women, once and for all."

"I don't suppose we'd like to hear it."

"That any woman is capable of anything," I said, more to myself than to her. I gazed at her proud, angry face and knew I'd had enough ambiguity for one day. For one lifetime.

"Good luck," I said. "Both of you."

With what I hoped was a show of dignity, I left the lovers there in the twilight.

I wasn't sure how I felt about them; I only knew I couldn't stand to look at them any longer.

I went back to Dinah's place. She'd left a note: she and Chester had set off for Oregon in her ancient Dodge Dart.

It was funny how I missed her that night.

36.

My dreams were scattered by a banging on the door.

As I feared, my visitors weren't selling Girl Scout cookies. They were U.S. marshals, selling a quick trip to the U.S. Attorney's office.

"Be there at eleven," they commanded. "Or else."

Already I had a problem. Guttman, the prosecutor in question, and I had a history. I'd jerked his cord a few times because I knew his son was Georgetown's leading supplier of designer drugs.

I could expect no charity from Waldo Guttman.

I still didn't know what to say. If I told the truth, the whole truth, and nothing but the truth, I was going to complicate Forrest's life. If I didn't, I might complicate my own.

I was nearing a moment of truth.

What would it be?

Help your friend?

Or fuck your buddy?

I didn't even call my lawyer, because I knew what he would say.

At ten o'clock, my moral compass spinning wildly, I called Forrest.

"I'm seeing Guttman in an hour," I told him. "Maybe we should get our stories straight."

I felt terrible. For all I knew this very phone call was a felony. What the hell was I supposed to do? Maybe I should just tell the truth and count on Forrest's shadowy intelligence agency to bail him out.

Yet, except for this man, this friend, I'd be fish food in the Gulf of Mexico now. Full fathom five Tom Tullis lies, those are pearls that were his eyes.

"I'll have to call you back," Forrest said. "Don't go anywhere."

"I'm due there at eleven."

"Wait for me!" he commanded.

Furious, I waited.

After twelve minutes he called back.

"Turn on your radio." He named an all-news station.

I turned Dinah's radio on.

Sirens, voices.

A disaster at the Southwest Marina.

A reporter live at the scene.

A cabin cruiser has exploded, he said, setting other boats ablaze and snarling traffic.

Fatalities feared.

The owner of the boat, James Atwood, prominent attorney, missing. Foul play suspected.

Meanwhile, on the West Bank . . .

I felt an odd mixture of satisfaction and sorrow. The son of a bitch tried to kill me. And yet I had persisted in liking him. He'd been sucked in by greed, the way a lot of people had.

"Forrest, are you still there?"

"I'm here."

"What the hell is going on?"

"My guess is the Colombians decided to get rid of him. It was that or get rid of us, and he was a greater threat to them. As far as we're concerned, I don't think the U.S. Attorney is a problem now. With Atwood dead, they can put Bobby and Rudy away on gun charges, if not for Swink's murder, and they won't worry much about what those two say. Just tell the truth. Except you don't know who was driving the cabin cruiser."

"Sure," I said. "Sure."

"So call me after you see Guttman."

"Sure," I repeated dumbly.

Something was bothering me. Something about the way I'd called him and he'd put me on hold and called back twelve minutes later with the latest news.

"Forrest?"

"Yeah?"

"You think the Colombians killed Atwood so he couldn't finger them?"

"It's possible."

"Would it make just as much sense for your friends to have killed him—your agency, I mean—so he couldn't cause you any more trouble?"

A long pause. "Tom, don't be so cynical. It's bad for your health."

And that was that. I hurried to the U.S. Attorney's office, where Guttman and I talked briefly. He seemed shaken by Atwood's death, and not much interested in what I had to say.

"Be well," he said in parting, a touch ominously.

Back at my office, Harriet complained that I should write something about Swink's death, that I was failing in my obligation to provide high-grade scandal for her readers.

"Damn you, leave me alone!" I yelled, so violently that she fled.

249

Grundy kept calling but I wouldn't talk to him.

Buzz Makito called and asked me to meet him for lunch at the Willard Room.

I accepted. The Willard Room is as close to heaven as I expect to venture. Nothing bad could happen at the Willard Room, not as long as the other guy paid the check.

We lunched, amid turn-of-the-century opulence, on oysters in champagne sauce, quail stuffed with *foie gras,* and chocolate-covered strawberries.

Our new masters do feed us well.

There was a certain air of unreality about our meeting.

The name of his late associate, Mr. Swink, was never mentioned.

Nor was the unhappy fact that the late and unlamented Mr. Swink had injected Japanese money into the presidential campaign, a fact that, if exposed, might bring down his country's government and cause God knows what chaos in our own election.

I cannot doubt that these things were on my companion's mind, but he was a subtle man, world-class subtle.

He talked about education.

About the enchanting year he had once spent at the University of Michigan.

About how young Japanese loved American universities.

About education as the key to the twenty-first century.

He was starting to sound like a commencement address.

Then, ordering more champagne, Buzz mentioned that Japanese businesses had endowed more than twenty chairs and professorships at major American universities.

I nodded gravely.

Most are in science or engineering, he noted.

Yes.

But he had a friend, a bighearted but publicity-shy industrialist, who wanted to endow a chair in journalism.

I blinked.

But where should this plum be located? Yale? Stanford? Rice? Georgetown?

Fine institutions all, I ventured.

"Tom, forgive me if I am too forward," my host continued. "But my friend has asked me to recommend not only a university, but the journalist who shall fill the professorship. And my thoughts return ever to you."

My mouth fell open.

"You could select the university of your choice. The initial salary would be one hundred thousand dollars a year. Plus expenses, of course. You would teach perhaps one seminar a week, and otherwise devote yourself to writing and lecturing. How does it sound?"

How did it sound? It sounded like the proverbial whore's delight.

But was I the whore?

It sounded like one hell of a sweet way for Buzz to keep me from ever whispering anything even remotely unkind about his countrymen and their ill-advised political contributions.

Which I had not intended to do, in any event; I'd had enough trauma for one year, without leaping into an international scandal.

What I wanted was peace and quiet. And perhaps a little self-respect.

I reflected yet again that the dapper Makito might have been a man from Mars, as far as my understanding him or his understanding me went.

I was immobilized.

Part of me wanted to accept his heavenly offer.

Another part wanted to cry, "Remember Pearl Harbor!" and break a chair over his nicely barbered head.

Unable to choose, I wordlessly rose and left him there.

Buzz Makito must have thought me mad.

That made two of us.

251

. . .

Back at the office, Harriet issued an ultimatum: publish or perish. I waved my arms, rolled my eyes, beat my chest, made guttural noises until Fay Wray fled the mad Kong.

Grundy, pretending to be a doctor calling from my stricken mother's bedside, got through to me. He was even more crazed than usual. He claimed that soon after I left for Florida someone—one of Swink's henchmen, he thought—had tried to gun him down outside his Fourteenth Street apartment. But there was so much shooting on his street normally that it was hard to know what to believe.

But now he had a worse problem than assassination. With Swink and Atwood dead, his dirty-money story was falling apart; he wanted to quiz me, but I feared him, feared he would somehow do me harm, and I stalled him.

A political consultant called, claiming to have a forties stag film whose star was now a celebrated Capital hostess. "I don't want your filthy movie!" I cried, and threw my phone across the room.

Was I cracking up?

Was I no longer fit for the gossip beat?

I knew too much, more than I wanted to know, more than any mortal should know.

The phone kept ringing. Like a fool I kept answering, hoping someone kind would call. But all I heard was endless scorn and jealousy and malice, pouring over me like a tidal wave.

I decided to leave, to wander the streets. I imagined myself homeless, huddled on a grate, freed from the bondage of journalism, the horrors of gossip, the endless human pettiness that is the underside of our occasionally noble and always necessary Capital.

The phone rang once more.

Hope springs eternal; I answered.

"Tom? Wally Love, calling from Parker County!"

I smiled to hear his raspy voice.

"What in the world's happening back there?"

I told him enough about the deaths of Swink and Atwood to satisfy him.

"I feel awful," Wally kept saying. "Those people used me."

"Forget it," I told him. "You liked Allworth and you helped him. Swink was playing his game, but that didn't affect what you were doing."

I calmed him down, and I was glad. Wally may have been a dupe, but he'd hadn't been a crook.

Then he got around to what he'd really called about. "Tom, I have this problem. Maybe you can help."

"What's that?"

"My boy Charlie, my editor. He's run off with some woman. Craziest thing I ever heard of."

"The flesh is weak," I said consolingly.

"I need a new editor. Maybe you know somebody. I need a man—or a woman, don't get me wrong—who can write, edit, do layout, the whole thing. I can't pay much—forty thousand, tops, but, by golly, there's no better place to live on this earth!"

My poor tormented mind spun giddily.

I thought of Dinah, headed for Portland.

I thought of my crazed publisher, shouting obscenities outside my door.

I thought of that wave of raw sewage that kept sweeping over me, day after day after day, tomorrow and tomorrow and tomorrow.

And I thought of Oregon, shut my eyes, and imagined green mountains and crystalline air.

It wasn't the Capital of the World, but it might be something better.

"Wally," I said, "I know just the man for you."

37.

Relax, Reader, there's more.

Yes, I went to Parker County.

The people were decent.

The streets were safe.

The air was pure, the mountains majestic.

You could go for weeks without encountering even a hint of depravity.

A bake sale was big news, a borrowed bike a crime wave, a furtive glance a scandal.

And I was *bored, bored, bored!*

No gossip, no Gloria, no girls of Thirty-first Street. No tales of rape, pederasty, incest, and addiction among the champions of Family Values. No crime, corruption, sleaze, malice, cynicism.

No fun at all.

I had traded Sodom for Brigadoon, and I missed my friends.

Dinah was no help; she made up with her ex-husband and vanished into a pink haze of Togetherness.

I began seeing a sweet, sturdy gym teacher who sang in the Methodist choir. She cried when I wouldn't go to Sunday school with her. So I went and then *I* cried.

There comes a time in life when one must look into the mirror and not blink.

I looked and what I saw was not pretty. Our corrupt, greedy, indifferent Capital is my home sweet home. I am a fish that swims happily in its polluted waters.

A gossip in his element.

People *do* things there.

They think big, spend big, lie big, steal big, laugh big, win big, and lose big.

And gossip big, God bless them.

So the Prodigal returned.

Harriet greeted me with open checkbook, for the *Vindicator*'s circulation had dropped alarmingly when I took my tattling elsewhere.

Crafty Harriet has a syndication deal in the works. Millions of Americans will soon see their Capital through my jaundiced eyes.

And why not?

My friend Forrest stayed out of town for a few weeks, but after Rudy and Bobby were put away on gun charges, he came home. We had a long talk about the Capital one night. Forrest has a theory that all great capitals, from Caligula's Rome to Hitler's Berlin, reach political decadence and cultural greatness at about the same moment. If that's true, our Capital should be a joy to behold in the Nervous Nineties.

My God, look at us! Greed is king, the economy is a ticking bomb, crime, drugs, and poverty threaten to engulf us, and don't even *think* beyond the year 2000.

All that matters is that the game go on.

As I write this, the presidential campaign is slouching into its final weeks.

No one should win this travesty, but Don Allworth may. He is rarely seen without sweet Polly at his side—she alone has given this campaign a hint of class. Don's luck held, and the other-woman rumors dried up without ever seeing print.

(Addie, by the way, reconciled with Mike, but I'm convinced it's only a gambit.)

I'm rooting for Allworth, of course.

Because he might be a good President.

Because at worst he's the lesser evil.

Because Polly would be a lovely First Lady.

And, what the hell, because it would be fun to be wined and dined in the White House.

Good parties, good gossip, a few more good years—that's all we dare hope for, in the lengthening shadows of these giddy twilight years, here in the Capital of the World.